WHEN LOVE COMES MY WAY

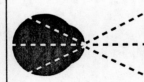

This Large Print Book carries the
Seal of Approval of N.A.V.H.

WHEN LOVE
COMES MY WAY

LORI COPELAND

THORNDIKE PRESS
A part of Gale, Cengage Learning

GALE
CENGAGE Learning

Detroit • New York • San Francisco • New Haven, Conn • Waterville, Maine • London

GALE
CENGAGE Learning®

LIBRARY OF CONGRESS CATALOGING-IN-PUBLICATION DATA

Copeland, Lori.
  [Fool me once]
  When love comes my way / by Lori Copeland.
    pages ; cm. — (Thorndike Press large print Christian romance)
  ISBN-13: 978-1-4104-5003-6 (hardcover)
  ISBN-10: 1-4104-5003-1 (hardcover)
  1. Large type books. I. Title.
PS3553.O6336F67 2012b
813'.54—dc23   2012021848

Published in 2012 by arrangement with Books & Such Literary Agency, Inc.

Printed in Mexico
3 4 5 6 7 16 15 14 13 12

To Sharon Kissiah Holmes —
I love you, girl.

To my Harvest House family,
especially Kim Moore,
who makes my stories stronger.

And to the lumberjacks of old. All the
Jakes, Andrés, Shots, Jims, Herbs, and
Rays who replanted pine trees so that
my children and grandchildren could
experience God's goodness.

ACKNOWLEDGMENTS

Writers are dependent upon research they have either read or experienced, so I wish to gratefully acknowledge four sources I relied on in creating the background for *When Love Comes My Way*:

- *Incredible Seney,* by Lewis C. Reimann
- *The Story of Logging the White Pine in the Saginaw Valley,* by Irene M. Foehl and Harold M. Hargreaves
- *Memories of the Minor Lumber Camps,* by Carl B.J. Minor
- *When Pine Was King,* by Lewis C. Reimann

When I was writing the book, my husband and I spent time in the beautiful Upper Peninsula of Michigan, visiting the old logging towns and researching how lumberjacks lived in the 1800s. I came away with a new respect and gratitude for those courageous men.

1

Michigan
Winter 1873

The front door of the office flew open, and Wakefield Timber camp foreman Jake "Big Say" Lannigan stepped outside. Sunshine blanketed the camp but did little to warm Michigan's biting winter air. Heading north, he strode down the planked sidewalk.

The blacksmith dropped his hammer on the anvil in front of him and stood up straight. "Mornin', Big Say. Got time for a cup of coffee?"

"Not right now." Jake's refusal was sharper than intended, but his mind was on other matters. Tess Wakefield — that woman had his undivided attention.

Heat crept up his neck as he walked to the camp store. It was a sorry day when Rutherford Wakefield was foolish enough to leave his vast logging empire in the hands of a willful, misinformed, spoiled brat! But that was exactly what the old man had done. He'd left Wakefield Timber, and everything else he owned, to his granddaughter, Tess.

The familiar jingle of harness filled the brisk air as wagons pulled into camp loaded with men looking for work. Jake made his way across the busy street, paying no attention to the commotion.

A new timber season had begun, and with it the merciless slaughter of white pine. Jake knew that half the greenhorns coming here today had no idea what they were getting into. Come summer, most of them would move on until the next cutting season.

Greed caused his headache. *The Gazetteer,* a popular tour book of Michigan, had sounded the news that stands of white pine on the Penobscot and Kennebec Rivers in Maine were being depleted and dry lumber was in great demand.

Maps of the mysterious western lands were being passed around to encourage the brave to seek their fortunes. An acre could be bought for sixty cents up to a dollar and a quarter. White pine was desperately needed for houses, barns, sheds, wagons, fences, bridges, boardinghouses, saloons, steamboats, railroad ties, and trestles. There were fortunes to be made in timber, and many opportunists were taking advantage

10

of the windfall.

Jake stepped up onto the porch of Menson's store and opened the door. He glanced around, searching for André Montague. The burly Frenchman was not only a good lumberjack, but he also wore many other hats in the camp, including being Jake's pencil pusher and good friend. The man was off shift, but Jake needed to talk to him. He spied André smoking a stogie at a table drawn close to the potbellied stove, playing poker with three other men. Jake closed the door and entered the warmth of the building. André glanced up from his hand and lifted a dark brow expectantly in Big Say's direction.

"Well?"

"She's going to sell."

André shrugged and stared down at his cards. "This does not surprise me."

Drawing a deep breath, Jake tried to tell himself he no longer cared what Tess Wakefield did with the business. He'd done all he could. The land was hers to do with as she pleased. Other than quit, he had no choice but to accept her decision, but there was no rule that said he had to like it.

He reached inside his jacket and pulled out a wad of crumpled paper. His anger flared anew when he thought of the time he'd spent corresponding with Tess over the last few months, trying to persuade her to replant the forests and refrain from selling her grandfather's timberlands. *Her* timberlands, he corrected, but the thought still left a bitter taste in his mouth.

With a flick of his wrist, he snapped open the first letter.

Dear Mr. Lannigan,
My, my, the budget increase you suggested for planting seedlings seems rather substantial. Couldn't you cut the seedling purchase in half and plant them farther apart?
You are running a business, not a charity. While planting little trees sounds like a worthy cause, we must show a profit or sell. I have recently opened a hat boutique here in Philadelphia, a dream that has always been close to my heart, so it's crucial that we trim the waste at your end, don't you agree?

Sincerely,
Miss Tess Wakefield

Jake opened the cast-iron door of the little stove and pitched the letter inside. With a great measure of satisfaction, he watched the fine-grained parchment with its ornate

12

handwriting writhe for an instant before turning into ashes.

Charity? She dared to call planting trees *charity?*

The word grated on him. Jake Lannigan had never asked anyone for charity in his life. Replanting the forests was not a philanthropic venture. It was a necessity, pure and simple.

He knew that if life wasn't given back to the land soon, the time would come when nature would refuse to provide. And he had written this to Tess Wakefield on three different occasions, but what did he get for an answer?

Dribble. Pure, unadulterated dribble!

He slammed shut the stove door and straightened the second letter.

Mr. Lannigan,
How nice — and unexpected — to hear from you again. My new boutique is causing quite a stir in Philadelphia! Everyone is commenting about my lovely creations. The replanting you keep suggesting will have to wait because, you see, I need to raise the capital to enlarge my thriving business by building more shops. And I simply must import lovely French lace and expensive Chinese silk,

which, as you must know, is quite the rage in ladies' hats.

Tess Wakefield

Jake jerked open the stove door once again and tossed the missive into the greedy flames. His intense gaze circled the room. This store was where the camp folks gathered to socialize. The women would buy their wares and the men would play cards and tell tall tales about lumberjacking. Here were folks who had dedicated their blood and sweat to Wakefield Timber. Now Miss Wakefield wanted to forfeit their futures for some French lace? How thoughtless of him! Why should future generations possibly matter when the little woman in Philadelphia only cared about hats? Every lady simply must have hats made of lace and Chinese silk!

He angrily flipped open the third letter he had received this morning.

Mr. Lannigan,
Your plea for more time is compelling, but my shop is simply booming, whereas Wakefield Timber is presently nothing but a drain on my resources. Although you've insisted that Grandfather's business will show a profit at the end of the

season, I think my fiancé is right. I should cut my losses and reinvest in something more profitable.

Therefore, I am writing to inform you that I am selling my logging business to Mr. Sven Templeton. I will be arriving soon to sign the papers and settle accounts with you. I'm sure you will join me in making this a smooth transition for all concerned.

T. Wakefield

With every letter the woman had grown more curt. He should have seen this coming. He wadded the sheet of paper in his fist and flung it into the fire. With a shove, he closed the metal door with the heel of his boot, the angry clank echoing throughout the store.

Sven Templeton — the most ruthless competitor in the timber industry! That merciless jackal would speed up the destruction. There would be no pine replanted. Tess Wakefield obviously didn't care a whit about anyone but herself. She was nothing but a coddled, willful, selfish brat. And Talbot Wellington-Kent, that fancy-talking, highbrow carriage maker she was engaged to marry, told her she needed to sell? How could the man know anything about the timber business when he'd probably never left the city of Philadelphia? Jake half growled under his breath with disgust.

André glanced up from his hand of cards.

"Miss Wakefield is not only selling the company, but she is also coming to pay us a visit."

"Oh?" André grinned and laid a full house on the table. "You are mighty touchy this morning, Big Say."

Jake ignored the good-natured jibe.

"When is our little flower from the East arriving?" André asked as he shuffled the cards. Cocking an eyebrow at Jake again, he proceeded to deal a new hand.

"The little flower didn't say."

"Maybe we ought to throw some sort of a welcoming party for her," the Frenchman suggested.

"Go right ahead and do that, André, but don't expect me to show up."

Two large store cats began racing around the store in a heated brawl. Yowling and spitting, they bounced off the shelves, sending canned goods clattering to the floor.

"They're fighting again! Somebody put those cats outside!" Henry Menson called and bent closer to the light, squinting at a piece of paper. "I'm trying to read Florabelle Melton's handwriting so I can get her grocery list filled. These varmints aren't helping." When the big calico hurtled past and Jake reached to grab it, the other feline was not far behind. It sprang headlong into the flour barrel, sending up a large puff of white fog. The cat Jake held hissed and clawed at him while he gently tried to calm it.

"Somebody, please, help me get that animal under control!" Henry swished his hand at the flour in the air. "This is the second mess this week I've had to clean up. If they didn't keep the mice out, I'd put them over in the bunkhouse with Old Sweets."

Chairs scraped against the wooden floor and bedlam broke loose when the men scrambled to catch the black-and-white streak darting wildly around the room. Jake all but smiled at the thought of the two pesky animals, in the middle of one of their outbursts, jumping atop the sleeping men.

The door opened, and into the midst of the fracas marched Bernice Trunksmore. She was the last person Jake wanted to see at that moment. Someone handed him the other squirming cat, and he walked to the front of the store, past Bernice, and released them.

The tall, heavyset woman was filling in for

the last school-teacher, who had abruptly left a month ago without taking her personal belongings with her. Bernice had stopped teaching a few years back and stated she never wanted to do it again. However, each time she was needed she temporarily, though reluctantly, took on the job, and Jake appreciated it. Right now, though, he knew she wasn't happy with how long it was taking him to find a replacement for the last woman.

Bernice turned and sailed toward him like a clipper ship in a high gale, and he braced himself for the inevitable tongue-lashing.

"Have you heard from the new teacher?"

"Now, Bernice, settle —"

"Don't 'now, Bernice' me, Jake Lannigan! When is Fedelia Yardley arriving?"

"Soon."

Her eyes narrowed. "Soon? Monday? A week from Monday? Two weeks from Thursday? And *what* have you hooligans done to those poor cats?"

Flour still clogged the air. He would regret the fib he was about to tell her, but he loved to pull her leg. "We put clothespins on their tails to see what they would do."

Bernice rummaged in her purse and pulled out a handkerchief. "No *wonder* the children of this town are such heathens!"

18

Jake exchanged an amused glance with André and tried to hide a smile. Bernice promptly returned to the subject clearly uppermost on her mind.

"When is Miss Yardley arriving?"

"Can't say. With winter setting in this early, it's hard to predict when the train will run and when it won't."

"It's your job to say. Are you incapable of doing your job?"

"I know it's part of my job, but —"

"I don't want excuses!" she snapped. "I want out! Is that clear, Jacob Lannigan?"

"Bernice." Jake swallowed his resentment. He didn't like being talked to as though he were a willful child. "I have made arrangements for a new teacher, but you're going to have to be patient long enough for her to get here."

"Hogwash. I've been patient for as long as I'm going to be. The party's over. There had better be a teacher here Monday morning, or you'll be up that well-known creek!"

"Now, Bernice —"

"Stop with the 'now, Berniceing'!"

Jake glanced again at André, but from the way his friend was grinning, like a mule eating green grass, he knew he wouldn't be any help. "Monday?" He couldn't believe the woman had just given him an ultimatum. The camp needed her to teach the children until Miss Yardley arrived. He needed to calm her down, but he doubted anything he said would do the trick.

He took in a deep breath and then let it out slowly. "Like I told you, I'm sorry, but I don't know exactly when Miss Yardley will arrive. Her letter said she would be here within the month. This is the middle of the month, so it can't be long now." He watched her jerk the strings of her bonnet as if they were her enemies, and her snapping blue eyes riveted him to the spot.

"I'm giving you fair warning. She'd better be."

Because Jake valued his life, he squelched the urge to grin. Why did he all of a sudden think the situation was funny? "Are the children giving you trouble again?" He knew he was in for it when hot color crept up the old schoolmarm's neck. Then she blew up like a load of dynamite.

"They're nothing but ill-mannered hea-thens!" She edged closer to wag her finger under Jake's nose. "I will not — listen to me — I will *not* spend another day past the end of the month in the classroom with those fiends, do you hear me? If Miss Yard-ley is not here by then — the end of *this* month" she emphasized, "the school will be closed. Do I make myself clear?"

"Yes, ma'am. Perfectly clear."

"That's less than two weeks."

"Yes, ma'am. I know that."

"Then you had better get busy."

Apparently convinced he fully understood the urgency of the matter, Bernice turned on her heel and marched to the door.

"The end of the month," she called over her shoulder. "Not a day longer!" She slammed the door behind her.

Henry glanced up from sweeping the flour and frowned. "She rattled every jar on my shelves. That woman has a temper, Jake. Even so, if she follows through on her threat, my little Modeen will be without a teacher again."

Nodding, Jake knew he had a problem. Bernice would be the eighth teacher to resign in as many months, and it was becoming almost impossible to fill the position. None of the other women in camp were qualified to teach. And even if they were, they wouldn't want the job.

"She sounds like she means it this time," Henry fretted.

Jake turned to warm his hands at the stove. Generally, few lumberjacks chose to subject their wives or families to the isolation of a logging camp, but Wakefield was a big operation, much larger than most. Along with timber operations to manage, Jake had sixteen households to oversee and nine children to educate.

If the five boys and four girls behaved like normal kids, it would have made his job considerably easier. They all had good, hard-working parents and were well-mannered children — except in school. He'd never understood why, but they were terrible scamps with the teachers.

"She's just upset because young Pud Wilkerson threw a skunk in the schoolroom," Jake said, wishing that was the only reason the woman was angry.

André swiped at his nose. "It took her all week to get the stench tapped down."

"Serves her right," Henry said. "She's too strict on those young'uns."

"Strict?" the men chorused.

"That woman's as fierce as a grizzly with a toothache."

Nate Waltrax chewed on the tip of his cigar and shuffled the cards for another game. "No one can blame her for wanting out. I wouldn't put up with those kids if it were me."

"Now, wait a minute, Nate," Henry said, wiping his hands on his apron. "My little Modeen —"

"Is the ringleader, Henry. She swears like a man and bullies anyone who gets in her way. She has a mean streak a mile wide." Nate bit off the end of his cigar and spat it on the floor.

"How many times have I warned you about spittin' on the floor when there's a spittoon right over there?" Henry complained. "Now, my Modeen isn't like that at home. She may be a little high-spirited, but she can be controlled."

"With a whip and a chair," André muttered under his breath.

Sy Melton reached for his wife's box of supplies and looked directly at Jake. "We'd all better hope Miss Yardley makes it here by month's end. If Bernice quits before the new teacher gets here, the womenfolk will be real upset."

Jake reached up to rub the back of his neck. All this commotion was making him weary. When his hand fell away, his fingers were covered with a fine dusting of white.

"You have flour on your neck," André said, snickering.

Jake didn't mind his friend's ribbing. It lightened the mood. "I'm not the only one. You look like a ghost." He glanced around the room. Everyone was covered with a film of white powder.

23

All of these men were his friends, and he hoped that after the sale of Wakefield Timber the camp would survive. He figured the place had about as much of a chance as the white pine had of avoiding Sven Templeton's crosscut saw, thanks to Tess Wakefield.

2

"Shadow Pine coming up!"

Tess snapped her head up when the train conductor sounded the call. Aware that she'd been caught dozing again, she glanced sheepishly at Fedelia Yardley sitting across from her. Fedelia never dozed. In fact, Tess could have sworn that the woman sharing this hideous ride hadn't shut an eye in the two days since they had left Philadelphia.

It was chilly in the drafty wooden train car. Tess pulled her wrap tighter around her shoulders and studied the other woman. Though pleasant enough, Fedelia had done little to reward Tess's periodic attempts to draw her into conversation. She seemed content to thumb methodically through textbook after textbook, enduring the tedious journey to the lumber camp with as few distractions as possible.

The steam locomotive pulled into Shadow Pine, and Tess disembarked and followed the other passengers into the small depot, noting there wasn't a private carriage waiting — but then, Mr. Lannigan didn't know the exact date of her arrival. Fedelia walked in front of her.

"Miss Yardley, do you know how we are supposed to get to Wakefield Timber camp? Surely they would have sent a buggy for the new teacher."

"No, I don't."

"Would you mind asking someone?" Watching the woman walk toward the clerk's desk, Tess realized there *was* quite a resemblance between them. Though the train conductor had mentioned the similarity, she'd thought it unlikely at the time.

Fedelia turned away from the clerk and approached Tess. "They sent a wagon to take me to the camp. It's waiting outside. You're welcome to come along."

"Wonderful. Thank you." Tess trailed her out of the building. She found herself liking Fedelia Yardley a bit more.

Then she paused when she saw the conveyance. "What is that?" She was appalled at the sight of the rickety-looking vehicle the camp manager had sent. Two warped planked seats were worlds removed from the plush padded seats found in Talbot's open-air carriages.

The driver grinned. "Haven't you ever seen a workin' wagon, miss? No, I suspect not from the looks of you and your sister."

Fedelia didn't give Tess time to answer. "We are not sisters, sir."

"No offense intended, ma'am. But you two look an awful lot alike."

Tess was certain the wagon ride would be worse than the train — cold, jarring, and most unpleasant. She should have insisted that Mr. Lannigan come to see her in Philadelphia. Then she could have granted him power of attorney in order to make the sale in her absence.

Sighing, she climbed onto the seat beside the schoolteacher and Walter Fedderson, a man she had met on the train. He said he was seeking work at the camp, but to her he looked too old to climb trees or pull a crosscut saw.

Waiting for the bags to be loaded, Tess readjusted the folds of her heavy woolen skirt. With more than a touch of pride, she reached up to pat her lovely hat. The ostrich plumes, coils of silk, and rows of fine English lace were fit for a queen — though admittedly it was all a bit out of place in these surroundings.

Her lovely little hat boutiques were her pride and joy. She sketched her breathtaking creations and then two seamstresses brought her ideas to life. It was all such wonderful fun. And Talbot was so proud of her!

The wagon hit a rut as soon as it took off, and Tess had to steady her hat as she sat up straighter. She realized then that hairpins had fallen loose from her hair, and wisps of curls fell to her shoulders when she swept off her bonnet. "I'll be glad to see this trip end," she confided to Fedelia.

Tess worked the thick tresses back into a soft cluster atop her head. The entire journey had been miserable, and she longed for a hot bath. She wished once she reached Wakefield Timber that she could go straight to a hotel and soak for hours in steaming perfumed salts before she sat down to a meal of delectable roast beef and a lovely dessert. Visions of a fine crème brûlée danced in her head.

Fedelia murmured something distractedly and continued to read. Tess studied her and decided her hairstyle made her matronly looking. She really needed do something about it. The dark blond mass was tidy, but it looked too severe pulled back from her face in a tight bun. Tess glanced at her elaborate creation on the warped board seat beside her. What a hat like that could do for a woman. She was certain that one of her designs would indeed work a miraculous transformation for Miss Yardley, conceding that Wakefield Timber's new schoolmarm, though not overly friendly, was pretty in a modest sort of way, but the serviceable brown traveling suit she wore, and the equally uninspired brown hat anchored firmly atop her pragmatic bun, cried dull, dull, and dull. She sighed again. Oh, that dreadful hat, so completely lacking inspiration.

After about an hour of traveling through an unending forest of tall white pines, Tess had had enough of the silence. "I don't plan to be in camp long," she remarked as if Fedelia had inquired — or was even mildly curious about the length of Tess's stay. The schoolmarm's eyes remained on the passage she was reading. Tess drew in another long, weary breath. "Not long at all." Her back ached from the uncomfortable wooden seat.

Having nothing else to do, she studied the trees. They towered sixty to eighty feet above the ground, and the pine branches grew so thickly that the sunlight never reached the ground. Though her grandfather had lived his entire life in these forests, Tess had not been back since she was a young child.

She'd often wondered how her mother, such a sophisticated city woman, had fallen in love with a dreadful lumberjack. However, when Clint Wakefield visited Philly on business all those years ago, he'd won her mother's heart, and she had followed him back to pine country.

Tess had never asked many questions about the situation because she saw the pain in her mother's eyes on the rare occasions when she'd mentioned her father. All she really knew was that Father had been killed in a logging accident when she was three and her mother promptly returned to Philadelphia and — in her words — a civilized life.

Tears welled in Tess's eyes as she took in the beauty that surrounded her. She could almost understand why her grandfather and father loved the pines so much. "It's breathtaking, isn't it?"

Fedelia finally looked up. A misting rain had started to fall. At times, the rain was mingled with sleet. "The weather is anything but lovely."

Tess smiled, aware of Fedelia's lack of enthusiasm for almost everything they had discussed. "You're right." She didn't want her beautiful hat to get wet, but because the wagon had no cover, she had to put it back on. Securing it in place, she asked, "What do you think about the talk on the train that the camp is lawless?"

"It's a concern, but I can't dwell on it. I have a job to do. I'll be fine."

"I'm sure Mr. Lannigan will see to your safety." Tess had always been shielded from anything remotely dangerous, but she was excited and couldn't wait to get there. She'd never witnessed an actual brawl.

Although Talbot had wanted her to complete the sale of Wakefield Timber as quickly as possible, she had to admit she was secretly starting to like the freedom she'd been enjoying since he had seen her off at the train station. In her twenty years, she had hardly been allowed to go anywhere alone. With the exception of opening her own boutiques, she had never been allowed to make even the smallest business decision for herself.

Her mother had died when she was eleven, and at that time Talbot had been appointed her guardian until she came to adulthood and her full inheritance at twenty-one. By then Tess was accustomed to him doing everything, didn't mind being under his thumb, and appreciated what her guardian — now fiancé — had done for her over the last nine years. He was very smart about

31

money, and she loved him, but now she was rather enjoying her newfound independence, and she imagined she would experience a tiny letdown when it came to an end.

Even so, she smiled when her fiancé came to mind. He was ten years older than she, and after her grandfather had passed and she had inherited his timber business, Talbot had been adamant that she quickly and efficiently dispose of it. He would have come to Michigan with her, but he had previous commitments that could not go unattended. Instead, he had thought to find her an appropriate chaperone, but after hours of pleading she'd finally convinced him she was capable of making the trip by herself.

Truth be told, at first she'd been a bit frightened, but now she was relishing her little adventure, and it wasn't over yet. "You're so lucky." Another sigh escaped Tess as the wagon clattered noisily down the uneven logging road.

Fedelia lifted her brows. "Lucky?"

"Yes," Tess whispered, taking care not to awaken the men who had boarded the wagon at the last stop. They said they were woodsmen traveling from the East to work.

Tess found the husky lumberjacks captivating. Fedelia had appeared to be repelled by them as soon as they scrambled aboard, their massive frames dwarfing the older gentleman on the back bench.

"Why would you say that I'm lucky?" Fedelia asked.

"Because you have complete control of your life. How intoxicating it must be to have not a single soul tell you where you may go, when you must smile, what you must say." Tess was thankful to have a man of Talbot's breeding and social position to look after her every need, yet how nice it would be to make a decision, one completely her own. Of course, she didn't envy Fedelia's reason for coming to the camp. Though Tess had been schooled at the most prestigious establishments, she knew she would be ill-suited for teaching young children.

Her teachers had been candid with her mother when she'd first started school, and her mother didn't fail to share those thoughts with her young daughter. Tess reflected on what her mother told her many times.

"Precious, though you are most personable, sadly enough your teachers have told me that my beautiful daughter is not overly gifted with scholarly pursuits."

No, she could never be a teacher, and she supposed it didn't matter whether she was

33

considered brilliant or not. In April she and Talbot would marry, and then her future would be secure.

Talbot Wellington-Kent. Most women were attracted to his large trust fund, but not her. Tess loved him for the man he was — funny, compassionate, and always protective of her.

The Wellington-Kent company had built the finest Philadelphia carriages available for more than seventy-five years. She was proud to say it wasn't Talbot's money she found attractive. She was wealthy in her own right as Rutherford Wakefield's only heir. No, it was Talbot himself. She felt comfortable with him. Though he could be a bit stubborn at times, he was dependable, and that was an important trait in a husband. She tended to be flighty — or so she'd been told.

Still, these few days of glorious freedom had made her start to wonder if she might delay marrying for a while and explore the world. She was lost in those daydreams when Fedelia's sigh pulled her back to reality.

Laying her book aside, the schoolmarm shook her head. "I must admit I wish I shared your outlook on my situation."

"You don't feel fortunate?"

"No. Merely apprehensive. As you said, there is talk that it's a bit rough in the camp."

"Oh, I shouldn't have mentioned that. Please don't let it worry you. It might be just rumor. And I'm sure the children won't be bad. It's probably just the men in the camp who are a bit unruly."

Seeming to want to change the subject, the young teacher said, "I should think you would want to keep the logging interest your grandfather left you. The timber business is quite lucrative."

"I know." Tess's smile faded as she looked again at the passing scenery. "Actually, at first I was in favor of keeping the business and letting grandfather's foreman run it for me."

"What changed your mind?"

"Talbot . . . my fiancé . . . thought it best to liquidate my assets and invest in something more promising. I've recently opened a third hat boutique. This is one of my creations." Tess smiled, lifting the hat from her head and holding it out for Fedelia's inspection. "Would you like to try it on? I wouldn't mind, you know."

"No, thank you," the teacher said flatly. "I couldn't, really."

Tess watched the mixture of awe and

revulsion in the girl's eyes and understood that Fedelia was probably not accustomed to such finery. "If I'd brought another with me, I'd be happy to give it to you, but since this is the only one —"

"That's quite all right," Fedelia said quickly, then smiling to soften her refusal. "What were you saying earlier? About why you changed your mind about keeping Wakefield Timber?"

"Oh." Tess set her hat back on her head. The poor girl might have plenty of book learning, but apparently she knew nothing about current fashion. "My fiancé's broker says the timber business has been in decline in recent years."

"Is your grandfather's foreman trust-worthy?"

"I think so. Mr. Lannigan and I have cor-responded over the past few months, and he seems to know the business. But he has this crazy idea of wanting to replant trees for future generations. Can you imagine?" Her gaze returned to the seemingly endless rows of pine. "I've heard it's estimated that enough timber is here to last for *hundreds* of years."

"Yes, I've read the same reports."

Tess glanced out at the hillside, where she was beginning to catch an occasional glimpse of fallen pines.

"But," the teacher continued, "I have also heard that logs with the slightest blemish are sometimes left lying on the ground to rot."

Tess viewed the passing landscape for signs of neglect. "They won't leave it like this. They're not finished here yet."

Fedelia gave an affirmative nod. "You are probably correct."

"I'm sure that sort of thing never happens in my grandfather's outfit." Tess watched the countryside grow more barren.

"One would certainly hope not."

Trying to stretch her weary neck muscles, Tess wondered how much farther it would be to the camp. She decided to inquire. "Driver, how much longer?"

" 'Bout a half hour."

"My goodness. It's farther than I thought." She rubbed the small of her back, sighing softly.

"You're to be married soon?" Fedelia asked.

"Sometime in the spring." Leaning forward, Tess proudly displayed the ring Talbot had given her. "See?" An envious look came into Fedelia's eyes as she gazed at the cluster of precious stones.

"It's lovely . . . and so large."

"Would you like to try it on?" Despite Fedelia's soft gasp of protest, Tess removed the ring and handed it to her. "Don't worry. Talbot will never know." The poor thing needed something to brighten her life.

Fedelia hesitantly slipped the ring on her finger and then moved her hand back and forth, openly admiring the way the diamonds caught the late afternoon light. Sadness entered her eyes, and Tess saw it. "Is there someone you care for deeply, Miss Yardley?"

"There was once, but I lost him before I realized how much I truly loved him."

"Oh." Tess reached out to gently touch the young woman's hand. "I'm so sorry. Was it long ago?"

Fedelia smiled. "Sometimes it seems as though it were a hundred years ago . . . but it has been only a few months. I'm afraid I've lost track of time. That's why I accepted the teaching position. I thought perhaps . . ." Her voice trailed as moisture welled in her eyes.

Clearing her throat, Fedelia quickly returned to an earlier subject. "This Mr. Lannigan you spoke of, I've also corresponded with him. He's the one who hired me. He doesn't think you'll regret selling your grandfather's business? It seems like a handsome inheritance."

"His feelings are really none of my concern." Though the foreman had not replied to her last letter, she wasn't surprised. From his increasingly sharply worded notes, she gathered that Mr. Lannigan was a stubborn man who could be quite rude when things didn't go his way. "But it wouldn't matter if he did. I want to please Talbot, and he feels my money can be invested more prudently."

"And you feel the same?"

"I have better things to do with my money than plant trees." Tess wondered if she really meant what she'd said, but before she could think on that too closely, she had to grab the side of the wagon for support. The old wooden conveyance had violently lurched sideways. Fedelia's stunned exclamation was ringing in Tess's ears as the young woman sailed out of her seat and onto Tess's lap.

"My goodness!"

Something was terribly wrong. Tess's heart jumped to her throat as she and Fedelia tried to regain their balance. What had just happened? Were they out of control?

The jolt had thrown Walter Fedderson onto the floor of the wagon bed. The burly men back there with him seemed to be faring little better. The older man struggled to pull himself back up on his seat. "What's going on?"

The wagon continued to pitch wildly. Tess could barely hold on. Abruptly, her world turned upside down. In the blink of an eye the cart tilted hard to the right. The team of horses broke loose at the same time Tess saw a wheel fly off, and then the wagon left the road and became airborne.

Helpless to understand what was happening, she continued to grip the wooden sides, desperately trying to hang on. The wagon tossed and jolted from side to side down a steep incline, hurtling toward a muddy, swiftly flowing river.

Fedelia screamed. Tess reached out with one hand to latch onto her, but her attempt met thin air. "Take my hand!" she shouted. She heard Fedelia shout her name before the woman was thrown out into the air like a rag doll.

"Dear God, please help us!" Tess called out when she saw Walter Fedderson follow the teacher. She could hear her screams blend with Fedelia's as the young teacher fell headlong into the icy waters. The churning river immediately laid claim to her flailing body, picking it up and carrying it swiftly along the icy current.

"Fedelia! Grab on to something!" Tess struggled to hold on as the shattered frame of the wagon bumped and slid its way down the frozen hillside. After what seemed like an eternity, though it was mere seconds later, it tumbled into the glacial waters, trapping Tess inside the wreckage. Bitterly cold water stung her skin and she choked, spitting water. Heart pounding, she tried to gather her bearings. She must have hit her head against something — it felt as though it would burst! She struggled to breathe as she thought about how she didn't want to die. In truth, she'd only begun to live. There was so much left she wanted to do. She wanted to marry, to have children . . . And her hats . . . her lovely hats . . .

Tess struggled fiercely to free her body, imprisoned in the frozen bowels of debris with her head just above water, and worried about her traveling companions. Mr. Fedderson — where was Mr. Fedderson? Had she only imagined that he'd been thrown clear, or was he trapped somewhere below her, fighting for his life? She searched the freezing water, seeking the older man. Nothing. And what happened to the other men who had joined them in Shadow Pine?

She realized she couldn't feel anything now, just a vague tingling where the tips of her fingers were supposed to be. She had to fight for her life. She tried to brace herself against the swift current that wanted to drag her under, her lungs aching for breath.

Oh, dear God, help me. She was going to die. Where were those woodsmen? They were strong; they could help . . .

Don't let me die like this. Don't let me die like this — she was aware she was losing consciousness, but she continued to pray as a terrifying blackness threatened to devour her. "Please, God," she sobbed. "I'm so s-scared . . ." Her words were a mere whimper now, her head pounding unmercifully. A mounting pressure in her chest sapped her remaining strength.

She was truly alone now, a thought that only an hour ago she'd found so exhilarating. Her hand slowly lost its grip on the wooden prison around her, and she felt her body growing lighter, weightless.

Please, God, if it must be the end, let it be swift. Watch over Talbot . . .

Then a warming numbness embraced her as an eerie silence took all sound away except that of the cold, rushing water and the pounding inside her head.

3

Cold air entered the office when André opened the door and poked his head in. "We are almost done with the new telegraph line, Big Say, but we cannot spare a crew to finish it right now."

Jake looked away from the lumberjack he was talking to and frowned. "How much longer?"

Shrugging, André shook his head. "You want the line finished or Mekin's timber order filled first?"

"Mekin won't wait. Fill the order and we'll worry about the line later."

The Frenchman pulled the door closed and Jake turned back to the man sitting in front of him. "It's not bad pay, Hugh."

"Three dollars a day?" Hugh Burton rubbed the heavy stubble on his chin.

Jake didn't want to lose this man. "I doubt Sven Templeton would match the wage. Better take what you can while you can." A river driver with Hugh's experience was hard to come by. The work was hazardous, and the working conditions were rugged.

Agile, fearless, and skillful, a river driver sent logs from the roll ways to the booming grounds, working from twelve to fourteen hours a day before getting back to camp each night.

"Well . . ."

"Three dollars a day, plus room and board." Jake was certain Templeton wouldn't be offering more. Rumor had it that when one of Sven's river hogs had been killed in last year's spring drive, Sven had docked the man's widow thirty percent of his pay because her husband had failed to complete the terms of his contract.

The man in front of him rubbed his chin again and sighed.

"I'd do more if I could, Hugh." Jake pushed back from his desk and reached for the pot of coffee on the stove.

"I was hoping for three twenty-five," Hugh admitted.

"I know you were." Jake filled Hugh's cup before replenishing his. "I heard they are hiring in Seney. You might try there."

The jack shook his head. "I can't move to Seney. The rumor mill says you're going to be leaving once the sale is final. That so?"

After placing the pot back on the stove, Jake walked to the window. He let the question go unanswered and hoped the man would let it drop. Although Sven had already approached him about staying in the area and working for him, Jake knew he couldn't. He was seriously thinking about yielding to his father's pressure to return to Lannigan Timber — then again, maybe he'd get out of the timber business altogether. Hugh's soft-spoken admission broke into Jake's troubled thoughts.

"My Nellie's real sick."

The foreman turned from where he'd been watching the sleet that had been falling all morning grow into large snowflakes. "I'm sorry about that, Hugh. We'd help if you'd let us."

He'd heard that Hugh's wife was seriously ill, and Hugh needed money to send her downstate to see a doctor who could possibly treat her lung affliction. In hardship cases like this, Jake and his crew usually dug into their pockets to help with the expenses, but anyone who knew Hugh was aware that he was a proud man, a man who wouldn't take anything he hadn't earned, a man who would prefer to work eighteen hours a day if necessary to provide the care his wife and family needed. "I won't take charity, but

I'm desperate, Jake. I'll take the job and as much overtime as you can see fit to give me."

"I'll do all I can."

Hugh rose, and when Jake offered a handshake, he noticed that the man's eyes were filled with quiet gratitude.

"I'm much obliged to you, Big Say. I promise I'll earn my keep."

Jake clasped the work-callused hand reassuringly. Hugh had run into a string of bad luck lately. First his wife's illness, and then his former employer's announcement that Barlow Timber was shutting down for good after last season. Jake was happy to do whatever he could. "Glad to have you aboard. Take your things to the bunkhouse and get settled."

Jake glanced up when the door to the office burst open, bringing with it a frigid blast of air. A grim-faced André stood in the doorway.

"You had better come with me, Jake."

"What's wrong?"

"There has been a wagon accident. It is serious."

Reaching for his wool mackinaw hanging behind the stove, Jake nodded his apologies to Hugh. He slipped into the heavy jacket and followed André out the door. "When did it happen?"

"Not sure, but not that long ago. I helped drag a woman out of the river. She is alive but near frozen. Doc Medifer is working on her now."

"The wagon team?"

"Broke loose. Some of the men spotted the horses up the road a piece. That is how we knew there was an accident and rushed down to the site. I had them put the team in the barn. Some of the men are down there now looking for more passengers."

"They'll never find anyone in that current," Jake said. "Better get some wires sent to figure out who these folks are. The train probably brought them to Shadow Pine and they boarded the wagon to come to camp."

"We cannot send anything. The lines are not up yet, remember?"

Jake shook his head as he strode toward the doctor's office. If it wasn't one thing, it was another. "Send them as soon as possible."

"To whom?"

"The railroad line. They will know what names were on the passenger lists."

André matched his strides with Jake's as the men braced themselves against the blustery wind off Lake Huron.

The logging operation lay in a deep harbor, protected on one side by a hundred-foot limestone cliff. The camp was a top-notch operation with land covered by beech, maple, birch, and deep stands of the coveted white pine. However, by mid-October the natural windbreaks did little to protect anyone from the fierce bite of the wind that could blow right through a man.

"How many were injured?" Jake asked as he and André made their way across the road and turned the corner.

"The driver managed to escape. He's banged up, but he'll make it. He said there were five folks in the wagon. Two women, an older man, and two woodsmen. The driver and one woman are the only ones we know survived. The others are unaccounted for."

"Where's the driver now?"

"He wanted to go back to Shadow Pine."

"Does anyone know who the woman in Doc's office is?"

"Not yet."

"Do we know how it happened?"

"Wheel came off. The wagon went down the embankment, broke apart, and then landed in the river. I'm surprised anyone got out of it alive."

The river had been up and running for days after heavy rains. Jake figured a strong man swimming against a swift current on a day like today wouldn't have much of a chance of making it to safety, much less a woman. "I've told Mingo a hundred times that he needs to replace those things he's calling wagons. I've been expecting an accident for years."

"The man is a miser," André said. "He will not spend a penny unless he is forced to."

"This accident will probably take care of that."

They reached their destination and stepped inside. A small group of men and women were gathered around the red-hot stove. Speaking in hushed tones, the men discussed the unexpected turn of events, shaking their heads amid grim predictions that the missing passengers would never be found alive.

Going to the curtained partition, Jake peeked into a dimly lit room where the injured lady lay. He could barely make out the outline of the doctor hovering over a small woman unconscious on the table.

He let the curtain fall shut and spotted Bernice heading straight for him.

"Jake, you're here. Do you know what's happened?"

"There's been an accident —"

"And do you know who is lying in there on that table, frozen stiffer than a wet sheet in a January wind?"

He had no idea who the woman was, but to his surprise Bernice seemed to be working herself into a lather. "Not yet." He saw that André had stepped inside.

"Fedelia Yardley, that's who!" Bernice wrung her hands and paced the length of the store.

Jake glanced at his right-hand man. "Is that the new schoolteacher?"

André nodded. "What little information we have points that way. The driver verified that Miss Yardley was in the wagon when the wheel came off. Of the two women, he was not sure which one she was, though. He could not recall the other female passenger's name. We suspect she might be the woman Burl Sutter has been expecting."

"The one he proposed to from East Saginaw?"

André put his hands close to the stove. "Yes. We are not positive, but Burl said she was due in sometime this week."

Jake glanced back at the end of the room where the young woman was lying. "Did she have any identification on her?"

"We found a couple of valises along the hillside with the initials *FY* on them," André replied. "The current must have swept the rest of the folks' personal belongings downstream — except for a few of Miss Yardley's textbooks found on the bank."

"Oh, merciful heavens!" exclaimed Bernice. "Why did this have to happen *now?* If that poor woman dies —"

Jake heard the woman's voice grow an octave higher when the appalling ramifications became apparent. He took a deep breath to calm himself. He didn't need Bernice's dramatic antics right now.

Slapping her hand against her forehead, she tramped back and forth across the wooden floor, picking up tempo as she went. "If she doesn't survive, you will have to close the school permanently because I simply will not be responsible for teaching those . . . those hoodlums!"

Jake cleared his throat. "Bernice, you should probably lower your voice. Whatever happens, you will not have to teach any longer than we discussed." He only hoped he could stick to that promise.

"Humph!"

He turned away from her and once again parted the curtain, but this time he stepped inside the small room. Doc barely glanced up. The man concentrated on the stethoscope he was holding to the woman's chest.

"How is she?"

Peering over the rims of his spectacles, the physician shook his head. "I was hoping she would have come around by now."

Stepping up to the table, Jake got his first real look at the injured passenger. The face of the soaking wet, bedraggled woman lying unconscious was pale as death. Fedelia Yardley, the long-awaited teacher, seemed to be at death's door.

As he looked at the woman's pretty face, from out of nowhere the name "Tess Wakefield" entered his mind. No, it was impossible. Miss Wakefield's last letter had just arrived. She couldn't have made the trip so quickly.

He focused on the mass of unruly hair, the small cupid-shaped mouth, pouty even now as she lay limp as a rag doll. He studied the patrician features that were characteristically Rutherford: high cheekbones, wide-set eyes, straight nose, and a chin of iron determination.

Could this half-drowned creature possibly be Tess Wakefield? He shoved the thought aside. He had enough troubles. He didn't need to be borrowing more.

"She's mighty lucky to be alive," Doc said as he walked to the medicine cabinet and pulled out a vial.

"Will she make it?"

"I don't think she's suffered any life-threatening injuries, and there appears to be no internal bleeding at this point. She took in a lot of water, though, and she's bound to have caught a chill. She has numerous cuts and bruises. I'm a little concerned about the fingers on her left hand. They are somewhat frostbitten, but I'm hoping she'll regain full use of them. I'm more concerned about her overall exposure right now."

"How long do you think she was in the water?"

"Not long, thank the good Lord. I think André got to her and managed to pull her out of the wreckage shortly after the accident happened." Doc put the stethoscope in his bag. "It's unlikely the others will ever be found."

Jake knew the doctor was well aware of the hazards of the river. At this time of year, the current could easily propel a body straight into Lake Huron, never to be seen again. André said they had recovered two valises bearing the initials *FY.* That was proof enough for him that Fedelia Yardley was indeed on the wagon along with perhaps Burl's woman.

André poked his face through the parted

curtain and asked, "How's she doing?"

The young woman on the table stirred, murmuring softly, "Please, Lord, help me . . . I don't want to die . . . please . . . God . . ."

"Looks like she's starting to come around." Doc moved back to the table, bent over his patient, and smiled. "Yes, she's coming back to us."

"Please . . ."

Jake watched as the young woman's eyes fluttered open. Eyes the color of rich chocolate stared back at him. He felt a swift flutter in the pit of his stomach. She took his breath away, with her striking dark eyes, golden hair, and soft, husky voice. She was far too appealing to work around men who didn't often experience her kind of beauty.

Jake had a hunch his job as foreman of Wakefield Timber had just been made all the harder. The lovely Fedelia Yardley was about to turn the logging camp upside down.

4

Tess's head throbbed when her eyes opened. She tried to bring the room and its occupants into focus. "What . . . where am I?"

"Try to relax, young lady. I'm Dr. Medifer. You've been in an accident, but you're going to be fine."

"An accident?" She focused on the tall, dark-headed giant with clear hazel eyes standing beside the doctor and tried to clear her senses. "What kind of accident?"

"A wheel came off the wagon you were riding in," Doc said, "and you were thrown in the river."

She brought her hand up to her forehead, trying to relieve the pressure in her brain. "Wagon? I . . . I don't seem to recall . . ."

Doc glanced at Jake and frowned. "Her memory may have been affected, which isn't unusual. Sometimes a blow to the head will leave someone feeling vague for a few hours or days."

She caught the movement of the tall man when he stepped away from the table, and then she heard his deep, resonant voice.

"Are you saying she has amnesia?"

The doctor gazed into her eyes. "Can you tell me your name?"

"Why, of course . . . it's . . ." Tess fought to clear the cobwebs cluttering her mind. "It's . . . no." She shook her head. "No, I . . . I'm not sure."

"Well, don't be concerned." Doc patted her hand reassuringly. "I'm going to give you something to make you rest. You've taken quiet a blow to the head, and the best thing you can do right now is sleep. Perhaps when you wake up your memory will have cleared."

Another man stepped into her line of vision, holding his hat in his hands. Were all the men here, wherever she was, massive?

"*Ma chère,* do you remember me?"

Tess peered up at the handsome man with a French accent, her eyes growing heavy with fatigue. Did she know him? Yes . . . no. She'd never seen this man in her life. "No. I'm sorry." She liked his gentle smile.

"I am André. You gave me quite a scare, *ma petite.* I am the one who pulled you from the river."

"Oh . . . it was you . . ." She felt weak as

she reached out to clasp his hand. "Thank you so kindly. I owe you a debt I can never repay."

Holding her hand as though it were a rare treasure, André smiled down at her reassuringly. "My pleasure, *ma chère.* You will feel better very soon."

The doctor lifted her head, and she willingly took a sip of the sedative from the cup he offered. She watched André step toward the dark-haired man who stood close by. When Doc eased her head back onto the pillow, she tried to smile. "Thank you."

"You're welcome. You should sleep for several hours."

André put his hat on his head. "Jake, I must return to work. The men are still looking for the others. You will check back with me later?"

The man André called Jake silently nodded. She wondered why he kept staring at her. She must look a fright.

"Lannigan, if I can prevail upon you to stay with Miss Yardley for a moment, I'd like to get a cup of coffee." The doctor rolled down the cuffs of his sleeves. "Do you mind?"

"No, Doc. I'll stay with her."

As Jake pulled up a chair, Tess struggled to stay awake, but before the curtain fell into place behind Doc, she felt herself losing the fight and drifted off to sleep.

Jake studied the small form on the table. *Well, hello, Miss Yardley . . . or could you possibly be Miss Wakefield?* What if she was? André and Bernice had everyone assuming that Fedelia Yardley had survived the accident, but what if they were mistaken?

He knew it was a logical assumption, considering the luggage found and the fact that Tess Wakefield had never provided an arrival date. Her latest letter mentioned she planned to come to Michigan, and for all he knew she could have left the same day. It seemed unlikely, but who knew what she would do? It would be just like the flighty woman to show up without bothering to inform anyone of her impending arrival.

He studied the sleeping beauty's features. She was too pretty to be that unlikable, so this couldn't be Wakefield's granddaughter. He shrugged. He really had no way of knowing who she was for certain.

He chuckled when he imagined how Miss Philadelphia-Born-and-Bred Wakefield would cotton to the job of trying to teach school to nine of the meanest children he'd ever met. Wouldn't that be proper payback for Miss High-and-Mighty?

58

He folded his arms, thinking about that. If she became the new teacher and then regained her memory, she'd be as mad as a wet hen. But he could honestly plead innocence with only a slight twinge of conscience because the thought had only crossed his mind.

His eyes narrowed, and he couldn't think of anyone who more deserved a lesson in humility. If this was Tess, it was high time a woman like her was introduced to the real world. Obviously, she didn't care about others' welfare. Still, if he found out for sure that she was Wakefield's granddaughter and had perpetrated a fraud, he'd have to answer to God as well as to her.

The thought didn't set right with him. He didn't hold with lying. Yet for all he knew, this *was* Fedelia Yardley, and until someone told him different he wasn't going to sweat it. The lumberjacks' workload was heavy, and though the camp needed the new telegraph up and running, he couldn't spare the manpower for that right now. Maybe in a few days they would be able to work on it again, and then the women's identity could be verified.

A grin pulled at the corners of Jake's mouth when he thought about Tess having to earn her way in the world for a change.

Wouldn't that be something? Miss Tess Wakefield believing she was Fedelia Yardley? A pampered little rich girl, who had probably never done a lick of real work in her entire self-centered life, forced to cope with the likes of Pud Wilkerson and Modeen Menson? He laughed out loud at the image.

The woman's eyes momentarily fluttered open. He quieted instantly. "Sorry, ma'am. I didn't mean to disturb you."

She smiled and drifted off again.

She would most likely regain her memory, but how long would that take? And what if the other woman's body washed up? It could take weeks before the remains were identified — if then.

The river had a way of taking care of debris. Miss Yardley's application had indicated she had no living relatives, so no one would be looking for her.

But Tess did. She had Talbot Wellington-Kent. He would be wondering what happened, and he would ask questions.

Jake's thoughts sobered. What if Tess Wakefield were dead? It would be a sad turn of affairs. Rutherford had always treated Jake right, and the old man had loved his only grandchild. But he was gone now, and until this mystery was solved Jake had his employees' welfare to consider. For as long as he could, he'd make sure their jobs were protected, and, in the meantime, he might plant a few pines here and there to prove to someone a hundred years down the line that at least one person had cared about the next generation.

Once Talbot Wellington-Kent found out Miss Wakefield was deceased, he'd sell the timber operation for sure. From everything he knew about him, Jake felt certain there would be no way of convincing the man of anything different.

The doctor returned to the cubicle carrying a steaming cup. "Everything all right?"

Jake smiled. "She seems to be resting quietly."

"That's what I'd hoped. Much obliged. I'll sit and drink my coffee and keep a close watch on the new schoolteacher." Doc lowered his voice. "Bernice is having an attack of the vapors worrying about her."

Jake nodded. "Bernice would bust a corset if anything happened to the new teacher."

5

Tess forced her heavy lids open and squinted against the sunlight streaming through a lone window. Her hand came up to protect her sensitive eyes.

She was lying in a room she'd never been in before. She cautiously moved her fingers. Through a dull haze she was able to focus on the young woman who stood beside the bed, pouring hot liquid into a tin cup. When the girl noticed her stare, she smiled.

"Good morning, ma'am. I hope you slept well?"

"Very well, thank you." Tess's gaze traveled around the unfamiliar room. Her head throbbed. A dull, pounding ache was centered deep in the base of her neck. The scent of vanilla drifted to her when the girl leaned down to fluff her pillows.

Tess eased into a sitting position. The effort left her head spinning. Next to her bedside table was a tray with a plate of thick sausage patties and a mound of golden-brown hotcakes swimming in syrup, and she put her hand over her mouth.

The young woman swiftly removed the tray and noted brightly, "Maybe we'd better wait a bit until your stomach settles."

Tess nodded gratefully, fighting waves of nausea washing over her. Her head sank back onto the pillow, and she closed her eyes. She felt so weak. "Where am I?"

"Wakefield Timber camp. The wagon that brought you here lost a wheel, and you were thrown in the river. Those old things have always been a worry, but Doc says you'll be good as new in a couple of weeks."

Tess slowly opened her eyes again, fighting sleep. Wakefield Timber. The name sounded vaguely familiar, but . . . "I don't remember." Actually, she couldn't remember anything except waking up in the doctor's office and then promptly going back to sleep after being given a strong sedative. "Were there others . . . ?"

The girl turned to pick up a third pillow. "I'm afraid the other passengers were swept downstream."

Heartsick, Tess gazed at the young woman. "I'm so sorry."

"The doctor doesn't want you thinking about that right now."

"I see."

The girl's voice brightened when Tess reached to squeeze her hand. "My name is Echo Burne. My husband is a river hog. I've been sent to look after you until you're on your feet again. You be needing anything, anything at all, Miss Yardley, and I'll come running."

"Thank you, Echo. You're very kind." Although comprehension was a chore, Tess sensed she'd just made a new friend.

Noticing that the light seemed to be bothering the invalid, the girl moved away from the bed to adjust the window curtain. Tess studied her. She was young, maybe eighteen or nineteen, with large, expressive blue eyes and a liberal sprinkling of freckles across the bridge of her nose. The simple cotton dress she was wearing was drab and threadbare but clean.

The throb in her head intensified when Tess struggled to recall the accident. Nothing came to mind. Even her name failed to register with her. Yardley? Somehow that didn't sound right, yet it had a familiar ring to it. "Echo, you called me Miss Yardley."

"Yes . . . oh . . ." Returning to the bed, Echo reached for her hand and held it. "Now, don't you be worrying your pretty head about a thing. Doc says you might be

64

a tad fuzzy about the accident for a while, but it's nothing to be concerned about."

Tess frowned, trying to remember. "That's my name? Yardley?"

"Yes, ma'am, that it is. Fedelia Yardley. You're the new schoolmarm."

"I am?" The frown deepened. Somehow that didn't sound right either. "Are you certain?"

"Yes, ma'am." Echo straightened the sheets. "The camp folk were sure enough relieved to learn you were spared."

Tess found the girl's words disturbing somewhere deep inside, but why? Her mind failed to register anything, yet she couldn't believe she was a schoolteacher when she didn't even know her name.

Echo went about her work as Tess tried to come to grips with her unsettling situation. She focused on the immediate situation. "What sort of place is this?"

"A timber camp. Not many of the jacks bring their wives to live here, but we do have some families. Mr. Lannigan sees that their kids get proper schooling. He says if children are properly educated, they will more likely get ahead in life."

"Mr. Lannigan?"

"Yes, ma'am. Jake Lannigan. He's Big Say — foreman of Wakefield Timber. He oversees the whole camp."

Tess sighed. So many strange names and faces, but she faintly remembered that Jake was the name of the giant she saw yesterday with the hazel eyes. "Well, I suppose it will be a few days before I'm able to take over my teaching duties."

"Yes, ma'am. Doc says in a couple of weeks you should be fit as a fiddle."

"Is there someone who could help until I've recuperated? The pupils shouldn't unduly suffer because I am indisposed."

Echo steadfastly refused to meet her gaze this time.

"Um . . . no, ma'am. Bernice, she quit teaching some years back, but she's been filling in lately, and she declares she don't want to do that any longer. Not ever, actually. She wants to stay home and take care of her Hubert. The weather's getting mean, so I'd say they'll close school until you're ready to take over."

"Oh? Well, maybe something can be worked out," Tess mused. "I wouldn't want to disappoint the children by having their studies interrupted."

"No, ma'am, but don't you fret none. I'm sure they'll do just fine — well, I don't know that for certain but . . ." She flashed a smile. "You just concentrate on getting your strength back."

Their conversation was interrupted when a knock sounded. The door opened and a man stepped inside. Tess immediately recognized the dark-haired man they called Jake. Echo's face broke into a bright smile.

"Morning, Big Say."

"Morning, Echo."

"Miss Yardley's doing real fine. I was just about to persuade her to eat a bite."

Jake Lannigan strode across the room toward Tess, his boots scraping the wooden floor. As she watched him approach her bed, she couldn't help but feel awed by such an impressive specimen of manhood. Large and uncommonly muscular, he carried his splendid steel-girded body with the authority of someone long accustomed to giving orders.

When he reached her bedside, their gazes met, and Tess felt a shiver race down her spine. Peering into his eyes, she wondered if she had ever met a more compelling or handsome man. His sheer size dominated the room.

"Good morning. I trust you're feeling stronger today."

His voice was deep and resonant, the way she remembered it from the day before. "Much better, thank you." For some reason, she wanted a mirror to check her appearance.

"I trust you're comfortable?"

"Yes, I am. Everyone has been most kind."

He extended his hand. "Jake Lannigan's the name. I was in the doctor's office yesterday."

His grasp devoured hers. "I remember." The brief contact sent a tingle up her arm. He quickly stepped back from the bed, but his warmth lingered on her skin.

"Is there anything I can do to make you more comfortable?"

"No. Echo's taking good care of me. I'll be fine."

"Your memory hasn't returned?"

"No."

"That's too bad. Doc thinks it will, eventually."

"I'm sure I'll have it back in no time at all." She heaved a sigh and then attempted to offer a smile. "It all seems so strange. Does anyone have any idea where I lived or where I taught or what my life was like before I agreed to come to Wakefield camp? Has my family been notified about the accident?" She looked down at her left hand. "I'm not wearing a ring, so I assume I'm single."

His gaze also shifted to her ring finger.

"Your résumé states that you are. Unfortunately, it also said you have no immediate family."

Her heart sank. Was she an orphan? There had to be someone who loved her. She'd know when her memory returned. She looked up and noted that the lumberjack's attention was still focused on her left hand, and he seemed to be deep in thought.

"Perhaps . . . perhaps my jewelry came off during the accident? A ring could be lying in the bottom of the river."

"I suggest you talk to André Montague. He could have more information. I wasn't at the accident site."

"André Montague? The Frenchman?"

"Yes. He was the one who pulled you out of the river yesterday."

"Of course. Thank you. I shall indeed consult with Mr. Montague. The man saved my life, so I must thank him from the bottom of my heart. He was very brave."

"Diving into that icy water took some grit," Jake agreed.

Her head was beginning to hurt, but she needed to address the subject of her students. "Mr. Lannigan, I was telling Echo that we'll have to do something about my pupils."

"What about them?"

"Well, I understand it will be a couple of weeks before I can assume my position. I would hate to think that school would be interrupted because of me."

"I wouldn't worry about it. Bernice will hold classes until you're feeling better. You rest up and get well."

"But I understand she is anxious to spend more time with her husband —"

"I've talked to her. She'll fill the position until the end of the month. You just concentrate on getting well. Meanwhile, I'll arrange for your living quarters. The last teacher preferred to stay with the Mensons at their store, but the arrangement cramped them. They don't have much living space." Turning to Echo, he said, "If she needs anything, stop by the office. If I'm not there, André will take care of it."

"Yes, Big Say."

Jake paused. "Has your husband been behaving himself, Echo?"

"Yes, sir. He's bein' real good."

"You're sure?"

Tess noted the way Echo's gaze avoided Jake's. The sudden change in his tone surprised her. It was sharper and more insistent.

"I'm sure."

Jake glanced at Tess and nodded. "I'll be

dropping by occasionally to see how you're progressing. You rest up."

His gaze focused on the third finger of her left hand once again, and she wondered why he was so mindful of the fact that she wasn't wearing a ring. A moment later the door closed behind him. "My, isn't he nice." Tess felt a sort of emptiness in the room after he had left.

"Yes, ma'am. He's a real gentleman," Echo agreed.

"I'm sure his wife must be very proud of him."

"Big Say isn't married."

"He isn't?"

"No, ma'am, but there are more than a few who would like to have him."

"Echo, I thought his name was Jake, so why do you call him Big Say?"

"We all call him that sometimes, but that's what his men call him because he's the boss."

She turned to fetch the tray as Tess settled her head on the pillow, wincing slightly from the pain. She could imagine the number of women who would like to have Jake Lannigan. She didn't find the thought all that disturbing herself. She'd never met a man as rugged or as overpoweringly male as this big lumberjack. Or at least she couldn't remember if she had. And he seemed good — perhaps he was even a man of God?

That was most important. She wasn't as good as she'd like to be, but she instinctively felt that she tried her best to obey the Good Book, and the man she would love would have to do the same.

Such silly thoughts. She was thinking about love and she didn't even know her own name. That blow had not just knocked her senseless . . . it had apparently knocked the sense right out of her.

6

"By yimminy, vhere is dat voman!"

Sven Templeton paced back and forth in Jake's office late Saturday afternoon, furious that Tess Wakefield still hadn't arrived.

"Doesn't she know dat Sven Templeton is a busy man? I can't spend half my life running to Vakefield Timber to see if she has finally gotten herself here. If dat young voman vants to sell her lumber company, den she had better be gettin' here!"

Leaving André to handle the volatile little Swede, Jake kept his head down and worked at his desk. Fedelia Yardley had been here for two weeks. She was finally well enough to move from Doc's house to her own quarters.

Was the woman Fedelia Yardley after all? Her mention of the lack of a ring had caught his attention that first morning he had visited her. If she was Tess Wakefield, she surely would have been sporting an engagement ring. Even though the river's current was swift, she hadn't been in it that long. He didn't think it would have stripped a ring from her finger.

"I do not know what to tell you, Sven," André said evenly. "I believe that Miss Wakefield will be here any day, but the weather has turned bad early. That could account for her absence."

"Vell," Sven jammed his hat back on his head, "if she ever decides to show up, tell her she has Sven Templeton in a pickle, by yimminy!" He slammed out of the office.

"I do not blame him for being upset," André muttered as he moved back to his desk. "What is keeping Rutherford's granddaughter? The weather is certainly a factor, but she should have been here by now."

Jake sent him a noncommittal glance and changed the subject. The longer it took for Miss Wakefield to show, the longer it would be till the business was sold. "Did you order the dynamite?"

André picked up a logbook and scanned the columns. "Yes, fifty pounds on Monday."

"That should do it."

"I do not understand this, Jake." André snapped the book shut. "You would think if she was so eager to sell Wakefield Timber

74

that she would be here by now."

Shrugging, Jake rose and reached for his mackinaw. "I'm in no hurry to see Sven get the property, are you?"

Sven Templeton lived by the round forty rule: Cut your own forty acres and all the forties around it. Jake had been pushing for legislation to make that dishonest practice illegal, but it was slow in coming.

"I cannot think of anyone who is eager to see Sven get his greedy hands on Wakefield Timber," André said, scratching his head. "But I still find it strange that Rutherford's granddaughter would delay for so long." He paused, frowning. "Say, *mon ami,* you do not suppose the other woman might have been her on that wagon instead of Burl Sutter's fiancée?"

Jake headed for the door. "Has Burl's woman arrived yet?"

"No." André chuckled. "And because we have not found a body, Burl is still a little . . . uneasy, shall we say? I think he's afraid it might not have been her. He admitted he was drunk and didn't know what he was doing the night he asked the lady from East Saginaw to marry him." André glanced up. "Going somewhere, Big Say?"

"I promised Doc that I would see Miss Yardley to her new quarters."

André's brows lifted. "Is she well enough to leave the doctor's care? She should not push her recovery."

"Doc says she's fully recovered except for her memory. Her fingers are still tender, but she's healed nicely."

Leaning back in his chair, André locked his hands behind his head, propped his feet upon his desk, and smiled. "Now, there is a beautiful woman, this magnificent school-teacher."

"If you say so." Jake had bigger problems at hand. The nagging thought that everyone could be mistaken wouldn't let up. What if it had been Tess Wakefield on that wagon? The notion had crossed his mind more than once the past couple of weeks, but there was absolutely no proof she was Rutherford's granddaughter, and there was proof she was Fedelia Yardley — if you could call a couple of bags with her initials and a few textbooks proof.

He should probably make the new telegraph a main concern. "How's the work coming on the telegraph line?" He'd saddled André with so much extra work the past couple of weeks that finishing the line had become low priority.

"Slow. The workload and winds are so heavy we've been unable to make much

76

progress on it." The Frenchman's grin widened. "Ah, you are avoiding my question. Do you claim you have not noticed the new schoolteacher's beauty, my friend?"

"Can't say that I have." Jake rested his hand on the doorknob. "Don't forget to put a couple of icers on the new south tote road tonight."

"This I have already done."

Even as they spoke, the requested sled was being harnessed to a team. Its square, strongly built wooden tank could hold up to a hundred gallons of water, allowing the teamsters to ice the sleigh road at night, making it easier for the work crews to slide the logs out of the forest the following day and for the men to get around.

"I shouldn't be long." Jake adjusted his wool cap, wishing he could stay in the warm office. Though the sun was shining, the day was raw and bitterly cold.

"I am happy to offer my services and show Miss Yardley to her quarters," André said, still grinning.

"There's no reason I can't."

"Where will you put her?"

"I had a couple of men fix up a small area this morning. It's not much, but it's comfortable." Comfortable enough, anyway. The Mensons had asked for different accommodations for the new teacher.

"Ah, *oui?* And where is that?"

Jake avoided his friend's eyes. "Does it matter?" The question went unanswered when Bernice opened the door to the office and stormed in.

"Oh, good. There you are," she said crisply.

Jake shot a glance at the still smiling André and then focused back on the woman. "I'm sorry, but I'm on my way out —"

The substitute schoolteacher ignored Jake's attempt at a hasty departure. "I assume you're on your way to assist Miss Yardley in getting settled?"

"Yes, Bernice —"

"Good." She removed her gloves. "Then Miss Yardley will be able to assume her teaching duties Monday morning."

"If the doctor —"

"I've already spoken to the doctor. He informs me the young woman is in robust health."

Jake eased a step backward when Bernice took two steps forward. He was trapped.

"I have done more than my share by consenting to teach these past two weeks, thereby allowing Miss Yardley sufficient time to recuperate."

"Yes, Bernice," Jake repeated, trying to be patient.

"Consequently, I shall expect to be officially relieved of my teaching duties this afternoon at the end of the school day."

"If Miss Yardley is prepared —"

"Of course Miss Yardley is prepared! She's a teacher, isn't she?"

Jake shrugged. What André said earlier had struck a nerve. He realized he'd been trying to convince himself the woman couldn't be anyone but Fedelia Yardley, but the truth was she could be Tess Wakefield. From the beginning he'd noticed the woman's fine looks and her slight resemblance to Rutherford Wakefield.

He almost grinned. If she was Tess Wakefield, he was fixing to house her in a place no woman would ever accept. He felt a sharp poke on his shoulder that drew him from his thoughts.

"Are you listening to me?"

"Yes, Bernice."

"Then it's settled. I assume you have provided comfortable quarters for the new teacher?"

"I've done my best." Jake said. He should amend that statement to say that he'd done the best his conscience would allow, under the circumstances.

"Very well. I'll be running along. I want to make my Hubert a nice supper to celebrate. Venison stew always brightens his day."

"Yes, ma'am."

Suddenly, Bernice was inches from Jake's face, wagging her finger at him. He knew a storm was brewing and drew back defensively.

"This afternoon is the end, Jake Lannigan."

"Yes, Bernice. This afternoon."

Straightening, she smiled. "Thank you." She began pulling on her gloves while she walked to the door. "I feel sorry for our dear Miss Yardley, you know."

"Oh?" Jake had never known Bernice to feel pity toward anyone.

"Once she spends a week in the classroom with those hooligans, I suspect she'll develop an affinity with the barracuda."

Jake lifted an expectant brow. "The barracuda?"

"Yes." Bernice snapped the door open and her eyes met his. "They eat their young."

7

Slowly turning in front of the mirror, Tess's eyes were fixed in horror on the dress she had just put on. It was so drab — and uninspired.

"Mercy me," she murmured. She couldn't imagine anyone actually choosing this color or material.

"The dress and coat you were wearing when André pulled you from the river were muddy and badly torn," Echo said as she folded a pile of discarded dresses and placed them back in the valises. "I tried to repair the garments, but I'm afraid they ended up in the scrap pile. You lost your shoes too. You weren't wearing any when André brought you to Doc's."

"Hmm . . ." Tess studied her reflection. "Do you favor this color, Echo?" Though the dress fit well enough, the fabric brought to mind a garment of dirt. Dirt with buttons.

"I . . . I can't say I care for that particular shade." Turning back to the bed, Echo said softly, "I'm sure going to miss you, ma'am."

"Why should you miss me? I'll still be here." Tess wasn't sure where her new quarters would be, but she was confident Jake Lannigan would make sure she was comfortable. He had been such a gentleman the past two weeks, stopping by to visit at least three times a week. Sneaking a final glance at the mirror, she edged away.

"Oh, I know I'll still be seeing you, but it won't be the same as coming here every day to take care of you." Echo's voice trailed off shyly.

Over the past couple of weeks she and the young girl had formed a solid bond, and she was beginning to believe Echo had been starved for friendship. The other married women in camp were older and had children. Echo and Waite had none.

Echo mentioned that Waite Burne was fifteen years her senior. From what Tess gathered, he was a possessive and jealous man who wanted his young wife to spend her time and energies on pleasing only him. Echo, being a gentle, simple girl, had no doubt been eager to oblige, yet she suspected that the days Echo had spent with her had made the young wife realize how much she wanted companionship with a woman close to her own age.

Tess crossed the room, put her arm around her new friend, and gave her a reassuring hug. "Don't worry. We'll see each other every day. Why, you're the best — and only — friend I have, Echo." The girl was so slim that Tess could feel her bony shoulders protruding from her slender body.

She offered a smile. "And you're my only friend, ma'am. Until you came here, I rarely visited with the other women. Waite isn't a churchgoer, so we don't socialize much."

"Now, haven't I asked you not to call me ma'am?" Tess made a playful face at her. "Friends call each other by their given names." She sighed. Her given name still sounded so odd to her. "Please, call me Fedelia." A timid but proud smile was threatening to overcome Echo's usually serious features. She was such a sweet girl.

"Yes, ma'am . . . Fedelia. I surely will."

The young woman had been a virtual godsend since the accident. Tess had been confused and weepy at times, terrified at others, but Echo had been her strong and reassuring anchor over the past couple of weeks. She had made Tess believe her words of encouragement, or she didn't think she would have made it through the long days and nights of uncertainty.

Echo went to the window and peered out. "Big Say is coming up the trail."

"Now?" Tess turned away from the mirror. Something about her clothes was so puzzling. "He can't be! It's too early!"

Every time the camp foreman came to see her, she grew more enamored of him. Though he rarely smiled, on the occasions when he did her pulse thumped as wildly as a trapped moth.

"He can't see me in this dress!" Glancing around the room, she spied the two half-filled valises. "Quick, Echo, hand me another garment!" Even as she said it, she knew from sorting through the valises that everything she owned was as unbecoming and drab as the dress she was wearing.

Echo rushed to retrieve something else, and a moment later the brown dress was hastily discarded in favor of a dark green. This color added an unbecoming yellow tinge to her skin, but she had little choice. She pinched her cheeks to add a bit of pink.

Jake's knock sounded at the door. Echo glanced to Tess for permission to answer, and she hurriedly nodded her consent. She waited for the young woman to open the door, but Echo's hand paused on the knob, her gaze anxiously skimming Tess's newest garment. "Ma'am . . ."

"Fedelia. Now, we mustn't keep Mr. Lannigan waiting!" Her hands came up to nervously fuss with her hair. "Oh, dear, I do so want to make a good impression."

The camp foreman could be a bit distant, and today Tess wanted him to show her even the tiniest sign that he recognized her as a woman.

Echo obediently opened the door. "Afternoon, Big Say."

Tess barely noticed the gust of icy air that followed Jake into the room. His mere presence made her feel warm and safe.

"Good afternoon, ladies."

"Mr. Lannigan, how nice to see you." She swept across the room graciously and extended her hand. "I'm afraid you've caught us dawdling." Giving him what she thought might be her prettiest smile, she confessed, "I hope you won't be inconvenienced, but I'm not quite finished packing."

He took the hand she offered and bowed from the waist. "I'm in no hurry. Please, take all the time you need."

As usual, the deep, rich timbre of his voice sent her pulse flapping. When he straightened, she was startled to see his gaze discreetly fasten on the front of her dress and then skip away.

85

Ugly. The garment was just plain ugly. Where was her flare? Her sense of taste? Why didn't she have one pretty thing to wear?

She soothed her wounded vanity with the satisfaction that at last she had captured his eye. "Aren't we fortunate to have such a lovely afternoon to make our move?" She allowed the smallest hint of flirtation to seep into her voice.

He nodded. "The weather could have been worse."

"I hope I'm not keeping you? I know a man like you must have better things to do than see me to my living quarters."

"No, I'm looking forward to it." He flashed a smile. "I hope you'll be comfortable."

"Well, if you'll excuse me, I'll only be a moment." She returned his smile, pleased he'd said he wanted to escort her.

"I'll wait outside."

His gaze briefly skimmed her again before he turned away. A moment later he opened the door and stepped through it. Leaning against the closed door, her eyes drifted shut and a long, wistful sigh escaped her. "Isn't he just about the most handsome man you have ever seen?" Being in the same room with this big man turned her insides to a quivering mass.

Feeling as if she were very young again, Tess clasped her fingers around her arms and whirled around the room. Had she ever reacted this way before? No, it was not possible. Jake Lannigan was not like any man she'd ever met, she was sure of it. "Do you think he noticed me, Echo?"

"Oh, yes. I'm sure."

"Really noticed me?"

Echo nodded. "Yes, ma'am."

She stopped twirling and felt her face flush. "Honestly?" To have a man like Jake Lannigan look at her — *really* look at her the way a man looks at a woman who has seriously piqued his interest — well, it would make the past two frustrating weeks worthwhile. Losing her memory had been unfortunate, but she wondered if it was possible that the accident happened for a divine purpose. Had God sent her here to find a husband?

Just as Jake's eyes had done, Echo's gaze dropped to the front of Tess's dress. "Ma'am, your buttons . . ."

Tess glanced down. Her jaw dropped and her cheeks flamed when she discovered the reason for Lannigan's attention. In her haste she had buttoned the dress incorrectly. The lopsided mishap was a sight to behold.

Groaning with embarrassment, Tess's hands came up to cover her face.

"Oh, don't you be worrying, ma'am," Echo soothed. "Big Say — he won't think anything about this. He's a real gentleman."

Tess wasn't worried about what he would say. She felt sure he wouldn't deliberately point out what an idiot she had just made of herself. She prayed for a hole in the floor to open up and swallow her alive. At this instant Jake Lannigan must be outside rolling in the snow with amusement, and she had to walk out there and face him. She hastily redid the buttons.

A few minutes later, draped in a heavy, shapeless brown coat, she reluctantly slipped out the doctor's front door. Taking a deep breath, she squared her shoulders and prepared to defend the ridiculous spectacle she'd just made of herself.

Jake was leaning against the trunk of a tree when she came out. When he saw her, he straightened and reached out to take the two valises from her hands.

"All ready?"

"Yes." Tess could feel the blood rushing to her face, but mercifully she managed to avoid his gaze. Moments later she found herself trailing behind him, trying to keep up with his long-legged strides. There was no need to worry about having to explain the unfortunate carelessness to him. The incident seemed to have escaped his mind. Apparently, he was intent on delivering her to her destination with as little socializing as possible.

She gradually became aware of her surroundings when she followed him down the planked sidewalk. "Echo tells me that not all logging camps are alike. She mentioned something about haywire camps. What does that mean?"

Jake slowed down a little to let her catch up. "Echo was talking about fly-by-night operations strung together with hay wire. Other operations are larger and better managed. Wakefield Timber is one of those."

Tess detected the note of pride in his tone. "Echo said this logging camp is almost a little town in itself."

"It's pretty good sized."

When they passed a small building, she read aloud a sign posted in the window. "Mitts, Woolen Socks, Tobacco, and Hinckley's Bone Liniment for Man or Beast."

Jake nodded. "Menson's Store. Everything a man needs. It's also the town gathering spot for the jacks when they're between shifts."

"What about the women?" she asked. His

89

gaze swung around to meet hers, and for an instant the atmosphere felt so charged that Tess forgot to breathe. Her footsteps slowed.

"There are not many women in camp, but a woman can buy necessities there. We have a few jacks who live with their wives, but this is mostly a man's world. You'd best keep that in mind."

She broke eye contact first to glance at the windows above the store. It looked as though living quarters were up there. "Is that where I'm staying?"

"No. That's my room."

He crossed the street and she followed without a word, mystified by his sudden mood change. He seemed a little grumpy now. She glanced at the half dozen buildings that lined the block as they walked past the camp office, the huge horse barn, the hay barn, the icehouse, the blacksmith shop, the pig house, the chicken house, and the root cellar. It seemed as though they were going in circles, but she continued to follow. Wakefield Timber was indeed a large operation.

Excessively cold wind whipped at her clothing, and she drew the heavy wool closer around her. She assumed that the next building they came upon was a cookshack because the air around it was filled with the mouthwatering aroma of pies baking in the oven.

Stepping off the sidewalk, Jake led her onto a small path that wound through towering stands of white pine. A tangy, spicy aroma from the woods filled the air as Tess scrambled to keep up with him.

Overhead, trees soared to breathtaking heights, their branches outstretched to touch the blue of the majestic sky. She glanced about in awe, fascinated with the sheer beauty surrounding her. The lofty trunks and Jake Lannigan's imposing height made her feel as if she were an insignificant speck dotting the forest floor.

After a while she noticed a steady chopping sound. Tess slowed and then stopped altogether to tilt her chin upward. She shaded her eyes as she squinted up into the bright afternoon light. A man was sitting in the top of a tree some two hundred feet off the ground.

Jake noticed that she had paused, and he followed her gaze. "He's a high climber. Ever seen one before?"

"I . . . no, I don't think so," she whispered. She heart was filled with childlike wonder.

Shielding his eyes from the sun, Jake said, "That's Lane Garrettson."

The man leaned back into a rope and

began to cut with sure, swift strokes. "What is the rope for?"

"That's called a life rope. It helps secure him. See what he's doing? That's called the back cut. He's using a one-man crosscut saw."

She stood transfixed, almost afraid to breathe for fear it would unseat the man. Prickles of apprehension shot down her spine, and her heart pounded in her chest as she watched the young daredevil go about his work.

She knew little about lumberjacking, but in the past weeks Echo had educated her some. The thought of hanging by a rope on the side of a tree that height made Tess light-headed. "How can he do that?" she murmured, moving closer to Jake and feeling protected when she was near him.

"Do what?"

Tess peered up at him in disbelief. "Climb a tree that size and . . . and start cutting it!"

"It's his job. Stand back."

She watched the man set his spikes deeper in the trunk and wait. The crown of the tree started to lean. The jack let the saw drop. "Timberrrrrr!"

"What's he doing now?" she whispered.

"He's waiting."

"For what?"

"For the tree to fall."

"Doesn't he know how dangerous that is?"

"He knows. If the crown doesn't sever completely and splits the trunk when it topples, his lifeline will pull him into the tree. That can break a man's back or kill him instantly."

"And he's up there knowing that?" Tess was horrified but powerless to turn away.

The air was filled with a sharp cracking and splintering as the top of the tree hurtled to the ground, propelling the young man outward in a violent thirty-degree arc. She clamped her eyes shut and put her hands to her mouth to stifle a scream. She was going to be sick. Why hadn't she looked away so she would have been spared the appalling spectacle of a man falling to his death!

Jake turned to face her. "What's wrong?"

Tess screamed out loud this time, and her terrified cry ricocheted throughout the thick forest, unaware that the noise would still axes and men would cease work to identify the strange high-pitched squeal reverberating through the woods.

She could visualize the broken, bleeding body of the fellow lying at the base of the tree. "He's dead, isn't he?" she asked, with eyelids still pressed closed.

Jake glanced back up. "Who's dead?"

Her lids flew open. She glanced at Jake, her mouth gaping with amazement. A man had plunged headlong to his death, and Jake Lannigan hadn't noticed? "That man who was . . ." Her voice trailed when she looked up to see the jack disconnect his safety gear, climb to the flat top of the tree and stand, his arms spread wide with victory as he gave a cocky grin to the crew working below him.

She gasped. "Why . . . he's alive!"

Jake continued down the path. "He wasn't ever in trouble."

"You mean that happens every time a man cuts off the top of a tree?"

"Every single time."

"I can't imagine anyone in his right mind willing to go through such a frightening experience!" She paused. Suddenly it seemed as though they had walked for hours. "How much farther is it? I'm very cold."

"Not much farther."

Why would any woman, who apparently had held a perfectly good teaching position in Philadelphia, have given up a warm and secure life? She purportedly had been of her mind as recently as two short weeks ago.

Tess wished she could remember. Had her life been so terrible that she'd decided to come to a remote Michigan lumber camp to work? A place filled with men who calmly faced imminent death every day?

She blew out her breath in a frosty plume. Apparently she'd lost her mind at some point prior to the accident.

8

Threatening clouds ballooned in the west when they finally reached Tess's new quarters. Jake set the two bags on the ground and waited for her to catch up. He listened to the heavy rustling in the thicket behind him, aware that Miss Yardley — who, he was becoming increasingly more convinced, was Miss High-and-Mighty Wakefield — was having a hard time keeping up with him.

Grinning, he relished the thought of how furious she'd be if her memory returned and she discovered she wasn't Fedelia Yardley. He'd wager Tess Wakefield could pitch a fit if she wanted to, and he had no doubt she would want to if she found out he'd had the slightest suspicions of her identity from day one and had not seen fit to mention them to her.

The more he was around the woman, the more he was certain his suspicions were right, that she was Wakefield's granddaughter, though he had no explanation as to why she wasn't wearing an engagement ring. Maybe she'd broken off the engagement. Maybe she'd left her expensive jewelry at home.

How she'd come here this fast he couldn't say, but he'd wager a month's wages this woman had never taught school a day in her life. She'd been confused when the doc had asked her to fill out papers for his files. He'd had to spell F-E-D-E-L-I-A twice for her.

"Are you okay, Miss Yardley? Do you need help?"

"Absolutely not!"

She sounded anything but okay. So many questions were going through his mind. Was he having a guilty conscience because he hadn't revealed the fact of who she might really be? Was he playing a game to keep the beautiful Miss Wakefield not knowing who she was so she wouldn't sell? He'd never thought of himself as a scoundrel, but now he had real doubts about his intentions.

If they were still betrothed, Talbot Wellington-Kent would be having kittens wondering what happened to his fiancée. The man wasn't stupid. And he was rich. He'd find a way to make inquiries with or without a telegraph line.

Then, and only then, would Jake tell her and her intended what he thought of their notion to sell Wakefield Timber to Sven Templeton. After that, he planned to walk out on her and leave her high and dry. She would be in one fine mess for weeks.

If this woman was Tess, maybe he could convince her that selling to Templeton was wrong. Then, when she regained her memory, she'd change her mind about pine. The thought was enough for him to keep silent. No real harm would be done to Miss Wakefield, and she might even learn a lesson in humility.

God, forgive me for keeping this to myself, but this earth is Your creation, and I'd like to keep it the way You created it.

He glanced up when she emerged at last from the thick undergrowth, muttering under her breath. Her hair was matted with pine needles, and the wind had stung her face a raspberry red. All signs of her earlier enthusiasm for the adventure had disappeared. He straightened when she glared at him, replacing his grin with a sober expression.

"I hope the walk hasn't been too tiring for you, ma'am." He'd taken her on a bit of a wild goose chase to see if she had any grit, and now he almost felt guilty for doing it. Almost.

"I'm getting a blister!"

"Please accept my condolences."

She stared down at her feet, and Jake knew she was trying to force herself to remain pleasant. Her face looked cold enough that if she tried to smile, her features might shatter into a million pieces. She ripped off her gloves and tried to blow warmth back into the tips of her stinging fingers.

"There was a shorter route," he admitted.

"Oh? Then why didn't we take it?"

"I thought you might enjoy a brief tour of camp."

"Camp? I didn't even see the camp. It was more like a tour of the entire Upper Peninsula." Snatching pine needles from her hair, she threw them to the ground.

She was right. If they had taken the normal route, they would have walked around the back of Doc Medifer's office and been at their destination in less than two minutes, but that would have been too easy on her. He wanted to make it as tough on the woman as possible. If she was Rutherford's kin, she'd handle it, spoiled or not. "Ever been in a logging camp, ma'am?"

"Never. And right now I don't care if I

ever see another one."

"You're unhappy with your new position so soon?" He stepped up to the heavy door to her new quarters . . . in the bunkhouse. "Well, I suppose most people don't know or don't much care where their lumber comes from as long as it keeps coming. They want their bridges, homes, barns, fences, and big, fine carriages. It doesn't matter to them that folks are destroying the land to get the timber."

The remark sounded a bit extreme, yet he was a man with strong opinions. She should, by this point, be feeling the same concern about the waste clearly in front of her eyes, but sore feet seemed to be the burning issue. She stood on one foot as she tried to rub the other.

"But then, I imagine timber would be the last thing you would worry about." He dismissed the subject and opened the door to reveal a tiny room. "Welcome home."

She squinted and then stared into the dim, confined, windowless space, and her reaction made him grin. But as soon as she glanced at him, he grew serious again.

"Excuse me?"

"I said welcome home. This is your new room."

My new room, she silently mouthed. He

wasn't sure what she had expected, but this wasn't it. Though a look of horror registered on her wind-chapped features, her beauty was still evident.

"Sorry I couldn't put you somewhere that would allow more privacy and space, but I guess you can always look at it this way" — his smile returned, and it felt almost friendly — "you'll have close neighbors."

She managed a wan smile in return. "I have no idea what you're talking about."

Picking up her valises, he motioned for her to go ahead of him. "You have a private door leading to the outside, but there's also a door going to the inside of the building. I doubt you'll use it, but it's there if you ever need it. Go on."

Giving him a look a teacher might give an unruly student, she obliged. The facial rebuke was so hard-hearted that he realized this very well might be the new school-marm. Once inside the room, he opened a second door to reveal the crew's sleeping quarters.

The room was long and narrow, with rough board bunks, three tiers high, set around the walls. Each bunk was filled with straw and covered with a heavy wool blanket. On every bed a grain sack served as a pillow, and by the thick lumps in them Jake supposed she would figure out that the jacks stowed their personal belongings inside the cases. A large, black iron stove sat in the center, and above it, a string of wire was stretched across the entire length of the room.

"You must be kidding," Tess murmured. Her gaze roamed the room.

He knew she wanted to be assigned private quarters. There were a handful of married women in camp, but she was the only single female. He had to accommodate families first. "I'm afraid there's no room for a single woman in the camp, so I made do with what I had." He followed her down the long rows of bunks, her eyes running the length of the rough log walls chinked with mud and moss.

"Echo told me a few women were in camp . . ."

"They're all married."

She paused before turning around to face him. "But this room houses *men.*"

"They won't bother you. I'll have André move Fred Massey to the front bunk. Fred's a former preacher. He has three daughters of his own and sleeps with one eye open. You'll be as safe as a church mouse." He smiled and started back toward her room. "This is the best I can offer in these parts, ma'am."

"I'm to live here . . . with your crew."

Continuing to walk, he shrugged. "Not in *here*, precisely. What sort of man do you take me for? You have four walls and a private entrance, but I thought an inner door would be handy. If you encounter trouble or need anything, you'll have a hundred and twenty-five big, strapping men to help."

"You, sir, have clearly lost your mind."

They reached the end of the room, and he saw her turn to look back.

"My room's not much bigger than a rat hole," she whispered. Her eyes suddenly noticed a large cat lying on a nearby bunk.

He followed her gaze to the black fur ball that looked comfortable as all get out. "I'm aware your particular quarters aren't spacious, but your résumé said you would settle for anything comfortable." He met her eyes. "Did I misread that?"

"Well . . . I suppose if I said that . . ." Her eyes centered on the cat. "Does he live in my quarters?"

"She. If you want her to. Do you like animals?"

"I . . . I think so. But I don't think I've ever lived with one."

"Then you're in for a treat. Speaking of rats, Old Sweets here keeps the population

103

under control. She can sleep with you, if you'd like." He turned away when he noted her cheeks growing pale. He told himself there was no real need for her concern. Number one, she probably wouldn't be there that long. Nevertheless, Jake had given orders that his men stay clear of the new teacher. Fred would enforce the command. He trusted his men, plain and simple.

Number two, the new telegraph line would be working soon. After that they would know for certain if it had been Tess Wakefield or the Yardley woman who had survived the accident.

In the end, it would likely take Tess's fiancé to make the long trip to confirm a solid identity, and winter was setting in hard and fast this year. If this was the new schoolteacher, nothing would come of his ploy to show Miss Wakefield the value of restoring her property. He would simply be educating Miss Yardley on the subject.

The schoolmarm wouldn't stick around long anyway, once she got a look at her pupils. Not a one of them ever had. But if this was Miss Wakefield, she might learn something from the experience, and he wouldn't lose a night's sleep over the deception. Until he knew the truth, his crew's jobs were safe from the likes of Sven Templeton.

"Refresh my memory," she said, interrupting his thoughts. "Why should residing with a hundred and twenty-five men not concern me?"

"Because I've told them to leave you alone."

She burst into hysterical giggles and marched back through the remaining rows and into her room. He liked the sound of her laughter. It lightened the dim space.

"And that's supposed to make me feel better? You told a hundred and twenty-five barbarians, who probably haven't seen a single woman in months, to not bother me!"

"There are other women in camp —"

"No single women."

"No single ones, but a woman's a woman. The men are used to seeing them."

She slumped weakly down on the end of her cot, and he wondered if he was pushing her too hard her first day out of Doc's care.

She reached up to remove her bonnet. "How far is it to the school?"

"No more than a five-minute walk." Jake crossed his arms and leaned against the doorsill. "The men are having supper now. You might want to get settled before they come back. Later, you can go on over to the cookshack. Cookee will see that you get something to eat."

"I've lost my appetite."

"If you change your mind and need anything, you know where my office is."

"Actually, I don't have the slightest idea. We wound through the woods for so long. How will I find you?"

"Easy. Ask anyone and they will point you in my direction." Reaching into his breast pocket, he extracted a piece of paper and handed it to her. "By the way, here are the teacher rules. You should memorize them."

Unfolding the paper, Tess read them aloud.

1. Teacher will fill lamps and clean chimney in schoolhouse each day.
2. Teacher will bring a bucket of water and fill the wood box for the day's session.
3. Teacher will make pencils carefully and whittle nibs to the individual taste of the pupils.
4. Male teachers may take one evening each week for courting purposes, or two evenings a week if they go to church regularly.
5. After school hours, the teacher may spend the remaining time doing les-

sons or reading the Bible or other good books.

6. Female teachers who engage in unseemly conduct will be dismissed.

7. Every teacher should lay aside, from each pay, a goodly sum of his earnings for his benefit during his declining years so that he will not become a burden on society.

8. Any teacher who smokes, uses liquor in any form, or frequents pool or public halls will give the school board good reason to suspect his worth, intention, integrity, and honesty. Termination may follow.

9. The teacher who performs his labor faithfully and without fault for five years will be given an increase of twenty-five cents per week in his pay.

She glanced up.

"Any questions?" he asked. He watched her shake her head. "No? Most newcomers have a few."

She glanced back at the list of rules and shook her head a second time, but he couldn't read what was behind the blank look on her face.

"All right, then. Breakfast is four thirty sharp, dinner at noon, supper at five thirty. Weekdays, class starts at seven thirty a.m. It seems to work well for the students. See that you're there on time. The kids get rowdy if you aren't."

She nodded. "All right."

"By the way, you have permission to use a hickory switch . . . if you think you're big enough." With that he walked out and closed the door behind him.

Tess sat down on the cot, stunned. What had ever possessed her to come to Wakefield Timber camp?

I must have family. Everyone has family.

She angrily swiped at the moisture rolling down her cheeks, resenting a terrible, overpowering feeling of loneliness and desperation. She might not know who she was, but this feeling that engulfed her seemed so foreign, so wrong.

André would help her. At least he seemed civilized. She'd have him notify her family that she'd changed her mind about teaching and wished to return home. They would immediately comply with her request, and she'd be free from this frightening situation in a matter of days. She could tolerate anything short lived.

Pounding the thin mattress, she vented her frustrations while trying to even out some of the lumps. Eventually she lay down, closed her eyes, and forced herself to be calm. She would wake soon. She had to believe that. She must, or she felt that she would lose her mind.

Dear Lord, make this a bad dream. Wake me up. My family will be standing over me and we'll laugh at the insidious nightmares I've been having . . .

A gut-wrenching, overpowering stench made her sit straight up in bed. She fumbled for a handkerchief to place over her nose and mouth. The odor was nothing she recognized. Her tiny room suddenly felt suffocating.

When the loud, raucous sound of men's voices reached her, she realized that she must have fallen asleep. With a sinking heart, she surmised that all one hundred and twenty-five of her "close neighbors" were home.

Sliding from the cot, she kept the cloth pressed to her nose and fumbled for the inside doorknob with her right hand. She burst out of the small room gasping for a breath of fresh air, only to find none available.

When she abruptly appeared in the bunkhouse, more than a hundred pairs of male eyes swiveled to focus on her. The noise in the overheated, smoke-filled, steamy room quickly subsided.

Peering over the top of the handkerchief, she stared wide-eyed at the burly, rough-looking woodsmen who stared back at her, slack jawed.

When the silence closed in, her gaze traveled slowly around the room, trying to locate the source of the revolting stench. It didn't take long to figure out that it was coming from the wire strung above the stove and across the room, heavy with wet socks, mitts, and shoepacs.

Tess's gaze returned to fix on the men. They were so big. She had never witnessed such massive and steel-muscled brawn assembled under one roof. Her jaw dropped when she focused. Some had already peeled their clothes down to their heavy woolen underwear, while others still wore plaid wool shirts caked with grime and sweat, baggy woolen pants cut off midcalf, and worn leather boots.

Feeling slightly sick to her stomach, she realized she had to say something — had to explain why she had violated the sanctity of their private quarters.

Allowing the handkerchief to drop slowly

away from her nose, she flashed the sea of giants a timid smile and said hesitantly, "Hello. Uh . . . Mr. Lannigan said to expect you."

"Big Say?" returned a handful of deep male voices.

André recovered first, hurriedly snapping his suspenders back upon his shoulders while others reached for their pants. "*Excusez-moi,* Miss Yardley! We were not aware a woman was nearby."

"I . . . I'm sorry, but Mr. Lannigan said that I live here now."

"*Nous sommes si désolés.*"

"He said we are so sorry!" a jack supplied.

"I live in here." She gestured helplessly toward the hatbox that was to be her new home. "Really." She nodded as if it would help to confirm what she'd told them. "That's what your boss says."

"Big Say put you with *us?*"

She nodded and wondered why the men didn't know she was going to be there when Jake had specifically said he'd told them to leave her alone. Even André didn't seem to know, and he worked directly with the man. And what about Fred Massey, the man who was supposed to sleep with one eye open?

She had a few questions for Jake Lannigan.

111

"Uh . . . men." André cleared his throat. The others continued to stare. "Permit me to introduce Miss Yardley, the new school-marm."

A polite chorus of "Nice to meet ya, ma'am" followed.

Art Medford was the first to edge forward, swiping his hand down his pants leg before shyly extending it to her. "Welcome, ma'am. You'll have to excuse us. It's a shock to find a woman in the midst of the bunkhouse."

"I understand." She accepted the gesture of friendship. "It came as quite a shock to me too."

The jacks crowded around then, offering their callused hands and words of greeting. Tess took each chapped hand, grateful that the men were willing to accept the uncon-ventional situation they found themselves in, but she still thought they should really do something about the smell.

"I cannot imagine Big Say putting you here with us," André exclaimed.

She sighed. "Nor can I, but here I am." Her eyes traveled to her space, separate from the large room, it was true, but so . . . close. "Please don't let my presence bother you. I'm sure some of you have sisters or daughters. I promise to be as inconspicuous as possible." She would make certain that the men would be up and gone before she emerged from her room in the mornings. In the evenings she would eat her supper and then retire to her rat hole. She would simply have to make do until her family could rescue her from this dreadful situation.

"I suppose if this is where the boss wants you . . ." The Frenchmen's smile was sincere, but she suspected he was as puzzled by Lannigan's choice of housing as she.

"Have you had your supper, mademoiselle?"

"No, but I'm not hungry. I'm so exhausted that I just want to go to bed." She glanced expectantly toward the men. "If that's acceptable?" She wasn't sure if there was some procedure she'd be expected to follow. She'd never lived with a hundred and twenty-five men before. Absent memory or not, that much she was sure of.

"Yes, ma'am. Make yourself to home," one of the jacks said.

"Thank you, gentlemen." She turned and then seemed to change her mind. She walked back to André. "Oh, Mr. Montague?"

"*Oui*, mademoiselle." He smiled. "Please, *ma chère,* call me André."

Various hoots and catcalls broke out, and she felt color creep up the back of her neck.

"Do not mind them," André apologized, shooting the men a look of warning. "They are imbeciles, but they mean no disrespect."

A man stepped forward, a towering man with kind eyes. "I'm Fred, ma'am. I'll be right proud to sleep outside your door if 'n you need anything."

Scratching his head, André smiled. "So this is why Jake had you change bunks." He began to chuckle. "That is why he is Big Say. He knows what he is doing."

Tess was relieved to hear Jake had at least halfway warned the men. Perhaps he was thinking of her well-being. Her doubts were put to rest, but she still had questions, but not for Jake. "Mr. Montague — André, Mr. Lannigan thought you might be able to shed some light on my past."

The lumberjack's forehead knitted into a frown. "Jake said this?"

"I'd like to talk to you about my family sometime tomorrow, if that would be convenient?"

"I do not know more about you than Jake does, mademoiselle, but your résumé says you do not have close kin."

"None? No one at all? I'm alone?" She frowned at the sea of still bewildered faces.

"This is what your application says. I am most sorry."

114

"Thank you, André . . ." She managed a smile. "I think I'll be going to bed now."

"Good night, ma'am," the men chorused politely.

"Good night . . . and listen, I don't want to disturb your privacy either. You will tell me if I get in your way, won't you?"

"Yes, ma'am."

"Now, let's see . . . breakfast is at four thirty?"

"Yes, ma'am. Four thirty," André answered.

She nodded, and then she turned, walked into her room, and closed her door. Rummaging through a valise, she found a pair of shoes. She took one out and wedged the toe beneath the door.

Just to make certain Fred Massey did his job.

9

"Has Lannigan lost his mind?" Jim Carten sprang down from his bunk. "She can't live with us!"

Fifty jacks joined him and crowded around André the moment the door closed behind the schoolteacher.

"Be quiet!" André motioned for the men to lower their voices. "She will hear you."

"Don't make any difference," another jack said. "How are we gonna be expected to live with a woman in here? Has Big Say lost his mind?"

"André, Lannigan can't expect us to live with a woman!" said another man. "Why, we won't be able to cuss or even scratch where we got an itch. It just ain't fittin' for a woman to share a man's quarters — for her or us."

The men fell silent when Tess's door opened. She set the cat down in the main bunkhouse and glanced up. "Is something wrong, gentlemen?"

"No, ma'am," Fred Massey said. "Just shootin' the breeze. Sorry if we disturbed you."

"Oh, I wasn't in bed yet. By the way, do you mind if the cat sleeps out here? I keep feeling the need to sneeze, and I think it's because of her."

"It's okay, ma'am. She likes to sleep by the stove."

"Thank you — oh, and the tobacco smoke?" She fanned the air beneath her nose. "I hate to mention it, but would you mind smoking your pipes and cigars out-doors? I would appreciate it ever so much."

Mumbles broke out in the room and the men shot glances at each other.

André spoke up. "I am sure this can be arranged, mademoiselle."

"Thank you. And good night again." She closed the door.

"Look at that!" Herb Jenson hissed. "She ain't been here fifteen minutes, and we can't smoke inside anymore. You better do some-thing, Montague! And quick!"

"Shhh! Calm down! I will do my best to get it straightened out with Big Say first thing in the morning." André snapped his suspenders loose. "For now, we sleep."

"Talk to him tonight!" A jack jerked his

head in the direction of the closed door. "How are we expected to go to sleep with a woman in the next room?"

"I am aware that Miss Yardley is attractive —"

"It wouldn't matter if her looks would gag a maggot. She's a woman, and most of us ain't been around a woman in months," Alex seethed. "It ain't fittin', and you have to do somethin'!"

"I understand that, but we cannot disturb Jake tonight." André stripped off his shirt. "It is late, and you know how he is when anyone disturbs his sleep."

"Well, I plan on disturbin' him!" Jim declared. "We're going to settle this thing right now!"

André climbed into his bunk. "It will wait till morning."

Jim turned and stormed out of the bunkhouse amid whispered calls of encouragement. Ten minutes later, he returned.

Jake followed the jack into the bunkhouse and faced his crew. He had wondered how long it would take them to confront him about the new turn of events. However, the matter could have waited till morning. The men crowded around him, all talking in low voices at the same time.

"What do you think you're doin', Big Say?"

"Is this your idea of a joke, Lannigan?"

"She doesn't want us to smoke inside anymore."

"And Sweets bothers her."

Jake lifted both hands to restore calm. "One at a time!" He glanced at Tess's closed door. She didn't need to hear the men's complaints. "Maybe we'd best take this outside." Jake turned on his heel and most of the crew followed.

Cold air whipped the men's hair when the door closed behind them. "Now, what's this all about?" Jake demanded. The jacks hunkered down against the harsh wind.

"You got no call to put a woman in our bunkhouse, Big Say. Ain't you got a better place for her?"

"Put her with you," someone suggested.

"Yes!" the jacks chorused.

Jake met their angry glares and tried to calm his own irritation. He knew when he decided this was the best place for the schoolteacher that there would be a ruckus. "If it makes you feel any better, men, this is only temporary."

André faced him. "How temporary?"

"I can't say for sure. You know as well as I do how long schoolteachers last around here. I don't expect she'll stay much longer than a few days." If she was Tess Wakefield, and she remembered who she was, she wouldn't even stay that long.

"The telegraph wire is still not completed. You keep me so busy with other things that I have not had the time or the resources to get it up. If she wanted to contact someone, she would not be able to." André shifted from one foot to the other. "Jake, if I did not know better, I would say you are deliberately stalling."

His friend was right. He was stalling. And God forgive him, it was for all the wrong reasons. "Fine. Take a crew and install the telegraph wire tomorrow."

André shook his head. "Better yet, I am going to ride to Shadow Pine and wire the train line for the passenger list for the past two weeks. Someone is surely worried sick about the two women and the men swept downstream."

"And how will you get those worried people here, André? With the weather getting worse every day, you know as well as I that it won't be long before nobody can get in or out of here. Besides, listen to what you're saying. It's only been two weeks. Those families aren't worried yet. They realize what time of year it is and that travel can be slow."

"Forget that telegraph line! What's the big idea of putting the woman in our bunkhouse?" Ray demanded.

"Because I have nowhere else to put her. You men know there are no available rooms or cabins in camp."

André shook his head. "Perhaps you could arrange for Bernice or Alice Waterman to put her up if she won't be here very long."

"I gave that some thought, but it's impossible. Bernice lives with her husband in one room. Alice has her husband and three children in two rooms. I could hardly ask them to sacrifice what little privacy they have in order to accommodate the new schoolteacher."

"Then why don't you keep her!" Ray grumbled.

It was the second time someone had suggested she stay with him. That wasn't going to happen. "She's fine where she is."

"It's not fittin' for a single woman to live with a bunch of men," another man complained.

"She is not 'living' with you. Her room is private, and you're not to go near it." His eyes traveled the men. "Not one of you, if you value your jobs. André, I expect you and Fred to enforce this rule. Chances are she won't make it a week in the school-house, and then, weather permitting, she'll be out of here."

"She won't *be* outta here if she can't *get* outta here. The snows are getting deeper now," a jack said.

A renewed chorus of complaints erupted.

"There has to be somewhere she can stay besides the bunkhouse," Jim argued.

"You tell me where it is, Jim, and I'll arrange it. I'm open to suggestions."

The men murmured among themselves, but as he knew, neither Jim nor anyone else was able to come up with an alternative. The jacks were stuck with her.

Jake faced his crew, trying to keep his voice low. "I don't want to hear any more about the matter. The woman stays where she is. And if I hear of anyone stepping out of line, he'll answer to me. If anyone thinks he can't abide by the arrangement, then I want him to pack his gear and see me in my office first thing tomorrow morning."

The men quieted. Silence indicated that no one was willing to lose his job over the dispute.

"Any questions?" Jake noted a few dis-heartened grumbles persisted, but no questions.

"By the way, while I have you all together,

there is one other thing I might mention."
He had their full attention. "I understand
that some of you are having a hard time
remembering the correct names of the
neighboring crews." His gaze directly pin-
pointed one or two in the crowd. "I hear
trouble's brewing because you've been
referring to our good friends to the north as
the 'Shadow Pine Prissies.' " Jake knew who
the rowdies were and watched as a few of
them shifted stances.

"Who's been complainin'?" Ed Holman
challenged.

"The Prissies have, and I want you to
knock it off before a brawl breaks out. You
know the rules. If you're looking for trouble,
you look for it on your own time. Do I make
myself clear?"

The men's enthusiastic compliance shot
frosty plumes in the cold night air, and the
"Yes, sirs" and affirmative nods were enough
for him. "Good." He glanced at André, who
had remained quiet during the last exchange. "It's cold and late. I think we'd better all turn in. Four thirty rolls around
early."

The crowd began to break up, and André
fell into stride with Jake as the foreman
returned to his room. "Are you insane, my
friend?"

"She stays where she is."

"Yes, but I fear this will not work."

"It's up to you to see that it does."

"Having Miss Yardley in the bunkhouse is going to make it difficult for the men, Jake. Why would you do this? It makes no sense. I have known and worked with you for . . . what? Nine years? I have never seen you be so disrespectful to a woman, a woman who has no memory of her prior life. Could not we build her something small, perhaps next to the schoolhouse?"

"Disrespect? You know good and well I have no place else to put her. We haven't had time to get the telegraph installed. How do you think we could build a cabin?" His head was a jumbled mess and he needed some rest. "It's late, André. Get some sleep. You're not going to change my mind. I know it will be hard on the men, but it'll only be for a short while."

André's footsteps slowed when they approached Menson's store. "Why do you do this?"

Jake shook his head and shrugged. "Call it a hunch."

"Do you know something I do not?"

Jake's gut feeling told him the woman in the bunkhouse was Tess Wakefield, but did he know it for sure? No. "Only that I'm going to bed." Jake nodded curtly. "And I suggest you do the same."

Tess sat straight up in her cot. There was that horn again. The long, doleful wail filled the darkness, shattering the silence of the cold Michigan night. Groaning out loud, she threw her hands over her ears. Why must they eat so early on Sunday?

The hours last night had dragged by endlessly. She'd tossed and turned on her cot, listening to one hundred and twenty-five men snore in various keys, discords, and harmonies. The heavy wooden door failed to block the sound of constant whistles, wheezing, and snorting. The concerto had left her ready to scream.

Sometime in the night she had climbed out of bed and rummaged through the valise for something, other than the shoe, to stuff under the crack of the door. Her effort had been in vain, and the symphony had gone on and on and on. Now there was the horn, or was it a snore in a different key?

Slipping off her bed, she cracked open the door to peek out. The men were getting up. Some were pulling on heavy pants, while others sat on the sides of the bunks, scratching their heavily stubbled faces and yawning in a sleepy stupor.

Fred noticed the door ajar and cleared his throat to alert the others. André glanced up and grinned when he saw her peering out.

Pulling his suspenders over his shoulders, he walked toward the door, smiling. "*Bonjour,* mademoiselle! Good morning!"

Easing the door open a fraction farther, she asked, "What's all the racket?"

"Racket?" André's expression turned blank for a moment. "Ah! You mean the chuck horn?"

She stifled a yawn. "Yes, that horn. Why must they blow it so early?"

"It is four thirty. Cookee is blowing his tin Gabriel. It is time to get up and eat."

She slumped against the door frame. It sounded as though Gabriel were trying to blow down the walls. "Is it morning already?"

"*Oui.* I hope you slept well."

She turned tired eyes on him. There was no need to complain about the men's sleeping habits. It was nothing they could help. "Like a log." Surely God would forgive her for such a small fib.

"Then you must be hungry." André leaned closer to the doorway and winked. "I have yet to meet a woman who can dress in ten minutes, but you will try? Big Say likes his crew to be on time."

"Oh . . . well, we wouldn't want to disappoint Big Say, would we?" She yawned again and turned back to grab the water pitcher on the stand beside her cot. "Would you be so kind as to bring me fresh water?"

"Fresh water?" The smile on André's face faded.

"Yes . . . water." Seeing that her request had taken him by surprise, she added, "So that I may wash."

"Wash?" His grin returned. "Now?"

"Yes. Is there something wrong?"

"But it is Sunday. We do not take baths on Sunday."

"We don't?" She glanced at the other men, who were all shaking their heads. They never washed on Sundays. "Well," she was almost afraid to ask the next question. "Exactly when do we wash?"

"On Saturdays."

Her eyes narrowed. "*Only* on Saturdays?"

"Every Saturday," André bragged. "Lannigan likes his crew to be clean!"

She handed him the pitcher. "Then Lannigan is going to love me. I shall be washing more often. Would you please see that I have a pitcher of fresh water outside my door every morning?"

"*Every* morning?" André said, clearly alarmed by such excessive bathing.

127

"If you don't hurry, I shall never make it to breakfast on time." She started to close her door but then suddenly turned back. "And tell that man to stop blowing that infernal horn!"

She closed the door and heard the men chiding André. She smiled at their teasing.

"Oh, André. Tell that terrible ol' man to stop blowing that horn!" a man mocked in a high, feminine pitch. The others broke into guffaws, and she stifled her own giggle. "Do not laugh," he warned. "We will take turns getting Miss Yardley's water."

The men were still snickering when he opened the door and marched out into the cold to fill her pitcher.

10

Tess lit a candle and then placed a piece of wood in the small heat stove that rested in the corner, hoping it would hurriedly heat the room. She was brushing out her hair when André returned.

He handed her the pitcher. "I am sorry for the ice floating on the top."

Eyeing the water, she shivered before murmuring a polite, "Thank you."

As she splashed the freezing water on her face, she could hear the men moving around in the other room. Trying to still her chattering teeth, she hurriedly slipped into a clean chemise and then pulled a blue wool dress over her head. She sat on the side of the cot and buckled her shoes, and then she quickly grabbed her hair and pinned it loosely on top of her head. She heard the men start to file out of the building as she reached for her coat and bonnet.

André was waiting by the outside front

entrance when she emerged from her room a moment later, still tying the strings of her bonnet. Because it was still dark, he carried a coal-oil lantern to light their path.

Extending his arm cordially, he smiled. "You look lovely this morning, *ma chère.*"

"You're much too kind," she said, taking his arm. She knew she looked as though she'd dressed during a buffalo stampede.

Snow was beginning to fall. Large puffy flakes clung like white cotton to the bushes and tree limbs. The air was so frigid it stung her lungs. She snuggled deeper into her coat and recalled the long walk the evening before. She couldn't imagine why the men who built this logging camp would have put the crew's quarters so far from the cook-shack.

Rounding the corner of the bunkhouse, she spotted Doc Medifer coming out of his office. The doctor glanced up to the sky before turning up his collar and heading for breakfast.

Her footsteps slowed when realization struck her. She glanced at André. "That was Dr. Medifer, wasn't it?"

André smiled. "*Oui.* He lives behind his office."

"His house is this close to the bunk-house?"

"*Oui.* Why do you ask?"

Eyes narrowing, she picked up her pace. What kind of game was Jake Lannigan playing? He'd marched her around in the cold for what seemed like miles yesterday, and now she learned that Doc Medifer's house wasn't more than spitting distance from the bunkhouse! Why had he put her through that when it wasn't necessary? She didn't know, but she was going to find out.

Men swarmed through the doors of the cookshack. Tess clutched André's arm tighter as she was jostled back and forth by men of all descriptions and nationalities. There were short men, fat men, tall men, handsome men, less-than-handsome men, grizzled veterans, men who smiled at her, and others who didn't. She recognized two of her "neighbors": Fred and a man called Joe.

She was grateful that André steadied her when she was propelled into a large room with row upon row of tables covered with oilcloths. Two big cookstoves with roaring fires lined a wall, and three burly-looking cooks were busy frying large skillets of potatoes.

Her pulse quickened when she saw Jake enter the room with two other men. Glancing briefly in her direction, he barely nodded in greeting before he walked to the head of the nearest table and sat down.

She was nearly knocked off her feet when four energetic, hungry young men scrambled frantically for a seat. She wanted to confront Jake right then, but it wasn't the time. She sighed, striving for patience. Her answers would come in due course.

André motioned for her to sit, and she claimed a place at the end of one of the long benches and watched wide-eyed as one of the cooks stirred pancake batter in a fifty-pound lard can. Clouds of smoke billowed from the grill through an open flue in the roof.

Tess had never seen so much food. Platters upon platters were piled high with potatoes, pancakes, sausages, and bowls of stewed prunes. There were also enough pies, cakes, and cookies to feed a small army.

Two wizened chore boys moved up and down the rows of tables, pouring cups of tea and coffee. The clatter of dishes being passed back and forth filled the room as the men heaped monstrous portions upon their plates. Tess was amazed at the sheer complexity of the operation.

"May I offer you some morning glories?"

She looked at André and saw that he was holding a platter of pancakes. "No, thank

132

you." She passed the platter on, realizing she had no appetite. She watched with horror when the men poured bacon grease and heavy maple syrup over their stacks of hotcakes.

In scant seconds, the room grew as quiet as a church. She glanced up, wondering what had caused the lull. Except for the creaking of a bench or an occasional cough or the clatter of steel utensils against tin plates, not a sound was heard.

Leaning toward André, she kept a close eye on the jacks at her table, who went about eating seriously but silently. "What's wrong?"

"Wrong?" She noticed André was whispering. Jake gave her a stern look from his place at the head of the table. Deliberately ignoring him, she leaned closer to the Frenchman and lowered her voice. "Why is everyone so quiet all of a sudden?"

"Talking is not allowed during meals," he murmured.

No one was allowed to talk? That was bizarre. The men had been chattering like magpies moments before. "For heaven's sake, why aren't they allowed to talk?" she blurted out in a voice that ricocheted like a stray bullet through the room.

At least a hundred heads turned, and the

cook standing at the grill shot her a sharp glance. She fumbled for her fork, scooped up a small bite of potatoes, and nibbled for a moment, trying to make sense of such a ridiculous rule.

Jake glanced down the long row of plates. Why was André sitting beside Tess this morning? He wasn't her keeper. Ordinarily, the ink slinger took his place at the head of the table the same as the foreman and scalar did.

His frown deepened when he saw André lean over to silently encourage her to take another serving of potatoes. She shook her head, but moments later he saw her lean over to whisper to André and then she stifled a laugh.

The man should know better than to let her talk! And he shouldn't be sitting with her, either. Jake forked another bite of hot-cakes into his mouth. Was he jealous? His irritation grew when he saw the Frenchman place a cookie on Tess's plate and then move closer to respond to something she'd whispered to him.

Jake's voice roared from the head of the table. "No talking at the table, school-teacher!"

Heat rushed into her face, and she was

sure it turned a thousand shades of red. She reached for the cookie and obediently brought it to her mouth.

Why, the nerve, scolding me in front of all these men!

André said quietly, "It is his job to see that the rules are obeyed." He returned his attention to his breakfast.

She sat through the remainder of the meal in silence. In doing so, her ears turned to the language of the jacks. If they did speak, it was to ask for something, and usually in one or two quiet words. Salt was called "gravel," ketchup was "red lead," pepper was "Mexican powder," pancakes were "morning glories," and sugar was "sand." It wasn't much, but she figured if she ever regained her appetite, the knowledge would help.

She pointedly ignored Jake Lannigan when everyone left the cookshack twenty minutes later. Giving him what could only be considered a snooty look, she hoped to convey the message that she didn't appreciate the way he'd yelled at her as though she were an unruly child. His humiliating tone still rang in her head.

If he understood her silent dispatch, he gave no indication it bothered him. When they exited the building, he brushed past her without a word.

She took André's arm again on their way back to the bunkhouse. "Why is that man so rude?"

"Big Say?" André chuckled. "He has a lot on his mind. The company is about to be sold, and he does not care for the new buyer."

"Is he concerned about his job?"

André threw his head back and laughed. "Lannigan worried about a job? Oh, *non!* His father owns a logging camp. And there are many outfits that wish to have him running their operations."

"Then what's he so prickly about?"

"He would like to see Tess Wakefield keep her grandfather's business and replant the trees we harvest. He has been concerned for years that the pines will run out and nothing will be left in these forests."

"Tess Wakefield?" The name sounded familiar.

"*Oui.* She is Rutherford Wakefield's granddaughter. Rutherford died a few months back, and she's the sole heir. Jake has written many letters to Mademoiselle Wakefield, urging her to keep the business at least until he can get a program of replanting underway."

"The request sounds reasonable enough.

Why won't she go along with it?"

"Who knows?" André shrugged. "All I know is that she plans to sell to Sven Templeton."

"And that would be bad?"

André nodded. "Templeton is not a good man. He cares nothing for the land, only the money. Mademoiselle Wakefield is expected to arrive soon, and Jake is not happy. I think he wishes the worsening weather will delay her until spring. If so, the sale would be postponed."

She turned to peer over her shoulder at the camp boss, who had paused to speak to one of his men. "Why doesn't he like me?"

"He likes you, *ma chère*." André smiled down at her. "Jake may be slow to warm to you, but once you know him, there isn't anything he wouldn't do for you."

She found that hard to believe. The man she was getting to know seemed cold as steel. "Is there a particular woman in Mr. Lannigan's life?"

"This I do not care to discuss."

Lannigan was so abrupt. Tess figured that most women would probably find it hard to converse with him, and yet a man with his extraordinary good looks should appeal to single women. He appeared to be a decent man, one who ran his camp with admirable morals.

But she knew so little about him . . . and she wasn't sure she wanted to know more. It wasn't for her to judge the foreman or his actions. Lost memory or not, she instinctively felt that was the Lord's place. However, her earlier attraction had worn thin now that she'd actually spent time with the man.

"Many pretty girls run after him," André offered. "But besides Marcy Wetlock, I don't know of anyone Jake . . ."

She glanced at the Frenchman when he paused, as if he realized he was revealing more than he should. "Marcy Wetlock?"

"Ah, *oui* . . ."

"Now that you've mentioned her, André, you may as well tell me who she is." She couldn't fathom why she wanted to know, but something made her curious. Was she trying to fool herself when she said she didn't care? The man was undeniably appealing.

"Ah, er . . . she is an acquaintance who lives in Shadow Pine."

He straightened his hat and changed the subject. "The sky pilot will be here soon for Sunday service. Perhaps you would like to attend his preaching, *non?*"

She turned to peer over her shoulder at Lannigan. *Marcy Wetlock. What kind of woman is she?*

Looking back at André, she brought up what had been uppermost on her mind this morning. "Last night I asked if you would be able to enlighten me about my background."

"I am afraid I cannot tell you anything other than that which is on your application, *ma chère.*"

Disappointment tugged at her heart again. She desperately needed help. "Nothing?"

"Your application says you lived in Philadelphia, you are single, and that you have no close family. You are welcome to read it," he offered. "Why don't you stop by after school Monday afternoon and we will look it over together? Perhaps something will help prompt your memory."

"Thank you. I shall do that." With any luck, the document might contain a useful clue. "André, earlier you mentioned the sky pilot would be here today."

"*Oui.* He goes from place to place and preaches the Good Book."

A preacher. Well, perhaps he could help her.

The older man arrived after daybreak. The

snow was deep enough that people had to travel by sleigh. Tess watched as road monkeys worked tirelessly to keep paths cleared in camp.

André told her Sunday services began at nine thirty. When she arrived at the schoolhouse, which doubled as a church, she glanced around the cramped classroom and realized that not everyone in camp came to hear the inspiring message read from the book of Acts. Those who did attend made the service a warm and enthusiastic one.

The service had already started when Jake stepped in and stood at the back of the room. Tess felt his presence before she saw him. When she turned her head and met his hazel-eyed gaze, she felt like a smitten schoolgirl. The man radiated power and authority. He shifted his focus from her to the preacher and remained standing, listening to the sermon, until he was called away.

Lunch was another ordeal. The cook stepped outside of the shack about eleven fifty and began blowing various trills and arpeggios on his tin horn. Immediately, the people in camp stopped what they were doing and came running.

Dinner tables were piled high with bowls of beef stew, slices of hot bread, bowls of rutabagas, the inevitable prunes, and more cakes, pies, and cookies. Tess was sure she would grow as large as the camp's prized horses if she ate half the portions that were offered.

She had observed that the cookshack didn't bustle like this on weekdays or Saturdays for the midday meal. Why today? She was sitting next to Fred Massey. The eating hadn't started yet, so she knew it was safe to talk. She didn't want another scolding from Big Say.

"Why all the fuss for lunch today, Fred?"

"Well, ma'am, usually the only thing we jacks get for lunch are flaggins. The cooks bring them to us by sleigh and hand them out when we're working in the woods."

"Flaggins? I've never heard of such." She saw kindness in Fred's eyes when she smiled.

"It's mainly bread and meat, Miss Yardley."

"That's all you get for lunch?"

"Yes, but they feed us plenty for supper, after the woods are dark and we come back to camp. They treat us real good here. Big Say sees to it."

The hush came over the room, and it wasn't long before the meal was over and the food and dishes cleared away. The men returned to the bunkhouse to write letters to their wives and sweethearts, sharpen their tools, or mend their socks.

Tess discovered that Sunday was also boil-up day. She watched as the men dragged their clothes and blankets outside and dumped them into large vats of hot water in an effort to delouse their personal belongings. Good-naturedly referring to themselves as crumb-chasers, the men went about picking lice and bedbugs out of their clothing.

Apparently the battle against the vermin was vigorously waged with tubs of boiling-hot water mixed with laundry soap and tobacco. She found herself in the middle of the action, helping the crew scrub sheets and blankets. At the end of the day her hands were worn raw, but she felt a sense of accomplishment and contentment. The idea that she'd slept with bedbugs disgusted her, and she vowed she wouldn't do that again.

The men had been courteous and pleasant to her, and that evening, in the bunkhouse, a man they called Deacon brought out his fiddle and sang funny little songs like "Six Whistles," "My Willie Oh!" "Tall Tales of Taylor," and her personal favorite, "Sixteen Men in a Pine-Slab Bunk." Everyone joined in on a rousing chorus of:

Beans are on the table
Daylight's in the swamp,
Hey, you lazy shanty boys,
Ain't you ever gettin' up?

Then Deacon struck a chord for a hoe-down. André pulled Tess into the circle of men who grabbed other men for partners. They stomped the pine boards of the bunk-house until she was certain the floor would give way.

Sundays in a logging camp would be her favorite day.

Late that night, as she snuggled down between extra clean sheets, she tried to clear her mind. She plopped her pillow over her face to drown out the noise in the next room, but tonight the men's snores weren't so bothersome. She knew the snorers a bit more personally now, and somehow that made the strange noises easier to tolerate. *Thank You, God, for the new friends I've made today.*

For some crazy reason, she wished Jake Lannigan had been one of them.

11

Monday morning, dressed in brown and with outward calm that belied the fact that her insides were roiling like the waters of Lake Huron, Tess watched her students file into the classroom and take their seats.

"Mornin', ma'am." A boy placed an apple on the teacher's desk. "Name's Scooter Wilson."

"Thank you, Scooter."

A little girl brought her a popcorn ball and then everyone settled down. "Good morning, children. First of all, I'd like to say how much I'm looking forward to having us learn together." She walked to stand in front of her chair behind her desk and studied her class.

Other than the fact that she didn't have the vaguest idea of what she was doing, Tess felt slightly more confident today. The small one-room schoolhouse sat within easy walking distance of the bunkhouse, and so far the children's eyes followed her with rapt attention.

If only she felt qualified to teach.

"Tirzah Reynolds?"

A small girl in the second row raised her hand.

"Thank you for the popcorn ball, and what a lovely name you have."

"Thank you, ma'am. It's Hebrew. It means cypress tree."

"I think that's beautiful. It's from the Bible, isn't it?"

"It's from my mom and dad."

Tess chuckled at the response. "And how old are you?"

Tirzah said, "I'm seven years old, ma'am."

Tess smiled again at the sweet child. Then she said, "Now, class, it would be nice if each of you would stand up and tell me your name and your age." She smiled at her small flock encouragingly. There were nine in all, five boys and four girls. A few grumbles broke out, but one by one the children rose to their feet.

"My name's Modeen Menson. I'm thirteen and my father owns the camp store." Modeen's tongue snaked out at one of the older boys before she sat back down.

"Uh . . . the name's Toby Miller. I'm eight years old."

"Pud Wilkerson. Fifteen."

"My name is Violet Ann Jump. I am eight years old, and my daddy says I'm the prettiest girl in camp." She tittered nervously before flopping back down on her seat.

"King Davis, sixteen. And Violet Ann's old man is full of it. Violet Ann's so ugly her pa has to tie a pork chop around her neck to get the dogs to play with her."

Tess's eyes widened as Violet gave an indignant gasp. She hoped this was first-day jitters and not how the children acted all the time.

A boy in the third row sprang to his feet. "Quinn Morrison, ma'am. I'll be eleven come Saturday. My pa's giving me a gun so's I can blow them heads off them sons-a-
. . ." he rattled off an expletive . . . "jackrabbits."

She quietly made a note in her journal: *Work on children's language.* Glancing up, she said, "Go on."

A shy, blue-eyed child hesitantly moved out of her seat. "My . . . my . . . name's . . . Ju-ju-Juice Tett-tett . . . er . . . son. I'm sev-seven . . . ye-years ol-old, and . . . I-I . . . sta-stam-stammer a lit . . . a lit . . . a little bit."

The younger children burst into giggles, and Tess quieted them with a sharp look.

"Juice. That's a unique name."

"Thank . . . thank . . . you. My moth-mother named m-me . . . aft-after an or-ange." The child gave a proud grin, revealing the wide gap of her missing two front teeth.

"Scooter Wilson, ma'am. I'm nine years old, but I'm mean for my age." He gave the other boys a pointed look and then dropped to his seat.

"Well." She smiled back at the children. *Merciful heavens.* She tried to ignore the attitudes in the room. "My name is Miss Yardley, and I think it's time we got down to work." Reaching for the spelling book, she said a silent prayer. *Father, please allow me to bluff my way through this day.*

"Can anyone tell me what page we're on?" Feeling for her chair, she seated herself.

"Page fifteen!"

"Uh-uh. Page twenty!"

"Fifteen!"

"Liar, liar, pants on fire!"

"Shut up, pig face. We've already done fifteen. We're on page thirty-two. Ain't that right, Pud?"

Amid the competing shouts of the children, a sharp crack sounded, and Tess felt herself falling. The chair she was sitting on shattered into pieces, pitching her to the floor in a heap. Chaos broke out as her feet flew into the air. Stunned, she lay flat on her back for a moment, trying to focus. She could hear the children snickering, and her temper flared. Nails and screws lay haphazardly on the floor. Someone had deliberately tampered with the chair!

Gathering her fortitude, she slowly pulled herself above the edge of her desk and leveled a stony look at the little hooligans. They would see who laughed last. "We will begin on page one."

By the end of the school day, she realized she'd have to study long into the night to prepare her lessons for the following day.

She felt certain she'd forgotten everything she'd ever known — about everything.

Early that afternoon, André strode into Jake's office and pitched a telegram on his desk. "Take a look at that."

Picking up the scrap of yellow paper, Jake's eyes scanned the message. "I see the telegraph line is installed."

"The work was completed about an hour ago. I wired Talbot Wellington-Kent first."

The wire from Talbot Wellington-Kent indicated he was upset over news of the accident and inquiring as to the whereabouts of his fiancée, Tess Wakefield.

"What do you make of it?"

"Sounds like Mr. Wellington-Kent can't keep track of the woman he's engaged to marry."

"Come now, Jake! This confirms that Tess Wakefield left Philadelphia a little over two weeks ago on a train headed for Shadow Pine. That can only mean one thing."

Jake got up to pour himself a fresh cup of coffee. "It doesn't tell us if Miss Wakefield was the woman swept downstream."

"Well, it could have been her!" André's face grew troubled as he walked to his desk to pick up his cup. "It would certainly explain why she has not shown up to close the deal with Sven. If this is true, someone will need to inform Wellington-Kent that his fiancée most likely died in that wagon accident."

Jake moved back to his desk. "I'm not telling him any such thing."

"Why? The man needs to know!"

"Because we could be mistaken. We don't know for certain the missing woman is Tess Wakefield. Have you sent Fedelia Yardley's kin a telegraph?"

"You know she has no family!"

"The dead woman could be Fedelia Yardley or Burl Sutter's intended —"

"Nonsense. Miss Yardley is here, teaching

this morning."

"The woman you want to *think* is Miss Yardley is teaching." His eyes met André's. "We can only speculate if she is the new schoolteacher. We haven't found a body to identify. It would be cruel to inform a man that his fiancée is deceased when we have no proof."

"It would be far crueler for Miss Wakefield to act as if she is a schoolteacher if she is not," André argued. He glanced up. "This is not good. What if the woman swept downstream was Fedelia Yardley?"

Jake shrugged. "André, we have no proof of who survived that accident. At this point, all we know for certain is that one of the two women in that wagon was apparently Tess Wakefield."

"*Alors!* How could this happen? Tip's granddaughter killed?"

"We'll hold off on getting Sven back to camp for a while longer. You should wire Wellington-Kent and inform him that he will have to come here and identify the surviving woman."

André whistled under his breath as he stirred his coffee. "This will be very bad news to the man. His fiancée is missing and most likely dead. And the early snows are making cross-country travel impossible."

"There you go thinking that Miss Yardley survived the accident and Miss Wakefield didn't." Jake shoved aside a brief pang of guilt. Tess was probably the one who survived, all right, and she was in that roomful of rowdies today for the first time. "Wire Miss Wakefield's fiancé what little information we know for certain. The wagon lost a wheel, and there were two women and some men on board. All but one woman and the driver were swept downstream. The surviving woman has no memory, and the driver doesn't know who she is."

"But if the missing woman was Mademoiselle Wakefield, Mr. Kent should be prepared."

Jake sat down behind his desk and focused on the journal sheet. "The message will give him warning that the missing woman could be his fiancée. Don't forget Burl is still waiting for his bride-to-be to show up. Who knows? Maybe Miss Wakefield decided she didn't want to get married and skipped out on Wellington-Kent. It's happened before. She could be anywhere right now for all we know. Or," Jake snapped the journal closed, "she could have been swept downstream."

André shook his head. "I believe it was her, Jake. And now . . . perhaps she is fish bait."

"Well, that's your guess, but I don't think we should be sending out news we can't substantiate." He glanced up when a lumberjack entered.

"Trouble at the roll way, Big Say, and something's going on at the skid way too. It's gonna take a while."

"Be right there." Jake stood up and reached for his coat. "I'll probably be out the rest of the day."

André waved him off. "Go, but what will happen now? With Rutherford's only heir missing, the business could be tied up in legal papers for years."

"I suppose it could." Jake pulled his gloves on. "Can you handle sending the message?"

"*Oui, oui.* Go now. You are making my head to pound."

12

Tess pulled on her coat late that afternoon and looked up to find Echo standing in the doorway. Overjoyed to see a friendly face, she beckoned her inside. "Hello!"

With a shy smile, Echo walked to the front of the schoolroom. "I was on my way home, and I thought we might walk together."

Tess sighed. "You don't know how happy I am to see you." She embraced Echo, and then draped her arm around her friend's waist while they walked down the row of desks. "You can't imagine the day I've had!"

"That bad?"

Tess paused to bank the fire and wrap a heavy woolen scarf around her neck. "Half the children in class should be in jail," she confided. "Or, at the very least, under lock and key."

Her friend flashed an amused grin. "It's been hard work to keep a teacher."

Tess followed Echo outside, closed the

door, and then drew her coat tighter around her. The sky was gray and the clouds appeared laden. "It looks like snow again."

"Snow has come early this year."

Echo's tone held a note of dislike, as if long winters bothered her. "Don't you like snow?" Tess asked when they began to walk.

"No. I'm looking forward to spring," she confessed. "A time when tiny flowers sprout up through tender shoots of green grass, and the birds sing oh so sweetly in the mornings. The sun is warm on your back, and the world seems so . . . good."

Tess glanced at Echo's coat. The material was threadbare and frayed, scant protection against the biting cold. The young woman's teeth chattered when the strong wind buffeted her frail body. Her coat, on the other hand, was thick and warm, and she felt guilty being so snug when Echo was so miserable.

"What have you done this afternoon, Echo?"

"Oh . . . I went to Menson's store."

"Did you shop?"

Her friend shook her head. "No, but I enjoyed the outing. I get lonely sometimes."

She stopped and took Echo's hands. "You know what? I have an extra coat that . . . that I have tired of." She was tired of everything in her valises, and Echo seemed in need of the garment. "The color would look lovely on you. Would you like to have it?"

Echo's head dipped shyly. "That's very kind of you, ma'am, but I don't think I should accept. I appreciate the offer, though."

Tess was surprised by the young woman's hasty refusal, but she recognized pride when she saw it. However, she also knew the coat Echo was wearing could not adequately protect her from the long Michigan winters. "You really are welcome to have it. I'd like to have new clothes, but I can't very well justify them if I keep the ones I have. You'd be doing me a favor if you'd accept it." It was becoming increasingly clear that, even with her memory loss, she had a practical side and was more than willing to use it.

"I surely do thank you," Echo said. "I'm sure your coat's very pretty, but I —"

"Your husband wouldn't mind, would he?" Tess wondered if that could be the cause for the girl's hesitancy. The men talked at night, and she heard the stories of Echo's husband and how he ruled the roost with an iron will. Most shook their heads and called him names a lady shouldn't hear.

Echo shrugged. "I don't think he'd mind."

"Good. Then it's settled. You will walk with me to the bunkhouse and I'll give you the coat."

Echo chuckled softly. "You surely are a stubborn woman, Miss Yardley."

She laughed. "Well, I'm not sure about that, but it appears I could be."

"Waite says I have a determined streak a mile long. Maybe that's why you and me take to each other. Thank you kindly. I'm sure it will be a real blessing."

"I thank you." Tess grinned and squeezed her friend's hands. "You haven't seen the garment yet."

Chatting with Echo about other things, Tess made her way carefully along the icy roads. They were forced to step aside whenever sleighs loaded with monstrous logs edged by them.

Occasionally one of her bunkhouse neighbors would call out a friendly greeting, and she would smile and wave. From the deep woods, she could hear the increasingly familiar sounds of crosscut saws, the splintering of trees when they began to fall, and the faint cries of "Timberrrr" as the giant widow-makers came crashing to the ground.

When they arrived at the door of her room, Echo asked, "Aren't you afraid staying here with all these men?"

"At first I was scared to death, but not anymore. They are very kind to me." Tess inserted her key in the lock, and they entered her quarters.

"My . . ." Echo's gaze roamed the room. "This is small."

"Very, but I try to think of it as cozy." If she thought of it any other way, she would claw at the walls, screaming. She reached for a valise and took out the coat. Shaking out the folds, she smiled. "This should fit you nicely." She slipped the heavy garment over Echo's shoulders. "Sometimes I wish I had a room with windows so light could get in. One with lots of hot water and bath salts and . . ." She took a deep breath. "Oh, well, it's useless to wish for the impossible. No one has their own room in this camp."

"Big Say does," Echo said, running her hands over the thick gray wool, smiling.

"He does, doesn't he." It was a statement, not a question. "Where is it again?"

"Above Menson's store."

"That's right. And how many rooms does he have?"

"I don't know. Probably only one, and it's pretty small, they say." She turned in a pirouette. "This is so pretty. I've never had anything this fine."

She was pleased her gift made Echo so

happy. Why, the woman's smile went from ear to ear. Tess had never seen her as carefree as she was at that moment. "Then you must wear it with joy. It looks beautiful on you."

"I will . . . and thank you again." Echo kissed Tess on the cheek. "I'd best be getting on home. Gotta fry up some squirrel for Waite's supper." The light left Echo's eyes. It was obvious to Tess she didn't want to leave.

"May I walk part of the way with you, my friend?"

Echo's eyes lit up. "I'd like that."

When they reached the fork in the road, Tess hugged Echo and the woman left for home. She, however, continued on until the road split a second time. It was late afternoon. The tall pines were casting off cold shadows, and darkness would soon overtake the light.

Up ahead, a giant bluff came into view, and she saw great piles of logs stacked horizontally upon each other. Tess began to wonder if she might be lost, but she knew she was in no immediate danger because she could see a crew of jacks working in the distance.

Wrapping her scarf tightly under her chin, she climbed to the top of the mound. The

158

wind sent a bone-rattling chill through her. Leaning over a wooden railing, she peered cautiously down the steep incline to the bottom, some five hundred feet below. The men above her were systematically feeding the logs into a wooden flume to send below to the banks of Lake Huron. Several jacks worked at the side of the wooden shoot, pitching shovels of sand on hot spots to prevent fire breaking out from the friction created by the logs zooming down the flume, one right after another. She watched for a long time until she heard a familiar voice.

"You're going to freeze your nose off up here."

She turned to find Jake standing behind her, cupping his hands as he blew warmth into his gloved fingers. A different sort of chill raced down her spine. He towered over her like the pine he harvested, only he took her breath away.

"Hello. I was getting a breath of air and I noticed the logs." She turned back to watch another one sail down the flume. He stepped closer so that he was beside her at the railing. The fabric of his coat sleeve brushed hers, and the unexpected contact caused her heart to flutter like the wings of a trapped sparrow.

"This is the roll way. The logs will stay here until the spring. The men on top of the piles handling the cant hooks are called top loaders."

She was fascinated by the scene taking place below her. The men, working high atop the decked logs at the base of the flume, would place a six-foot pole with a loose dangling hook on its end against a log. Then they would bear down on the handle to give it a pull, and the log would cant over. Just like everything else she'd seen in the camp, the job looked dangerous.

"Those men must be extremely sure-footed."

"A good cant hook man has to be," Jake said in a tone that was almost cordial for a change.

"What happens to the logs?"

"With the first sign of the spring thaw, they'll be sent downstream to the booming grounds. There they'll be sorted according to company marks, gathered together into rafts with rope and hardwood pins, and then sent to the sawmill."

Her gaze was riveted on the action below. "It's all so fascinating."

He nodded, moving to lean against the railing beside her. "Any small error in judgment during a log jam could prove fatal for the men, bringing tons of timber down to crush them into pulp."

"My, that's a terrible thought." She was beginning to understand just how greatly these men put their lives at risk every day for their employer. She respected their loyalty. "What are those symbols on the end of the logs?"

"They are company marks. That's how the sorters at the booming grounds know which pen to pull them into when they come through."

Squinting, she could barely make out the initials *WT* encased in a tight circle on the bottom of each log. Of course, Wakefield Timber. She should have known. She wasn't sure why, but she had no inclination to seek the warmth of her room. It felt so right standing beside Jake. As though it was something she'd done all of her life, as though it would be something God intended her to do for the rest of her life. A shiver rocked through her as the wind blustered and howled.

Jake stood to his full height. "You'd better be getting back to the bunkhouse. It'll be dark shortly."

Turning, she followed him down the incline. "I'm not sure I know how to get back," she confessed. "I thought I did, but now I'm confused."

"Miss Yardley, you shouldn't stray away from the familiar. It's easy to get disoriented, and if you get lost it could mean your life."

She bristled at his slightly scolding tone. There was no, *I'm sorry you're confused,* or *It could be from your head injury,* or *Oh, that's a shame, Miss Yardley. Let me escort you back to your room.* No, the best Jake Lannigan could muster was a clipped "You shouldn't stray away from the familiar."

Her day had been taxing enough without his adding to it. Why did she even want him to walk her back?

"I'll be tied up another few minutes, but if you want to wait, you can walk with me," he said.

"Thank you," she said briefly. "It's ever so nice of you to offer." She huddled deeper into her coat and watched snowflakes whirl around her while Jake spoke with a couple of his men. She sighed. She couldn't deny that she had enjoyed their few moments alone on the hill, even if he was short with her.

Though he would consider the walk as nothing more than a duty, she'd find it a bit more memorable. When she fell in love, she hoped it would be a man similar to Jake

162

Lannigan, only more cordial. She didn't care for his gruffness, but the air around him was certainly charged, even electrifying. When he walked into a room, she felt his presence before she saw him.

Had she ever been in love? Surely she hadn't, because she was certain that the occasion would be so memorable that nothing, not even a blow to the head, could erase that memory.

A few minutes later, Jake stepped from the shadows. "I'm afraid I'm taking longer than I expected. I still have to check on my crew downriver. I could arrange for you to ride in a sleigh with one of the teamsters."

"I don't mind walking." Though she was numb to the bone, she was willing to endure the cold to be with him.

They fell into step. She wasn't surprised that he had very little to say to her. Racking her brain for something to chat with him about, she was painfully aware that they had little in common. He cut trees and she taught school, though she hoped he was better at his job than she was at hers.

Today was only her first day back to work, but she was appalled to note that her students caught on faster than she did. By late afternoon one of the boys sat next to her desk and worked on an arithmetic problem with her. Neither one could come up with the right answer. Maybe the head injury had knocked her stupid as well as stealing her memory.

She hurried to keep up with Jake's long strides, taking two steps to his one. He must have noticed, and she was pleased when he slowed his pace for her.

"Are you cold?" he asked.

Snow had begun to fall. "Yes . . . a little." She was pretty sure that if she stumbled, she would crack apart. Tess wondered yet again why anyone of sane mind would choose a place like Michigan to teach school during the winter.

She was shocked when Jake took off his heavy jacket and draped it around her shoulders. "Mr. Lannigan, I can't take your coat!" Then the heavenly warmth from his body enveloped her. The feeling was quite intimate, and she drew the coat closer around her.

He shrugged. "I'm accustomed to the winter here."

His scent lingered, and she found it comforting. He didn't smell the way the other men did, strong and disagreeable. He smelled of woods and pine and, unless she missed her guess, soap. He must wash more often than just on Saturdays.

She found herself wondering what it would be like to have big Jake Lannigan as her husband. She'd heard talk in the bunkhouse that as foreman of Wakefield Timber, he had to be able to whip any man in his camp, if the need arose. And apparently it had, many times.

His strength was respected among the crew, and from what she'd overheard in the bunkhouse, he never picked a fight unless he had just cause, and he'd never been bested in a fair battle.

She glanced at him from the corner of her eye. The fabric of his plaid shirt couldn't begin to hide the tight ridge of muscles in his massive arms. She wondered what it would be like if he swept her into those arms and held her tightly. His strength could be frightening, for she knew he could probably snap her in two with his bare hands. Yet she would bet that when Jake Lannigan wanted to be, he was as gentle as a lamb.

She laughed softly when she thought of how she'd just mentally compared this tall, powerful giant to a lamb. His voice broke into her thoughts. Surely — in her former life — she'd had no such scandalous thoughts about the opposite sex.

"Did you say something?"

Her face flooded with guilt when she realized he'd caught her thinking about him. She shuddered when his question seeped in. Was she talking out loud? She was horrified, although she would never let him know that. "I beg your pardon?"

"I thought I heard you ask me something."

"Um . . . no." She smiled. "I'm too cold to ask anything."

"How did your first day at school go?"

"Oh." She drew a deep breath of icy air because she suddenly felt extremely warm. "It . . . it went okay."

"Did the children give you any trouble?"

She noticed his guarded tone and wondered why. Did he think her incapable of performing her job? She glanced up and smiled. "None that I couldn't handle." Thinking back at the day's events, she wondered how long she'd be able to tolerate it.

Someone had taken the screws and nails out of her chair. Scooter Wilson had turned all the girls' coats inside out after recess. Toby Miller threw a pile of horse dung into the stove, and the ensuing stench had nearly caused her to cave in and dismiss class early, but she'd grimly soldiered on, refusing to knuckle under to her students' pranks.

She'd continued the history lesson with a handkerchief pressed over her nose. Then

166

she calmly announced, at the end of the day, that she was assigning the boys the unpalatable task of memorizing the prologue to *Romeo and Juliet.* When she told them they were to recite it orally during class the following morning, King Davis had released a string of cuss words that made the hair on her arms stand straight up, but she'd held her ground.

"Good," Jake said. "Let's hope it stays that way."

The chuckle that followed sounded almost sinister. As if he knew something she didn't. She glanced up into his mesmerizing hazel eyes. "Did I say something funny?"

His demeanor instantly sobered and he turned his gaze away. "No, ma'am. Just clearing my throat."

"You don't have to keep calling me ma'am." He never called her by her given name and she wanted to hear him say it. "My name is Fedelia." The name still seemed foreign on her tongue, but it was a nice enough name. Fedelia. She would rather it be Alice or Rose. Rose would have been nice. Fedelia sounded . . . stuffy.

A shout from the side of the road diverted their attention, and they paused when three men of Jake's crew ran out of the woods. One of them was carrying another man over his shoulder, and blood streamed from the man's injured leg, leaving a bright-red trail in the white snow.

"We need help here!" someone shouted.

Jake broke into a run, and Tess was close behind. Two jacks put the injured man on the ground, and she quickly averted her gaze when she saw the deep, bloody gash in the man's thigh. The sight made her light-headed. Suddenly the woods tilted. She took a deep breath and willed herself to focus.

Jake dropped to his knees. "Frank."

She watched as Jake wrapped his strong hands around the man's leg, trying to stem the flow of blood. The poor man was writhing on the ground, his face contorted with pain.

"What happened, Frank?"

"Ax bit into me . . ."

Her heart pounded hard in her chest. *Oh, God, please help him.* Mercifully, before he could finish telling his story, Frank passed out. "Thank You, Father," she whispered.

"I need a tourniquet . . ."

Jake started to unbutton his shirt, but she was already reaching under her skirt to tear a long strip from her petticoat. An instant later she handed it to him. The foreman worked quickly to stem the flow of blood, but it was gushing out of Frank into red pools.

"Jake, he's gonna bleed to death," a jack warned as he peeled off his coat to cushion the injured limb.

Leaning back on his haunches, Jake drew a skinning knife from the leather sheath fastened to his belt. "We have to get him to camp to see if Doc can save this leg. I need somebody to hold that gash together."

The man holding the jacket grew paler by the moment. Then he turned away from the gruesome sight.

"Sherman?" Jake barked.

"I can't do it, Jake. I'll puke for sure."

She closed her eyes. *Help me be strong.* She reached out and put her hand on Jake's shoulder. "I'll do it," she said softly. Jake glanced up. She knew her face was probably as white as the strip of petticoat she'd handed him, and yet she hoped he saw a determined spark in her eyes.

"Are you sure? It won't be pleasant."

She nodded. "Just tell me what I need to do."

"Let me cut a bigger piece off of your petticoat. We need a lot of tension to stop the blood flow. It's going to hurt like the blazes when I tighten it, and he isn't going to like it."

She modestly lifted her skirt so that he could cut a long, wide piece of cloth. Then she let his coat fall from her shoulders and knelt down beside him. With his brief instructions and all of her strength, she held down the powerful man while Jake placed the cloth around his leg and tied it. He reached for a tree limb, put one end under the dressing, and then twisted the tourniquet tight.

Tess felt sorry for the man, who was drifting in and out of consciousness and screaming for mercy when he was awake. His agonizing cries shattered the quiet hillsides, and tears rolled down her face. She willed herself not to faint.

Occasionally she leaned over and gently cradled Frank's face against her breast, crooning softly to him while his tears soaked the front of her coat. He was so young — maybe twenty or twenty-one — and so afraid.

"My leg . . . don't cut off my leg, Jake," Frank begged. His cries echoed across the frozen countryside.

"I won't, Frank, but Doc might have to. Otherwise you could bleed to death."

"Let me die then. Just let me die. I don't want to lose my leg," he pleaded. Speaking to the sky, the young man pleaded, "God, please let me die."

She knew his physical pain was excruciating, but the agony in his heart seemed ten times worse. Glancing down at the wound, she realized Jake had all but stopped the bleeding.

"We're going to have to get him to Doc Medifer so he can get that sewed up, if he can, and get blood flow back into that leg."

Snowflakes clung to Frank's wet lashes, and he stared vacantly up at the growing twilight.

"Can you hear me, Frank?"

Frank barely nodded.

"You've lost a lot of blood, but we're taking you to Doc's now to see what he can do. Don't give up on us."

When he met her gaze, the strain in Jake's eyes tore at her heart. Tess knew he cared for every man on his crew, but his tender words showed her a side of the man she hadn't yet seen.

"Do you think you can hold this stick in place and keep the tourniquet tight while we transport him?"

"Yes."

He turned to one of the jacks. "See if you can flag down a sleigh." The man took off at a run, and Jake focused on the other jack.

"Let's get him to the road. We need to hurry."

She took the tightly wound stick in her hand and fought to keep it from springing loose. It was harder to hold it in place than she had expected. She rose to her feet when Jake and the second jack lifted Frank in their arms, as gently as they would a baby, and carried him to the already waiting sleigh.

A man took the stick from her hand and held it in place as Frank was laid in place. She was so cold and exhausted she didn't know if she could take much more. She just wanted Frank to keep his leg and live a long, productive life.

Someone handed Jake his coat, and turning to her, he draped it around her shoulders once again. She was nearly frozen, but she was proud. She hadn't complained once.

"Are you all right?"

She nodded, numb to the bone. "I feel so terrible for him that he might lose his leg."

"He's alive, though. If he loses his leg, at least he'll have his life," Jake said gruffly. "Thank God for His mercy."

Her face wet with tears, she studied his grim expression. "And that's enough?"

Jake stood beside her, watching the sleigh

carrying Frank slowly fade out of sight. "If a man has no other choice, it has to be."

13

Walking to Menson's store one afternoon a few weeks later, Tess was amazed to realize how commonplace the camp routine now felt to her. Even so, she still shuddered when she recalled the tragic afternoon when Frank Kellier was hurt. His injury had been too severe for recovery, and Doc had been forced to remove his leg. Her heart broke for the young man. She had visited him often during the bleak, dark days of his convalescence. The loss of the limb had left Frank in a deep depression.

Every day for more than a week she'd stopped by Doc Medifer's house after school to read to Frank from the works of Charles Dickens, but he failed to respond. She knew it would take a long time for both his wound and his heart to heal.

During the days, the winter winds whistled around the eaves of the tiny schoolhouse, accompanied by thick layers of snow, which fell with monotonous regularity. Two weeks ago she had turned the page of the desk calendar to November.

Teaching was still such a challenge. The coal-oil lamp sitting beside her cot burned long into the night as Tess struggled to prepare lessons for the following day. Over and over the question came back to haunt her. Why would she have chosen to teach when she apparently had no talent for it? The most basic English grammar problem had her pacing the floor and wringing her hands in frustration.

The cramped schoolroom wore on the dispositions of both the students and teacher. With each passing day, she knew something should be done about the learning conditions. A larger schoolroom desperately needed to be built, and the children . . . well, the children were intolerable, and if she'd had anywhere to run, she would have after the first day. Unfortunately, she had nowhere to go.

But it hadn't taken long for her to reach her first firm decision. Having children was out of the question. She seemed to vaguely recall someone saying that children were a blessing sent from above, but if the children of Wakefield Timber were an example of parental bliss, she would happily forgo that hallowed state and buy a goat instead. She figured she could always sell the goat if it got out of hand, but she didn't have the same option with children — though, goodness knows, at times she was sorely tempted when it came to her students.

Yet her days weren't all bad. There were times when she found herself almost happy. She had formed a satisfying, close relationship with Echo, and the men couldn't have treated her with more respect.

Whatever Jake had said to them about leaving her alone worked. They implicitly heeded his warning, and now she considered them all loyal friends.

Every night some sat around playing cards, while others were already snoring away in their bunks by seven o'clock. A number of them would lie in bed reading Western novels and outdated pink copies of the *Police Gazette* as the rancid odor of drying socks, melting shoe grease, and pitch pine scented the air.

A few gathered around the old-timers, listening as they spun their tall tales about Ho-dogs, Paul Bunyan, Johnny Inkslinger, and snow snakes. From a far corner someone would strum a guitar and softly whistle "The Red Light Saloon."

Men were a funny lot, Tess had decided.

They liked to think they were the stronger sex, but she knew otherwise. Though their brawn made them seem indomitable, they had a simple honesty and concern for their fellow workers she admired. She knew the jacks would fight one another at the drop of a hat, going directly for physical satisfaction, using fists, boots, and sometimes teeth to settle a dispute, but she'd also seen a gentler side to them.

To those who treated him fairly, the timber worker was a square dealer and a true friend. He might have a rough exterior, but he also had a heart of gold. Tess would find herself smiling while she listened to a man brag about his record cuts in the woods, the amount of whiskey he could drink, the fights he'd fought, and the women he'd loved. Yet she knew this rough bear of a man could have his heart touched by a friend's anguish, the love of a good woman, or the brush of a child's hand.

But with every rule of thumb, there was an exception, and she happened to run into one on a late Saturday afternoon. She'd headed for Menson's store to buy material to make a hat. The thought had suddenly occurred to her that morning. She had no idea if she could fashion one, but the idea intrigued her.

The camp store was bustling with activity. Christmas was just weeks away, and Henry had his hands full waiting on customers. Tess browsed through the piece goods trying to decide what she wanted to purchase. The ribbons and laces were eye-catching. Tess thought about buying one or the other for Echo, but she knew her friend's clothing supply was limited and a fancy hat would look silly worn with a simple cotton garment.

Three jacks burst into the store, talking loudly and shoving each other like small, rowdy boys. The odor of their dirty, unwashed bodies cast a pall over the few ladies present.

Henry glanced up from behind the counter and looked none too happy to see them. It was obvious the men had been drinking, a vice strictly prohibited in camp during cutting season. Although a few of the crew piled into sleighs and made the trip to Shadow Pine on Saturday nights to carouse, they knew they had to be stone-cold sober by the time four thirty Monday morning rolled around.

The bell over the door tinkled again, and Tess's pulse leaped the way it always did when she saw Jake enter the store, André following. In the weeks since the accident involving Frank, Jake hadn't been quite as reserved toward her, but she sensed he was still going out of his way to avoid contact.

As the big foreman strode to the counter to make his purchase, André spotted her and walked over.

"*Bonjour,* mademoiselle!"

"Afternoon, André." She wished she could find the sight of the brawny, dark Frenchman as stimulating as the sight of his reticent boss. André was good-looking enough to attract any woman he chose. Not only was he handsome, but he was polite as well. She knew that most women would give their eyeteeth to have him show the smallest amount of interest in them, but it was Jake Lannigan's attention that made her heart race. For the life of her, she didn't know why, but for some reason his standoffish nature intrigued her.

Lannigan was a head taller than the Frenchman. His eyes were a little brighter, his lashes were a little longer, his hair was a darker chestnut, and his close-mouthed, knowing smile made him more intriguing than any other man in camp.

And in the midst of such superb masculine specimens on which to base her opinion, that was saying something.

"Are you going on the sleigh ride tonight,

ma chère?"

Tess snapped out of her daydreams, returning her attention to André. "I don't know anything about a sleigh ride tonight."

"It is an annual event this time of the year. We meet after supper in front of the bunkhouse. A few of the men have sweethearts in Shadow Pine, and they join us. There are ten — maybe fifteen — sleighs, and we stop along the way to cut the camp Christmas tree." André snapped his heels together and bowed. "You will find the evening quite enjoyable, mademoiselle, and I would be most honored if you would permit me to escort you."

She glanced wistfully at Jake as he paid for his purchase. "It sounds like fun, André, but I'm afraid I won't be able to go." There was a geography test first thing Monday morning, and she knew she would have to spend the entire weekend studying.

"Oh? You do not like sleigh rides?"

"It sounds delightful, but I'm afraid I have work to do." Her eyes drifted back to Jake. If by some miracle he had been the one to ask her, would she have cast her responsibilities aside and gone?

"Can this work not be postponed?" André's smile had turned boyishly coaxing.

"The holidays come but once a year, *ma chère.*"

Tess sighed. "I know, and I would love to go, André, but I really mustn't."

"Such a shame. For one so lovely to be stuck in such a small, stuffy room, with only the smell of drying socks to keep her company while others are skimming across the countryside, having a marvelous time! Are you *sure* this work cannot be postponed for only a few hours?"

"Why do you cut the camp tree so soon? The holiday is still more than a month away."

"Ah, we celebrate earlier and longer than others. Come with us!"

She was about to refuse again when her attention was diverted to the three men who had entered the store earlier. Their playful remarks were beginning to contain offensive language.

Jake's harsh glance must have been a discreet reminder that women were present. The jacks quieted momentarily, but shortly one shouted a ribald joke to the other, and the three burst into snickers. The foreman stepped over to confront one of the men.

"Waite, you, Ben, and Jess need to take it outside," he said quietly.

"Hey, Jake, we was jus' havin' some fun,"

the most inebriated of the three scoffed.

"Have your fun somewhere else. There are ladies present."

"Ladies?"

Waite Burne glanced around until his drunken gaze focused on Tess. It was the first time she'd seen Echo's husband. His mouth spread into a leering grin that repulsed her.

"Well, you're right. There shore is. Lookee here, Ben. There's a right purty woman among us!"

"Waite," Jake kept his voice low, but the tone was firm. "You know the rules. No drinking in camp. You and your friends see me in my office when you sober up."

"We're jus' havin' us a little Christmas nip," Waite said. "You can't really consider that drinkin', Jake."

"Move on, Waite."

"All right . . . I'm goin'. But I'd like to wish this purty little woman a merry Christmas first." Waite edged past Jake. "Hello there, honeybunch."

His bleary-eyed gaze skimmed her up and down, and he swayed unsteadily. His voice lowered to a conspiratorial whisper when he leaned closer to her. The smell of hard liquor turned her stomach. Poor Echo.

"If you've been a good little girl, ol'

Waite'll give you a little sugar in your Christmas stocking."

Jake stepped into Waite's path. "Leave now."

Tess noted that the warning held a note of finality. An uneasy silence fell upon the room as the two men faced each other. They were both large and formidable examples of manhood.

"I don't mean no harm —" Waite began.

"Go," Jake said.

Ben and Jess eased forward. "Com'on, Waite. Let's git on over to Shadow Pine. We don't want no trouble here."

Waite's eyes shifted to Tess and then slowly back to Jake. "Shore, Ben. Big Say knows I'm just liquored up — don't mean no harm." Waite winked at Tess, and then he began to move toward the doorway. "Merry Christmas, ma'am, and a right fine New Year to you."

She turned away and a moment later the door rattled shut. Without a word, Jake followed on the heels of the three men.

"I am sorry you had to witness that," André apologized.

As the shoppers resumed their browsing, she addressed the Frenchman. "So that's Waite Burne?" She was appalled by the fact that the unkempt man was Echo's husband.

André nodded and looked out the window. "Yes, that is Waite."

"Is he like this often?"

André shrugged as he turned back to her. "Normally Waite would not hurt a fly. When he is sober, he can outwork any man in camp, but when he drinks, he is crazy like a loon. He is always very sorry afterward, but I do not know how Echo puts up with him." Dismissing the subject, he returned to their earlier conversation. "You are sure you will not change your mind about the sleigh ride?"

"Thank you, André, but I'd better not. We have an important test on Monday."

He shrugged good-naturedly. "You will miss the fun."

"My loss. Perhaps another time." Picking up a bottle of lemon toilet water, Tess made her purchases and left the store.

When she stepped outside, there was no sign of Jake or the other three men. She tried to shrug off the disappointment that cast a shadow over her day. She realized she'd been hoping Jake might have had business near the bunkhouse so they could walk together, but, of course, that was silly. Jake Lannigan would never wait around to walk Fedelia Yardley home.

Wrapping her scarf tighter under her chin,

she started to cross the street just as loggers were bringing their horses into camp. With her mind still on Jake, she glanced up to see eight or nine of the horses galloping in her direction.

Stunned, she froze as the animals thundered down on her in a quest to reach the watering trough. She would have been trampled beneath iron hooves if a pair of strong arms had not snatched her quickly out of harm's way. Startled, she looked up to see a pair of handsome hazel eyes just inches from her own. A moment later Jake set her gently on her feet, but he kept his hands on her arms until he seemed sure she could stand on her own.

"You might start watching where you're going, Teacher."

Tipping his felt logging cap politely, he walked on as a heated flush rose to her cheeks. Oh! The man was insufferable! He saved her life and then chided her?

Jerking off her bonnet, she stuck her tongue out at his retreating back before she turned and marched back to the bunkhouse, happy to have that out of her system.

14

Creaking harness and melodious sleigh bells brought an envious smile to Tess's face as she stepped from the cookshack later that evening.

Row upon row of horse-drawn sleighs sat waiting to be boarded. In a jovial mood as they piled aboard, the wild woodsmen broke out into hearty choruses of "Jingle Bells."

French–Canadians, wearing colorful headgear and bright scarves, hoisted wives and girlfriends into the sleighs. Blond Finn giants already had their women snuggled beneath furry lap robes, waiting for the festivities to begin, while men from "down below" — southern Michigan — piled into the remaining sleds. All seemed prepared to put aside their good-natured rivalry to have a good time.

She could hear the friendly ribbing when men shouted back and forth to one another. The French–Canadians were dubbed

"Frogs," the men from across the pond were called "greenhorns" and "Hunkies," and the Saginaw toughs were "the valley boys." She had stopped trying to keep them all straight long ago.

Lars Rurik, a big congenial Swede, spotted her. She grinned and started backing up when he stood up in his sleigh and shouted at her to climb aboard.

Waving back at him, she called, "I can't. I have work to do!"

The man waded through the maze of bodies and jumped out of the sleigh, shouting, "No vone vorks the night Lars cuts the Christmas tree!"

Before she could stop him, the burly woodsman descended upon her. Amid her shrieking protests, he caught her up in his Herculean arms and carried her to the waiting sleigh.

"Lars, put me down!" she demanded halfheartedly, though by now she was longing to join the merriment.

"Vork later, voman. Tonight ve have fun!" Lars boomed.

Bells merrily jingled and laughter filled the air when the loaded sleighs began pulling out of camp. Tess made up her mind that the test could wait. For once, it wasn't snowing. And overhead, a full moon lit the snowy countryside almost as brightly as day when the sleds raced through the center of camp.

The view took away her breath, as did the sight of Jake coming out of his office with André at his side. The two men paused to watch the lighthearted shenanigans.

The crew waved as they passed, amid friendly shouts of "Hey, Big Say!" "Hop a sleigh, Big Say!" and "There's a seat for you, Montague!"

Jake grinned back at the crew, waving the friendly invitations aside. "You might as well go, André. We're through for tonight."

"No, I think I will go to the bunkhouse and pay Miss Yardley a visit. She is studying for a test and I will help —"

At that moment the sleigh carrying Tess swept by, and Jake saw the smile on André's face dim when she stood up and waved merrily at them. Pulling his hat out of his pocket, Jake grunted when the sleigh raced around the corner amid a loud, cheery chorus of "Deck the Halls." "I thought you said she wasn't going on the sleigh ride."

"She wasn't," André murmured.

A smile lit Tess's face when the sled whisked by Jake and Lars shouted for the driver to turn around.

Jake and André were still standing on the planked walk when the sleigh she was in barreled back around the corner. When it reached the two men, three jacks leaped out. Jake's grin warmed her heart.

"Don't even think it," he warned, but his words fell on deaf ears.

The lumberjacks picked up the boss as if he were a sack of flour and pitched him into the sleigh, landing him headlong in Tess's lap. He immediately found a seat of his own and then met her gaze with his beautiful eyes.

"Merry Christmas, Big Say!" she said happily.

The sound of bells filled the brisk night air as they raced along the icy roads to catch the others. Tess saw that a woman from Shadow Pine latched onto André, who had also been manhandled onto the sleigh.

The madcap ride took them over hills and hollows, through tall stands of pine and across a frozen pond. It amazed Tess at how the road monkeys kept the pond mostly cleared of snow so the folks in camp could ice-skate if they wanted. It was one of the more fun things they could do to pass the time, even though not many took advantage of it.

She laughed until her sides hurt. The

lumberjacks played as hard as they worked. Jake stood now in the middle of the sleigh, exchanging friendly banter tit for tat with his crew. His deep baritone boomed out the old, traditional carols as heartily as anyone's. She began to see a new and encouraging side to the handsome Jake Lannigan.

The ride went on for more than an hour before the sleighs finally pulled into a large field covered with fir trees. Everyone piled out, and the search for the perfect tree was on.

Moose Bentson, head cook, announced, "I will award a Christmas goose to the one who finds the camp tree this year! The tree must be large, at least twenty feet tall, with broad boughs."

She found herself running breathlessly beside Jake as they scoured the hillside for the prize. The wind blew off icy Lake Huron, and she prayed the good weather would hold for the festivities.

When she spotted the tree first, she squealed. Motioning for Jake, she watched with bated breath as he examined it. The magnificent pine stood more than twenty feet high, and the branches were arched in perfect symmetry. What a lovely sight it would be, standing in the center of camp, dressed in tinsel, shiny ribbons, and bows!

Jake smiled admiringly at her. "Looks like the pretty lady from Philadelphia wins the goose."

She grinned back at him, her heart beating wildly in her chest. Who wanted a goose? The greatest prize of all was to hear him say he thought she was pretty!

Eventually everyone gathered around Tess's tree, and after Lars felled it, it took seven men to carry it back to a sleigh. Amid shouts and laughter, they secured the heavy base to the side with thick ropes. The moon crept higher when the crowded sleds took off, but Tess didn't mind. She was wedged so tightly against Jake that he was forced to put his arm around her on the ride home. Sighing with contentment, she snuggled against his broad shoulder, drinking in his warmth.

Once they reached camp, the tree was set up in the center of their community. Hot mugs of cider started circulating, and carols broke out again. Tess knew she had shamelessly trailed Jake all evening, but until he said something to discourage her, she didn't plan to stop. Wherever he went, she wasn't far behind, and should she momentarily stray, he seemed to pop up nearby.

"Cookie, ma'am?" Jake offered.

She turned from speaking to Bernice and

smiled. Camp cookies were the size of stove lids. Curtsying politely, she replied, "Why, thank you, sir." She selected a nice, tasty-looking one and bit into it.

"I thought André said you had a test to study for."

"I do . . . did," she corrected. She'd have to study extra hard tomorrow to make up for tonight's fun, but it would be worth it. "It seems the jacks don't know how to take no for an answer. May I get you a cup of cider?"

"Thank you. You'll join me?"

Tess's pulse hammered in her throat. Yes, she would gladly join him in a cup of cider. She went in search of the beverage before he could change his mind.

Her stomach was still jumpy when she hurried back with two steaming mugs a few moments later. When she turned the corner, she saw that one of the women from Shadow Pine had cornered Jake.

The diminutive woman was uncommonly pretty, with sparkling emerald-green eyes and auburn hair. Her hat was darling and most fashionable. Tess's heart sank when she saw the way Jake was looking at her, as if they were more than casual acquaintances.

Jealousy welled up in her throat. A painful knot formed in the pit of her stomach, where only moments ago butterflies fluttered, as she watched the woman rise on her tiptoes to place a brief kiss on the boss's lips. The kiss might have been casual, but the look in the woman's eyes was not. Tess started to tremble, and hot cider spilled over the rims of the cups.

Jake glanced up. When he fixed his eyes on her, he murmured something quietly to the woman and she merged back into the milling crowd. Summoning up her brightest smile, Tess walked over and handed one of the cups of cider to him.

"Thanks. That smells good."

They sat on one of the fresh hay bales that were placed on the planked sidewalk. She longed to ask him who the woman was, but she had no right. Deep inside, she had a feeling it was Marcy Wetlock, the woman André had said Jake occasionally visited in Shadow Pine.

He broke the silence. "Bernice stopped by the office this afternoon. She thinks it would be nice if the children had a Christmas program this year."

"Then let Bernice come and organize one." Tess had figured out the first day why the woman was so anxious for the new schoolteacher to take her place.

He drew back in mock surprise. "But

that's *your* job, Miss Yardley."

Shrugging, she sipped the hot drink. "Tell me, Mr. Lannigan, did the shepherds watching their flocks use crude and offensive language with one another? Did they fight with their fists, spit tobacco on their sheep, try to brain each other senseless with their staffs, and repeatedly refer to the Virgin Mary as a common trollop? You see, I also thought a Christmas program would be nice. I've even had the children busy working on one this past week, but you have just heard the results of such wishful thinking. The little heathens did all the things I described and more."

"Well, maybe a Christmas program isn't the best idea," he admitted.

She enjoyed the few minutes they sat in easy silence after that, until a burst of merriment broke out in the crowd. Lars, Angus, Ray, Mort, and Jim bounded in the direction of her and Jake with devilish grins on their faces. It was plain to see they were up to trouble.

"Here we go again," Jake muttered.

Then Tess spotted the clumps of mistletoe clasped in their hands, and she frowned. Scooped her off her feet, she was kissed so many times in the next few minutes that she lost track.

Everyone joined in the melee, and soon chaos reigned. Tess tried to keep track of how many women Jake kissed, and how long the kisses lasted, but it was difficult. The handsome foreman of Wakefield Timber had no trouble attracting the opposite sex, but she noticed he generally made the embraces brief and casual, in keeping with the light-hearted holiday spirit.

It was only when Tess saw Marcy Wetlock heading in his direction that she broke from Ed Holman's clasp, snatched his clump of mistletoe, and ran.

"Hey, woman! Bring that back here! You've disarmed me!" Ed bellowed.

She didn't want to seem overly anxious, so she slowed her pace to casually saunter past Marcy, and then she headed straight for Jake. By the time she reached him she was breathless, but she had her mind set on a course of action.

He appeared momentarily startled when she rushed up and came to a sudden halt in front of him. Taking a cautious step backward, he shook his head. "Now, don't be getting any wild ideas, school lady . . ."

"Merry Christmas, Jake!" Before she lost her nerve, she bounded onto the wooden sidewalk to give herself an advantage in height. She thrust the mistletoe above his head, took a deep breath, threw her arms around his neck, and shamelessly covered his mouth with more than a schoolmarm's kiss.

Staggering backward, he caught her to him and she pressed closer. It was a reckless, indiscreet attack, and she was certain that sometime later she'd wish she had tried to control her impulse. He would probably think that, besides her memory, she had lost her mind — and perhaps she had.

Jake Lannigan had never encouraged any sort of personal attraction between them — quite to the contrary — but her attraction to him drove her. She was tumbling hopelessly, wildly, madly in love with this handsome, brawny woodsman, and at that instant her propriety was completely misplaced.

Her heart sang when she felt his arms begin to accept her, and she poured her heart and soul into the embrace. She was powerless to contain herself. He was everything she wanted, though it seemed she was the last thing he needed.

For one heart-stopping moment, she thought he might not respond. Dropping the mistletoe, she brought her hands down to clutch the lapels of his thick jacket and moved closer against the width of his chest, her mouth pressed against his. His arms caught her closer.

He momentarily broke the kiss, and their eyes met. The world around her disappeared, and they gazed with new awareness for each other. "Just kiss me, Jake Lannigan," she whispered. "Don't try and talk yourself out of it. You know you want to."

An impertinent grin spread across his handsome features. "Who said I didn't?"

Happiness bubbled within her as she was lifted in the cradle of his muscular arms and kissed like she'd never been kissed before. She was drowning deliciously in the way the rough fabric of his coat tickled her cheek, in the clean smell of his soap and shaving cream. Her senses were heightened, and she felt giddy and lightheaded and wonderful. And then the kiss deepened . . .

But a ring of laughter intruded. Jake glanced up, and she groaned when she saw that at least half of his crew had paused to watch the spectacle with growing amusement.

Clearing his throat, he casually lowered her to her feet, though his hands remained possessively around her waist. "Don't you baboons have anything else to occupy your attention?"

The crowd broke into a hearty round of applause, bringing a rosy flush to her cheeks.

The men rapidly dispersed with Jake's none-too-subtle suggestion, but she'd gotten her kiss — and what a kiss it was!

15

"Miss Yardley?"

Tess glanced up from her desk late one afternoon to find King Davis standing in the doorway. School was over for the day, so she was surprised to see him still there. "Yes, King?"

"Mr. Lannigan says for you to git yore bee-hind over to his office."

"Were those Mr. Lannigan's exact words?" Her tone held its usual note of disapproval of the boy's crude vocabulary.

"Close enough."

With a sigh she closed her grade book, realizing the message was not a courtly summons. "Thank you, King."

The boy disappeared as she stood and went to bank the fire. Yet even a coarse message was encouraging. Her hopes soared when she reached for her coat. Jake wanted to see her — she was making progress.

Maybe the kiss they had shared a few

nights ago had finally broken the ice between them. Perhaps the reluctant Mr. Lannigan was ready to admit that an undeniable attraction between them did exist, one he could no longer ignore. She had recognized it from the first. Jake Lannigan was destined to be hers.

The shadows were beginning to lengthen when she left the schoolhouse. A pale sun sank in the west, its watery appearance the first in many long days.

The ridges of deep snow cracked beneath her boots as she hurried along the sled path. Thoughts of being with the foreman made the bone-chilling walk much easier to tolerate today.

Her mind wanted to play guessing games. Jake had summoned her because he wanted to invite her to a private supper in his room. Would that be improper? Maybe she should stop and ask Echo, but then her friend didn't seem to be the type who would be familiar with such niceties.

She longed to know so much more about the big, rugged lumberjack. Did he read for pleasure? Did he like cream and sugar in his coffee, or did he drink it strong and black? She sat so far away from him during meals that she couldn't observe his eating habits. Did he have brothers and sisters?

Did he get his strong, aristocratic features from his mother, or did his dark, stunning good looks come from his father? What made him laugh? Who made him laugh? Who touched his heart?

She felt safe and warm and incredibly happy whenever she was near him. She wondered if somewhere, in the dark, mysterious part of her life, there had ever been a man who had made her feel this contented, this at peace with herself. She didn't think so. She was sure feelings this strong came but once in a woman's life. She didn't need her memory to remind her of that.

Climbing the steps to the lumber office, she paused a moment to take stock of her appearance. She was glad she'd worn the blue wool today. She turned the doorknob and walked in. Relieved to see that Jake was the only one in the office, she welcomed the few moments of privacy. She closed the door. "King said you wanted to see me?"

Jake glanced up from the ledger he was reading. His gaze ran over her in a way that made her heart rise in her throat.

"Have a seat. I'll be with you in a minute."

Disappointed that his greeting wasn't a little more cordial, she removed her mittens and bonnet and then walked over to stand beside the stove. Trying to keep her eyes off of him, she waited patiently as he finished what he was doing.

Finally he laid the pencil aside, reached inside the top drawer, and removed a small pouch. "I trust your day was productive?"

She smiled, making it one of her prettiest. "We're about to study the continents. I never realized that there were so many — five!"

"Five? I believe there are seven."

Her smile faded. "Seven? Honestly?" That rotten King Davis had lied to her again.

"I know you're wondering why I asked you to stop by."

He stood, and his towering height made her feel small and insignificant. Summoning her sunniest expression, she said, "Not really. I was glad to have the opportunity —"

"This isn't a social visit, Miss Yardley."

She realized how transparent she must seem and quickly tried to cover her eagerness to be with him. "Oh . . . no, of course it isn't. Exactly why did you send for me, Mr. Lannigan?"

Jake handed her the pouch he'd taken from the drawer. "It's payday."

Tess took the pouch and opened it, dumping the contents into the palm of her hand. She shook her head. "I'm sorry, but how much is this?"

"Seven dollars."

Viewing the paltry sum with growing horror, she heard him explain.

"I know it's small, but let me remind you that you'll receive a twenty-five-cent raise in five years if you perform your job faithfully and without fault, provided the raise is approved by the owner of the company."

Her gaze lifted slowly to meet his. Amusement flickered in the eyes that met hers.

"Something to aim for, isn't it?" he said, smiling.

Speechless, she nodded. She wanted to kick him in the shins for thinking this funny.

"That will be all, Miss Yardley." Turning back to his work, he dismissed her. "You'd better run along. It will be dark in a few minutes."

The few coins in her hand were discouraging enough, but the realization that his summons had not been of a personal nature was even more upsetting. Dropping the money into her purse, she squared her shoulders.

"Don't spend it all in one place," he murmured.

She started to the door when his voice stopped her.

"Miss Yardley?"

"What?" She didn't bother to turn and

face him.

"Thanksgiving's coming up. Have a nice one."

"The same, I'm sure." She hoped he had the courtesy to flinch when he heard the door slam shut behind her.

Thanksgiving and Christmas came and went with barely a notice. Supper Christmas night had nine big turkeys and all the fixings on the cookshack tables, and later the men sang Christmas carols in the bunkhouse. André read the apostle Matthew's account of the Christ Child's birth before he blew out the lantern.

Tess had lain in her small room and listened. Every word touched a chord in her heart, and she was certain she'd heard the story many times before, though she couldn't place the source of where or when. Her job application indicated she had no family, but deep inside she had a sense that somewhere, someone tonight was missing her. Maybe even longing to hold and comfort her, or kiss away her lonely tears.

On New Year's Eve an ice storm hit the logging camp, rendering the crew idle for two days. Tess sat in her windowless room trying to study, but the men developed a severe case of cabin fever, and shouting matches broke out in the bunkhouse. It was hard to concentrate with tempers flaring.

On the third morning, to pass the time, she struggled through knee-deep snow to purchase items at Menson's, and in the evening she worked in her tiny room, fashioning another hat.

As she stitched the finishing laces and bows, she sat back on her cot and admired her creation. She couldn't imagine how she'd thought of the design. The women in camp never wore such finery, but she'd wanted to make a new hat for each and every one of them. However, that would take time, so she decided to wait until they were all finished to give them the gift. Until then, she intended to tell no one of her secret project.

She remembered when the idea had first sprung to her mind. It was during a spelling bee one long afternoon. One minute she was doodling in the margin of her speller, and the next moment she was sketching a hat. A large elaborate design made of lace and silk and ostrich feathers. She snickered. That particular one would have to go to Bernice.

Of course, Menson's didn't carry ostrich feathers and silk, and certainly not the intricate lace she had drawn. The camp store had a small selection of ribbons and buttons and such, but she'd substituted where she could. She'd gone in search of crow feathers in the forest and found a few in the snowdrifts.

I have a knack for this sort of thing. Where did I get this gift? Perhaps I inherited it.

She knew the talent was God given, and she appreciated it.

Holding the completed hat in front of her, she sighed. Lovely. Simply lovely.

The ice thawed, but lakefront snow persisted. The men went back to work. The middle of January turned bitterly cold, and the children grew more unbearable with each passing day. And it snowed and snowed and snowed. And snowed.

Drifts mounted to alarming heights, and the road monkeys were having a hard time keeping the paths, roads, and planked walks cleared. Tess fell asleep at night listening to the wind batter the log bunkhouse. She might not recall her past, but she was convinced she didn't like cold and snow.

Not in either life.

The door to the schoolhouse slammed shut when Scooter Wilson ran outside. Tess stepped to the window and heard his feet thundering purposefully down the ice-covered path. He hurriedly unbuttoned the front of his pants while making a beeline for the outhouse.

Four of the children had complained of having bellyaches after eating their lunch. King Davis had passed out dried apples all morning, and Tess was beginning to wonder if he wasn't playing one of his pranks again. She'd wisely refused the treat, saying she didn't feel well herself. She had learned she could trust King about as far as she could throw him.

Tirzah Reynolds's hand shot up in the air and frantically waved.

"Yes, Tirzah?"

"It's hit me again!"

"Scooter, Quinn, and King are all using the —"

"I can't wait!" Tirzah's pained expression convinced Tess that she would have to make an exception this time. Ordinarily, only one child was allowed out of the room at a time.

"All right, Tirzah. You may be excused —"

Tirzah shot out of her seat and bolted for the door. Cautioning the class to settle down, Tess continued with the lesson. "And George Washington was who?"

Five minutes later, the door opened, and Quinn stuck his head in.

"Guess who has her tongue stuck to the outhouse door handle?"

Tess glanced up. "Who?" she asked, as if she didn't know the answer.

"The ol' cypress tree. You'd better come get her. She's screaming her fool head off."

She laid her book aside and stood up. "Thank you, Quinn. You may return to your seat."

Quinn went to his desk, and a moment later Scooter burst through the doorway and scrambled back into the room. Slipping into her coat, Tess called over her shoulder, "I shall expect your best behavior while I'm gone."

The newest crisis failed to disturb her, and neither did the persistent hammering that had suddenly started on the outside of the schoolroom door. The children's incessantly bad behavior tried her patience hourly, but she learned that it was far better to try to outwit them than give in to them.

While she was putting on her mittens, an eraser whizzed by her head and smacked the door, creating a fine sheen of chalk dust to powder her face. Ignoring the deliberate provocation, she calmly reached for the door handle and gave it a pull. The door refused to budge.

She tugged harder, and the children

started to snicker. Undoubtedly, one of the boys had tricked Tirzah into touching her tongue to the metal handle on the outhouse, and Quinn had then been sent to inform her of Tirzah's plight while King nailed the front door shut. King. Tess realized she hadn't seen him eat any of the apples, so he had fooled her into thinking he was feeling poorly in order to pull off this shenanigan.

It was hard for her to control the knot of building anger in her throat. This was going to be a long afternoon. Being stuck inside in a tiny room with no ventilation, the windows frozen shut, and seven children, four of whom were suffering from a roaring case of intestinal fright, was not going to be pleasant.

Taking a deep breath, she removed her mittens and coat, and then she dragged the slop jar to the far corner behind the wood pile for privacy.

"Please open your poetry books." Pained groans filled the room, which she ignored. They were going to do their work no matter what. "We shall read from the works of Robert Burns loud enough for both Tirzah and King to enjoy while we wait."

"Oh, horse feathers!"

"Do we have to read that 'My love is like a red, red rose' stuff?"

Hostility rose in the boys' voices.

Juice Tetterson's hand flew up. "I-I . . .
ha-have . . . to . . . thunder . . . Miss . . .
Yard-Yardley!"

Motioning her permission for the child to
leave her seat to use the slop jar, Tess summoned a brave smile. "Yes, we might even
have time for Elizabeth Barrett Browning's
sonnets." She gazed off pointedly. "How do
I love thee?" she quoted. "Let me count the
ways . . ."

16

Jake walked into the office late in the afternoon, stomping snow off his boots and heading straight for the stove to thaw out. He noticed that André was deeply engrossed in a wire he was reading.

"What has you so preoccupied?"

"We just received another telegraph from Monsieur Talbot Wellington-Kent."

Jake shrugged out of his coat and hung it on the peg. "Oh?"

"He is worried sick about his fiancée, Jake. He is trying to get here, but the weather has brought train travel to a halt. I am afraid he is thinking the worst."

Reaching for his coffee cup, Jake walked back to the stove, parroting his usual answer when the subject of Tess Wakefield was brought up. "We've told him everything we know. The rivers are frozen solid. It would be a miracle if any bodies were found now. When the weather clears, he can come and confirm Miss Yardley's identity."

The Frenchman shook his head. "You can see why he is upset. Miss Wakefield has not contacted him since she left Philadelphia. Talbot says here that her engagement ring alone was worth more than ten thousand dollars." André laid the telegraph aside thoughtfully. "I sympathize with the poor man."

Jake walked to the window to stare out at the falling snow. Tess wasn't wearing a ring, nor had she been the day André fished her out of the water. He'd checked — but the ring could have slipped off during the accident. He frowned as his conscience pricked. What if he was mistaken and the schoolteacher was in fact Fedelia Yardley?

A sick feeling formed in the pit of his stomach. If he was mistaken, he was deliberately driving her away — not to mention he was getting mighty attracted to the woman, whoever she was. He shook his head to clear his brain.

The woman in that schoolhouse had tenacity. He had watched her struggle to perform a job he suspected she wasn't trained to do without a word of complaint. Her predecessors had been in his office every hour on the hour demanding to be replaced, but this woman, facing an overwhelming task, was quietly gritting her way through it.

When we find out her true identity, let her be Fedelia Yardley.

Jake could deal with falling in love with a stranger, but not Wakefield's granddaughter. And yet, in his heart, he knew who she was.

Tess had adjusted to living among one hundred and twenty-five rough, barely civilized woodsmen, and only rarely did she show signs of losing her sunny disposition. Her aristocratic behavior and refined breeding were making gentlemen out of the burly lumberjacks, an enviable accomplishment for anyone.

The crew had even ceased their constant harping about her not allowing them to smoke in the bunkhouse. They good-naturedly bowed to her wishes and had taken their pipes and tobacco outdoors.

He was beginning to be deeply ashamed for what he was putting her through. That feeling had grown ever since the afternoon she helped him take care of Frank Kellier's leg. Though her face was pale and her hands shook, she had worked beside him even when grown men hadn't been able to render assistance.

He'd watched her sit by Frank's side like a mother hen, sharing her strength until the man found his own again. And the way she was standing her ground with her students — he had to hand it to her. Everyone knew that took perseverance.

Jake moved to his desk, sat down, and tried to get his thoughts off the woman who had come unexpectedly into his life. Staring blankly at the mound of paper before him, he admitted he knew she was falling in love with him. And he was feeling the same. The concession left a bitter taste in his mouth.

Under other circumstances, he would have welcomed her attentions. She was so beautiful. She possessed a cloud of flaxen hair, arched brows, long blond lashes, a pretty mouth, and ivory skin, yet there was more to Tess than mere superficial beauty. She had an inner strength he found compelling.

Her ability to accept whatever came her way without complaint, her kindness to offer a helping hand to anyone who needed it, her willingness to pray for those afflicted — those were the qualities he was discovering about her. He should have known she would be a special kind of woman, especially because she had Tip Wakefield's blood running in her veins.

What would she think now of Jake's dream to replant the trees? Somehow, he knew what man was doing to the land was starting to gain her attention, and he'd bet she shared his concern about the future.

He was starting to dread the day Tess regained her memory. What would she think of him then? She was drawn to him, yes, but she had no idea she was engaged to marry another man, and her eventual discovery that he had suspected her identity but done nothing to confirm it would surely alienate her.

He'd tried to discourage her attentions, but he couldn't deny he recognized love shining brightly through her eyes whenever she looked at him. And he couldn't deny that it gave him a certain sense of pride to see it there.

Rubbing a hand over the back of his neck, he tried to concentrate on his work, but his mind kept drifting back to her.

She had a way of popping into his office on her way home from school, and he found himself looking forward to the daily visits. These impromptu calls were usually short and served no practical purpose. He usually ended up walking her back to the bunkhouse, and they talked about the day's events.

The kiss they had shared the night of the sleigh ride had left him restless, thinking what it would be like to be her husband.

What would her hair feel like if he could loosen the pins and bury his hands in the shiny, sweet-smelling mass? He dreamed of this, yet at the same time he realized that Tess was in love with another man — now forgotten, but surely when her memory returned . . .

It was a mess, one big mess of his making, and he could see no clear way to correct it. Once she regained her memory, she would leave Wakefield Timber and return to Philadelphia to marry Talbot Wellington-Kent.

If he told her now he suspected she was Tess Wakefield, she would find a way out of camp despite the heavy snow, despising him for his part in the charade. If he waited until her memory returned, she would still leave, despising him even more.

God, I don't know what I was thinking . . .

"Do you mind?"

Jake glanced up blankly. André was looking at him as if he expected an answer. "Mind what?"

"Do you mind if I ask her to go?"

"Who?"

"Fedelia. Where is your mind, Lannigan?"

Snapping back to the present, Jake picked up the work sheet on his desk and shook it irritably. "It's on my work, where yours should be."

"My, my," André said with a curious look. "The man is edgy."

Jake realized his guilt had put him in a defensive mood. "Sorry. What was it you asked?"

"I want to know if you thought it would be improper for me to ask Miss Yardley to go for a walk Sunday afternoon."

"Yes. It would be improper." Jake got up to file the document.

André twirled his pencil between his fingers thoughtfully. "You claim to have no interest in the lady, but your actions of late would indicate otherwise. Am I not correct?"

"You're correct, but her contract states she isn't to socialize with men."

"*Mon ami,* are you serious? She has the run of the town and you know it. Besides, I do not believe you have been overly concerned about her following the rules. I seem to recall the Christmas sleigh ride and the many times you have walked her home lately."

"I haven't walked her home," Jake dismissed curtly. "We happened to be going in the same direction at the same time."

"Ah, *oui.* Every afternoon at five you just happen to be going to the bunkhouse — not that you live there or have any particular business in that direction — but every afternoon, around five?"

Jake met his skeptical gaze. "So what?"

The Frenchman shrugged. "Your behavior appears questionable."

Jake returned to his desk. He wasn't in the mood to talk about the subject and was glad for a few minutes of silence.

"Are you telling me to stay away from Miss Yardley?" André inquired at last.

"No."

"Then what are you saying?"

Jake sighed deeply. "I'm saying it isn't any of my business what she does. If you want to ask her to go for a walk with you, do it and stop bothering me."

"I think you are saying you are interested in her and for me to back off. Is not that more like it?"

"If that's what I was trying to say, I would say it."

"Would you now?"

Jake glanced up. "Montague, how would you like to be head chickadee from now on?"

André grinned. "Now the man threatens to have me shoveling horse droppings off the roads. Could this not possibly lead me to conclude that our lovely Miss Yardley has done what no other woman has been able to accomplish? Has the new schoolmarm captured big Jake Lannigan's heart?"

Reaching for his coat, Jake slammed out of the office.

17

The office door opened late that afternoon, and a rosy-cheeked Tess sailed inside. The wind had stung her face a bright red.

"Does it ever stop snowing around here?" She reached to brush the snow from her new hat. Steadying the brim, she then tried to blow feeling back into her numb fingers.

Jake turned back to his desk. André got to his feet. "Hello, *ma chère.* Allow me to get you a cup of coffee to ward off the chill."

"Thank you just the same, André, but I don't care for coffee today." Though she glanced at Jake, he refused to look her way. Recognizing he was in an aloof mood, she ambled over to his desk and perched on the corner. Resting her hand over his, she greeted softly, "Fine day, isn't it?"

Reaching out to prevent a bundle of papers from spilling to the floor, he grunted something that possibly could have been "ifyoulikeyourweathercold."

She couldn't help but smile. "Are you busy?"

"Yes."

She sighed and absently swung her feet, noticing he'd fixed his gaze on the hat she was wearing "Do you like it?" she asked. "I made it myself!"

"Really."

"I did, and I'm rather proud of the result." She sighed. "I'm discovering all sorts of interesting things about me. Losing one's memory isn't so bad. You can assess your natural gifts with complete objectivity, and if you don't care for what you see, you're able to change without the slightest hesitation and become someone you really enjoy." She met his gaze. "Correct?"

"If you say so."

"If there were one thing that I could change, it would be my chosen profession. What a day I've had! Tirzah, Scooter, Quinn, and Juice had frightful stomach issues, and wouldn't you know it, Tirzah stuck her tongue to the frozen outhouse handle, and then King nailed the school-room front door shut from the outside."

André whistled sympathetically under his breath. Jake bent lower to his work.

"It was horrid, but the dismal day finally ended. King knew he couldn't leave us nailed in the schoolroom forever, so a little before four he removed the nails. Tirzah had managed to get her tongue loose from the door handle sometime during the afternoon and set out for home, bawling. I'm going to have to stop by and explain the situation to her mother."

She paused, taking a deep breath. "So, needless to say, I'm glad to see this day over." She glanced at Jake and smiled. "I thought if you had business near the bunk-house, we could walk there together."

Jake shook his head. "I'll be tied up here at least another hour."

"Oh." Tess frowned when she saw André shoot Jake a grin. "You work too hard, Jake. Can't you finish whatever it is in the morning? I have something very important to talk to you about."

"No, it can't wait."

André raised an eyebrow. "You can go."

She glanced at André, who now was walking over to Jake's desk, still grinning. "Whatever it is, Big Say, I will finish it for you. I have not a thing to do but polish up my chickadee skills." André's grin widened.

Jake's jaw firmed. "No. I'll do my own work."

"You heard Miss Yardley. You work too hard, and she has something very important

222

she wants to discuss with you."

Persuasively, she smiled at Jake. "Come on, grump."

André reached for Jake's jacket and shoved it into his hands over his protests. "Bundle up tight, Big Say. It's cold out there."

She was fairly bubbling when they stepped outside the office. "Let's go skating!"

Jake paused to look at her as if she had completely lost her mind. "Ice-skating?"

"Yes. We could both use the distraction." Grabbing his hand, she pulled him along the planked sidewalk. "I spotted skates at Menson's store, and I couldn't resist buying us each a pair."

"You could afford two pairs of skates and a new hat this month?"

"Well," she said, sending him a sly smile, "Mr. Menson put your pair on your bill. He knows your size and I don't. I hope you don't mind."

"Mind that you spend my money? Yes, I mind that you spend —"

She interrupted. "And my hat cost practically nothing." He glanced at it again and frowned, but she cheerfully continued. "I went by the pond on my way home. With just enough snow cleared away, it's perfectly lovely today."

"Suppose I don't know how to skate?"

"I'll teach you."

"Suppose you don't know how?'

"I thought of that, but I'll take my chances."

"Suppose I'm not willing and I don't care to learn?"

"I *suppose* that would be too bad." She paused, giving him her sternest look. "Suppose we stop talking about it and just skate?"

"Suppose I send André to pacify you?'"

"I'm very fond of him, but I don't want to skate with him. Now face it, grouch. We're going skating."

"It's getting dark."

"I'll stop by the bunkhouse and get a lantern."

He was still grumbling after she had retrieved the light, taken his hand again, and dragged him through the woods down the long, snowy path leading to the pond.

"Some folks have work to do, Fedelia. What will I tell the crew if they see me sashaying around with you, ice-skating, of all the crazy things? And who gave you the authority to charge skates to me? If I had wanted a pair of skates I would have bought —"

"Stop being such a fussbudget," she called over her shoulder. "You make a lot more money than me, so you can afford a pair of skates. Plus, you're dying to go. Admit it. It will be fun. You'd think I was asking you to jump off a cliff."

"If I fall and break my neck, you'll be jumping off the cliff."

They reached the pond before dark. She set down the lantern and then took a seat to clamp on her new skates. "See? Isn't this fun?"

"I can think of a hundred better ways to have fun than getting out there on that ice and breaking a blasted leg."

Tess sprang to her feet and reached over to tickle him under the chin. "You won't break a leg or your neck. If you want the truth, you're going to be in more danger of harm if you don't relax and have some fun for a change." She wobbled and then straightened when she regained her footing. "That I can promise."

Shrugging her hand aside, he sat down, his gaze fixed on her as she skated gracefully onto the thick ice. She was surprised to note she was an excellent skater, skimming more artfully across the frozen pond than she knew she could.

"Come on! It's wonderful out here!"

Jake shook his head and stayed put. "What is it you wanted to talk to me about?"

"I want you to build a new schoolhouse!" Her grin widened when she saw his expression turn to astonishment. She spun in a tight circle, forming a perfect *O.*

"I don't think so."

"What?"

"I said no. I will not build a new schoolhouse."

"For me? Please?"

"Especially for you. You won't be staying around long."

"Why not?"

"Maybe because I'm not going to build anything. You have a perfectly good schoolhouse now."

"The teaching facility is insufferable! Why, even the rats won't spend more than a few minutes a day there! That's why the children are so unruly. They need more room. Their desks are piled on top of one another."

"They are not there to have fun. They are there to learn."

"Why can't they learn *and* have fun? I think they don't want to learn because of the terrible surroundings they are forced to endure." She skated passed him, wrinkling her nose as the blades of her skates showered him with ice.

"You're going to bust your backside."

"Derriere, Mr. Lannigan. Backside is

226

much too crude!" She whirled and dipped and made faces at him until he was forced to turn away in an effort to conceal the amused grin she saw forming at the corners of his mouth.

"Come on, coward. Put your skates on and we'll settle this thing. If I can knock you off your feet, you agree to build me a new schoolroom. Nothing elaborate. Just four walls and lots of nice, big, airy windows. On the other hand, if you, by some miraculous stroke of luck, manage to make me lose my balance, then we'll forget the whole thing."

"Ha. You're going to knock me off my feet, while I just have to make you lose your balance?"

She whizzed by, her skates sending another shower of ice flying at him. "Are you afraid?"

"Suppose I really don't skate? What sort of match would it be?"

"I don't skate very well." She spun in a tight circle, spiraled upwards, leaped and landed on one foot and spun like a top. When she stopped, she paused and grinned. "It's a fair match."

"Forget it. I don't have either the time or the extra men to build a schoolhouse. The one you have is good enough."

Her grin turned even more impish. "Come out here and tell me that."

"If I come out there, you'll be sorry."

"Ha!"

"All right, but remember . . . you're the one who asked for this."

She skated past him, sticking her tongue out. She was having fun. Back and forth she skimmed across the ice, waiting while he clamped and tightened the blades to the soles of his heavy boots. A beautiful, light snow was coming down, creating a perfect setting.

"Tell me when you're ready, and I'll come and help you," she called.

"That'll be the day." He stood up, and his legs bowed comically when he wobbled onto the ice.

Tess broke into laughter, her clear, sweet notes filling the crisp air.

"Laugh, Miss Smug. We'll see who's laughing in a minute."

"I told you I'd help you." She glided over and latched onto his arm. The would-be helpful gesture sent them both reeling, threatening to spill them onto the frozen pond.

"Let go of my arm!"

"Just hush up and lean on me!"

He grudgingly put his arm around her

waist, and they steadied each other.

"Are you ready?"

"Does it look like I'm ready?"

They made their way cautiously out and took a few, hesitant glides. "Now, see?" She faced him, skating backwards, and grinned. "It isn't all that difficult."

"This is a foolish thing to do. If I break an arm . . ."

"First you worry about a leg, then your neck, and now your arm. If I cause you to break *anything,* I'll take full responsibility."

"And how will that help me when I'm laid up with a broken neck, busted arm, and shattered leg?"

"You'll have the satisfaction of knowing you told me so."

"Wait a minute — hold on — not so fast!"

She turned around to skate by his side again, and their strides gradually formed a smoother gait. Tess was enjoying herself enormously as they moved slowly around the pond perimeter. "Isn't this nice?"

"Simply thrilling. When do we settle the matter of a new schoolhouse . . . that you're not getting?"

"Anytime you think you're ready."

"All right. Let me get the rules straight. You knock me off my feet, I build you a new schoolhouse —"

"The *children* and me a new schoolhouse," she corrected.

"I knock *you* off balance, and we forget I ever took part in this idiotic contest?"

"Correct, but you can't knock me off balance because of your clumsiness. It has to be fair and square, and you can't be rough or clumsy. You have to play nice."

"We'll see who's clumsy —"

Jake's skates locked with hers, and they both went down in a wildly flailing entanglement of arms and legs. He managed to struggle to his feet first. She was laughing too hard to do anything but lie there.

He took her arm, pulled her up, and they started out again, taking a second spill that sent her skidding across the pond on her seat. The fall knocked the pins out of her hair, freeing the mass to tumble loosely down her back. Her new hat landed somewhere in the deepening shadows.

"Just look what you've done to my hat and my hair, Jake Lannigan!" she yelled before dissolving in a fit of mirth and falling to her side, watching him struggle to get up. He made such a funny sight, all six foot three, two hundred thirty-five pounds of pure muscle, helpless as a new fawn on the slippery surface of the pond.

She got to her feet and skated over to peer

down at him with an air of self-righteous superiority. "Want to concede right now?"

"Concede to you?" He bounded lithely to his feet. "Fun's over, lady."

Startled, she skated off, and he came after her. Their feet flew across the pond, the blades of their skates cutting deeply into the frozen ice. The moment he'd begin to gain on her, she'd dart around him, laughing gaily.

"I want pretty pink curtains at the new windows," she taunted, "tied back with lovely satin bows!" She squealed and darted off again when he barreled toward her. It occurred to her that he was skating as well or better than she. Skidding to a halt, her hands came to her hips as she watched him race around the pond, skating backwards, sideways, turning, flipping, jumping, and spinning.

"Jake Lannigan! You fibbed! You can so skate!"

He sailed by her, deliberately covering the hem of her dress with a shower of ice from his skates. "I did *not* fib."

"You said you couldn't skate!"

"I said *suppose* I can't skate. I didn't say I *couldn't* skate." He winked at her. "I was skating when you were still wearing diapers."

His playful flirtation sent her pulse racing. "I hardly think I was still in diapers at twelve years old!"

He skated to the end of the pond and flipped around. Her heart sank when she saw the glint of combat filling his eyes. He was like a bull fixed on a red flag. "Shall we get on with the wager, my dear?"

Squealing, she turned and fled toward the bank, realizing she was no match for Jake Lannigan on or off the ice. Straight as an arrow, he skimmed over the pond. With a tremendous lunge, he managed to latch on to the hem of her skirt as she scrambled onto the bank, skate blades digging ice.

They tumbled roughly to the ground, and Jake's arm came around her waist, cushioning her fall against the broad expanse of his chest.

She broke out laughing when he rolled her over onto her back and pinned her firmly in the snow with the massive bulk of his other arm. "Help! Someone help me!"

"Your cries will do you no good, my lovely. There isn't anyone around." He gazed into her eyes and then said smugly, "I believe I have knocked you off balance."

"You cad! Your arm is crushing me!"

He grinned, flashing white teeth in a winter-tanned face. Dimples appeared in his cheeks, and she suddenly wanted him to kiss her.

"You like it."

"I do not!"

"You do too. I see it in your eyes."

Tess struggled to break free, but he grabbed her wrists and pulled her arms above her head, holding them easily with one large hand. "Oh, no you don't. You asked for this."

"Jake, please —"

He began to tickle her, and she burst into laughter again.

Their merriment started to recede when their eyes met. Snowflakes lit gently on her lashes and stayed there. Jake's eyes grew lazy as he traced a finger softly over the line of her cheek. She was very still beside him, afraid to break the moment. He gazed at her through half-closed lids.

"I don't want you stirring up trouble over this schoolhouse nonsense," he warned in a voice that had grown strangely husky.

"Umm, maybe . . ."

He released her wrists and gently shook her. "I want your promise, Fedelia."

"It wasn't a fair contest. How was I to know you'd take to the ice like a penguin?" His nearness intoxicated her. The warmth of his breath on her face ignited her feelings for him, and she wanted the moment to last forever.

"Promise me you won't get the camp riled up about this. I have enough trouble without taking on more."

"Oh, poor baby," she mocked.

His mouth moved closer to hers. "Promise me."

"Only if you kiss me," she whispered boldly.

His eyes openly caressed her face now. "No."

She smiled when her fingers pressed the fabric on his shoulders and then flitted over his neck. She loved to touch him. When his expression changed from mildly amused to one of growing concern, she relented.

"Yes," she said. "I give you my promise." Something passed between them. A moment she couldn't identify, but she knew that moment forever changed their relationship. She gazed deeply into his eyes.

"A woman shouldn't be asking a man to kiss her," he said.

She smiled, and she realized it was scandalous for an unmarried woman to permit her love to show so brightly. "What if a woman knows that, but she still longs to kiss you?"

"You have no shame," he murmured.

Her hands gently cupped his face. "If you're trying to scare me, you might as well stop. It's time you knew the real Jake Lannigan, and that man finds me attractive."

"You don't know me or what I'm capable of doing."

"I know you well enough to see a good man, one who would not take advantage of a lady who merely asks for a — mmph."

Her words were stopped when his mouth met hers.

She closed her eyes and gave herself freely to his kiss, wrapping her arms around his neck as his arms came around her to hold her close. She felt a new awareness he brought alive in her. She would gladly spend her life with him, mending his clothes, cooking his meals, soothing his hurts, bearing his children, and loving him fiercely until one or the other of them drew a last breath.

When their mouths parted at last, he didn't let her go but fixed his gaze on the soft fullness of her lips. "Go home, little one."

Tess wasn't sure she had heard him right. She laughed softly. "Go home?"

"Yes," he murmured. He looked into her eyes then. "Now — tomorrow. You don't belong here. Go back to Philadelphia and forget you ever heard of Wakefield Timber."

"No . . . no! I want to stay here with you, Jake. I have nothing to go back for —" She felt bereft when he released her from his arms and sat up.

"Go back to Philadelphia and try to put your life back together," he said softly. "You don't belong here."

"You're here."

"I'm here, but *you* shouldn't be. Not now." He shoved himself to his feet and didn't look at her. "You can't stay here with me."

She shook her head, stunned by his abrupt mood change. "Why? What have I done —"

"Heed my advice and leave. I'll arrange for one of the men to take a sleigh and get you out of camp. You'll have to stay in Shadow Pine for a while. The train can't get through, but the minute this weather clears, you're out of here." Darkness set in and the snow fell harder. "We need to go. I've wasted too much time as it is," he said curtly.

The unexpected, sharp rebuke caused tears to well up in her eyes, but she quickly turned her head to hide them. "All right," she murmured. "We'll go." But she wasn't leaving camp. She refused. He could argue all he wanted, but she wasn't going anywhere. Not without him.

Despite his brusque manner, he reached down a hand and gently helped her to her feet. After fetching her hat for her, he sat beside her as they removed their skates in silence. The memory of his kiss still sang in Tess's mind. She was sure he had enjoyed the embrace as much as she. She couldn't imagine what she had done to upset him.

"Are you ready?"

She glanced up as the snow silently fell around them, her heart brimming with anguish. "Yes, but I'm not leaving camp. You'll have to tie me up like a turkey and carry me to Shadow Pine."

"Have it your way."

He wouldn't dare. In few days he would simmer down and realize he was fighting personal issues, not her.

Refusing to meet her gaze, Jake said, "We're losing light."

"I'm right beside you."

And as far as she was concerned, that's where she would stay, regardless of his insistence that she go home.

18

"In conclusion, ladies, I think the only sensible course is to force the men's hand on this matter."

Tess had dismissed class early, hoping the mothers of her students would participate in this very important meeting. She was thrilled to see that the response was one hundred percent, yet guilt nagged her.

She had promised Jake she would let the matter drop, but she couldn't. Something inside wouldn't let her. A new schoolroom was important, and wasn't it right to fight for the important things in life? The children grew more restless and intolerable with each passing day, and were it not for the last blizzard, at Jake's insistence she'd be in Shadow Pine by now. She had a feeling God was handling matters in His way and His time.

For now she was stuck. Not even the sleighs were traveling far. She couldn't leave camp if she wanted to . . . and she didn't want to. So on impulse she had called this meeting, and before she went home she would stop by Jake's office to retract her former promise.

He wouldn't like it, but she was discovering she could be mulish when an idea was stuck in her head.

"And how are we supposed to force their hands?" Gert challenged. "I can't get my man to wipe his feet before he comes through the front door!"

"I know. I put up with a hundred and twenty-five men just like him." The bunkhouse front entrance looked more like a muddy swamp than a porch. But Tess was determined not to give up. On Sundays enough men turned out to have a decent-sized church service in the schoolhouse. There was no question the room was simply too small to accommodate the camp's needs — either as a school or church. Jake wasn't concerned about the matter. The only thing on his mind was getting her out of camp.

Various murmurs of agreement sounded and Tess tried to restore order. What she was going to propose was unorthodox, but she knew the women in camp were more than capable of carrying it through.

"Ladies, please, there are numerous ways of persuading your men to see our viewpoint without bruising their egos."

"But the Good Book says wives are to be submissive to their husbands," someone pointed out.

"I am not asking anyone to disobey her spouse," she clarified. "The Good Book is the final word, but that doesn't mean we can't slightly alter the degree of our submissiveness, does it?"

"I think it does," the same woman said.

"Why should we take your word on the matter, Miss Yardley?" Bernice blustered. "How would you know about submission? You're not even married!"

Laughter broke out, and Tess smiled. "Which makes me all the more dangerous, Bernice. Now, shall we get down to business?"

"What do you suggest we do?" Selma Miller appeared more than ready to get on with it.

"Well, for starters we'll need a good, strong name for our society," Tess proposed.

The women exchanged puzzled looks. She was certain half had never heard of a "society."

"What's a 'society'?" Gert asked.

"I guess you could say it's a group of interested citizens working together for a common goal," she explained, noting that the women stared vacantly back at her. "In our case it means the women of Wakefield Timber are about to take it upon themselves to get that new schoolhouse!" Gert's flabbergasted expression brought another round of laughter, and Tess almost smiled herself, but she wanted these women to take her seriously.

"I've never heard the likes of a female doing such a thing."

"Because you haven't heard of it doesn't mean that we can't explore the issue. I know we, as women, simply accept man's authority over the weaker sex, but I say it's time we formed a union and demand a voice in these matters!"

Beulah Morrison sprang from her seat. "I second that!"

"Sit down and close your lip, Beulah!" Bernice exclaimed, seizing the floor. "Being a teacher myself, I understand what you're saying, Miss Yardley. However, I don't know what we're going to do about all these Philadelphia, high-falutin' ideas you've been comin' up with. You know good and well the man is the head of the household."

"Of course he is, but does that mean a woman has no value to her husband beyond having his babies, cleaning his house, cooking his meals —"

"Chopping his wood, mending his socks, emptying his spittoons," Selma chimed in.

The women were clearly warming to the idea of having a say in things. She had them thinking now. "All we're asking is that your — no, *their* children — have a decent place to learn. I promise you, ladies, if we stick together in this matter we'll accomplish our goal. And I also promise that each of you will earn your husband's grudging respect in the process."

The women murmured with one another, and Tess realized the idea still sounded risky to them.

"But why us? There are only sixteen married women in camp. Sixteen women can't fight all those men!"

"I've already considered that. Obviously you will have the most power over your husbands, but in turn that will spread through camp to the other men." She started to pace in front of her desk. "Work your man. Maybe a nice, tasty apple pie will appear on the dinner table unexpectedly, an extra brush of your hand on his now and then, maybe a smile when he's least expecting it, possibly an extra love pat before he drops off to sleep. Of course, we'll try to settle this with as much decorum as possible."

"What's that?"

"Decorum? It means with as much grace and dignity as we can." She frowned. How did she know the meaning of "decorum"? It wasn't a word often used, at least not here. She shrugged. "Remember, ladies, that subtlety is the name of the game."

"And what will *you* be doing while we're baking all these apple pies, Miss Yardley?" Beulah inquired.

"I can assure you that I will be doing my share. And, if subtlety doesn't work, we'll use other means."

"Well, I guess it don't matter none. I don't have the foggiest idea what 'subtlety' means anyway," Beulah conceded.

Tess wasn't sure how she knew all these fine words, but they seemed to just pop out. "To be subtle means to be delicate, elusive, you know. You have to learn to work your man while still obeying him. In the meantime, I will be conducting a campaign of my own with the single jacks in the bunkhouse. I won't have the obvious advantages you will have, but I should be able to drop a few hints here and there, and hopefully I will win over Shot Harrison and Herb Jenson. Once I have those ringleaders on my side, the others won't be far behind."

"What about Big Say?" Bernice eyed her

knowingly. "He's gonna have a conniption fit when it dawns on him what you're up to."

"You leave Jake to me." *Please,* she silently added. He was her man, but she wasn't sure she could get him to recognize it. "Now, then," she said, strolling down the row of desks thoughtfully. "We will need a name for our society. It needs to be strong, purposeful, and credible enough to make the men take us seriously." Silence fell over the room as the women racked their brains.

"How about Women Hoping for a New Schoolhouse?" Beulah suggested.

"Sherman would laugh me out of the house," Selma declared.

"How about The Women's Society for Forming Future Citizens of Wakefield Timber?"

Expressions puckered and heads started to shake before Gert could finish. She shrugged. "Sorry. I ain't ever belonged to one of those women's 'societies' before."

"What about Builders of Our Children's Future?" someone suggested.

The women glanced at one another and nodded, indicating that the name didn't sound bad. Tess sighed. It was strong and purposeful, and the men would surely have to take a name like Builders of Our Chil-

244

dren's Future seriously.

From the back of the room a voice said softly, "Ladies, why beat around the bush? Why don't we call it what it really is? Women Against Senseless, Pigheaded Shanty Boys."

Laughter broke out, and Tess turned to see who would have the nerve to call the organization what it really was. Her amusement faded when she saw Echo standing in the doorway. She had been hoping her friend would come today, yet she wondered how Waite would react to Echo taking part in such open rebellion. Yet she could hardly hurt her friend's feelings in front of the other women by turning her away.

"That won't work," Tess mused. "It's catchy, but too long."

"Then shorten it. We'll be the WASPS."

Tess tested the name on her tongue. "WASPS?" She grinned. "Appropriate. How about it, ladies?"

The women applauded their enthusiastic, unanimous approval as she walked to the back of the room to take Echo's hand and squeeze it encouragingly. "It's perfect, Echo."

The young woman didn't crack a smile. "Thank you, ma'am. I'm right proud of myself."

Letting go of Echo's hand, Tess turned back to face the women. "It's even better that we use WASPS. The men will go nuts trying to figure out the meaning, especially if we drop the *B*." She winked mischievously and then smiled when hoots and cheers followed.

The meeting broke up, and after most of the ladies departed, she filled the lamp, made the pencil stubs for the following day, and then banked the stove. Echo stood in the back of the room, waiting.

The angry fingers of a cold north wind snatched at their coats as they stepped outside. The blustery day promised blizzard conditions by dark.

"What do you suppose Big Say will do once he finds you have all the womenfolk stirred up like a hornet's nest?" Echo asked.

Tess groaned and paused to pull her wool scarf closer to her neck. "I don't know. I'd be happy if he'd say anything to me." More than a week had passed since they had gone skating, and Jake had steered clear of her since, sending André to remind her that as soon as the weather broke, she could leave. That struck her as cold and impersonal. She'd stopped going by his office in the afternoons because he was never there anymore. She was starting to feel that he

246

would never warm to her.

"I think you're sweet on him," Echo noted.

Tess's mouth curved in a self-conscious smile. "Maybe."

"I think he's sweet on you too."

She sighed. "I'm afraid he's not."

"Yes, he is. I've seen the way he looks at you."

"Name one time."

"In Menson's store last week."

"He wasn't even aware that I was there."

"Yes, ma'am, he was. He stood in the corner and pretended he was talking to one of the jacks, but his eyes never left you once."

Tess grinned. "He did not."

Echo smiled back. "He did so."

They turned and headed for the nearest tote road. Tess decided it was a good time to broach the subject of Waite. "Echo, there's something I'd like to talk to you about."

"Okay."

"It's rather . . . personal. I hope you won't think I'm being forward."

"I won't think that."

"I know I have no right —"

"Please." Echo paused and turned to face her. "Say what you need to say. You won't be buttin' in where you're not wanted, and if you do, I'll tell you so."

This was not going to be easy, but Tess felt compelled to carry on. "Thank you." They resumed their walk. "I'm concerned about your taking part in our efforts to nudge the men to build a new schoolhouse."

Echo's face clouded. "You don't want me to be in your soo-ciety?"

"I want you to be in it, but I'm concerned, that's all."

Echo breathed a relieved sigh. "No need to be."

For a brief moment Tess toyed with the idea of coming right out and confronting Echo about her husband's drinking. She knew the other women were in no danger of causing any serious family friction as a result of their harmless crusade for a new school, but she was worried that if Echo's taking a stand in the dispute upset her husband, it might trigger another one of his drinking sprees.

"I wouldn't want your participation in our society to cause you difficulties at home." She paused, looking straight into Echo's eyes.

Her young friend directly met her gaze "You don't think the other women are going to have 'difficulties at home' from their participation?"

"I'm sure they will," she hedged, "but —"

Echo turned and began walking again, apparently dismissing the implication in Tess's tone. "I'm beholden to you for letting me be in your soo-ciety, ma'am. I ain't ever been in one of those. Never thought I'd have the chance."

"Don't change the subject." Tess was overstepping her bounds, but she couldn't ignore a potential problem, not where her friend was concerned. Even though Echo had avoided the subject of her husband's problem and had never asked for help of any kind, she couldn't in good conscience overlook the woman's situation.

"Echo, I think we're both avoiding the issue. You know I care about you. I don't want to cause trouble between you and Waite, that's all. The other women know this is all in good fun, and if it should get out of hand we'll stop immediately."

"You don't understand, Fedelia."

"No, I don't. Help me understand."

"Waite is my husband till death do us part," Echo said simply.

"I'm aware of your loyalty to him, and I applaud it, but should he ever mistreat you, you must come to me. My room is tiny, but we'll make do."

"No, ma'am. I can't do that." Echo

stopped her.

"Why not?"

"Because I belong with my husband and I don't want to leave him." Echo paused and turned to look at her. "Don't be worryin' about me, really."

"He doesn't hurt you, does he? I mean when he's drinking . . ." She couldn't bear the thought of someone harming this lovely creature. "If he ever does, you must let me help you. You're not alone. I will help you. Jake will help you —"

"He has never hurt me."

Color crept up the young woman's neck, and she seemed to struggle to find the right words. She only hoped Echo was telling her the truth.

"Waite's a good man. He drinks too much sometimes, but he's not mean to me or anything like that. He . . . he likes to relax with his friends and have fun once in a while." Her eyes met Tess's before darting away. "You'll see. I'll be just fine. Please let me be in your soo-ciety."

Tess sighed, wrapping her arm protectively around Echo's shoulder. How could she help someone who insisted she didn't want to be helped? "All right. You can be in our society, but you must promise to let me know if Waite gives you any trouble over this."

Echo's face broke out in a happy smile. "Oh, thank you, ma'am! Thank you muchly!"

Tess wasn't convinced she'd done the right thing, but the smile on her friend's face was worth the risk.

19

"Looks to me like you're progressing very well, Miss Yardley." Doc Medifer laid his stethoscope aside and smiled at her. "Any twinges of memory coming back?"

She shook her head. "None." Another week had passed without the slightest sign of her memory returning.

"Well, there's nothing to be worried about. I'm sure it will one of these days when you least expect it."

"Has there ever been a case where it didn't return?"

"Yes, many such cases. And it's a possibility you might want to consider, but it's far too soon to tell yet."

She rose and put on her hat. "I'm not worried, Doctor."

"You seem to be adjusting to camp life well." He flashed a grin. "I've heard you have the women all fired up to build a new schoolhouse."

Tess fished inside her purse for a coin to pay her bill. "I certainly have. The one we have is totally inadequate."

Doc chuckled as he waved her coin aside. "Put that in your coffer, young lady, and stay on those men. I hear the women are close to bringing those jacks to their knees."

She grinned. "We're trying our best, but how do you know we're succeeding?"

"Folks talk a lot when they're feeling poorly." He returned her grin. "Keep it up. It wouldn't hurt anything to bring some of these knuckledusters down a notch or two."

Or three, she lamented silently when she caught sight of Jake striding past the window.

"We're close, ladies, very close, but we're not home yet. Next, we move toward more devious measures. Downright shameful."

Several pairs of eyes rolled with disbelief as the schoolteacher faced her fellow WASPS the following week. By now the women knew the meaning of the word "devious," but some openly voiced that they weren't sure this was going to work.

A frail-looking woman rose in the back of the room. Her hands were red and work worn, her dress shabby, and her hair a mess, but she had an honest face. "Miss Yardley, let's talk sensible. I'm all for trying to get my man to help build a new schoolhouse, but we all know this ain't gonna work. Women don't have any say in such matters. Why, last night my husband said for me to shut my piehole because we got a good schoolroom, good enough for anybody. And that was after he had polished off three slices of blueberry pie!"

"That's man talk, and we know it," Tess argued. "If we want our children to learn and become bright, productive citizens, it's up to the community to provide the proper educational facilities. It isn't as if we're asking for the impossible! A large basic room with a few nice-sized windows is not an unreasonable demand, and on Sunday mornings there would be more room for church attendance."

She saw several heads in the crowd nodding in agreement. She knew the ladies' home lives were not completely ideal of late, but they would be proud of their accomplishment once the goal of a new schoolhouse was realized. And she had to hurry to get it finished. If the snow ever let up, Jake was going to ship her out of camp like the logs he sent down the flumes.

"Tell us what's next," Freda Davis suggested. "We've come this far. We can't back down now."

"No, we can't," Tess agreed. "We're going to have to tighten the screws. For starters, you will begin a work slowdown." An audible gasp filled the room. "Do you know what that means, ladies?"

They shook their heads.

"You mention that you're feeling poorly and you can't cook. And if you're forced to cook, be sure the meal isn't edible. You don't do the wash as often. You don't make the bed or sweep the floor every day. You sit in a chair, stare off into space, sigh, and cry a lot." Her eyes narrowed. "This is serious business, fellow WASPS. Face it. The only way we're going to win is to outsmart the enemy!"

Bernice shook her head. "Lannigan's going to string you up by your heels."

"I'll take care of Big Say. Now, at first your men will bluster and blow, but once they get sick of their own cooking and grow weary of having to pick up after themselves, they'll come around to our way of thinking."

"Are you *sure* you know what you're askin'?" Selma Miller demanded. "You not being married and all?"

"Absolutely. Living with the jacks has provided me certain advantages. I hear the men talking at night when they think I'm studying." She moved closer, lowering her voice to a whisper. "We must attack their weakest link, and you're close, ladies, very close. According to my information, some of the men are already tired of haggling over the matter. They want the nice, serene home lives they were accustomed to. Of course, there are always the diehards who keep insisting that they hang on. Those men will never give up unless we make them. I've given this considerable thought, and I'm positive you ladies are smart enough to use any means you have of bringing your men around to your way of thinking."

She straightened with a triumphant grin. "And, in order for me to do my part, I must now request a small concession from you. I have a plan — a very unconventional plan that is bound to turn a few heads, but you must bear with me. No matter what you see or hear, you must go on as if nothing inappropriate is happening. I can assure you, no matter how unorthodox my actions may appear, I shall be conducting myself with the *utmost* decorum."

"Oh, goodness. There's that word again," Bernice muttered. "What's she gonna do now?"

"Remember, ladies. We are working for a

common goal. As fellow WASPS, we are committed to uphold each other in our struggle for equality!"

An enthusiastic cheer went up. They could not weaken now. Tess stood before her audience, her face set in determination. "We must stick together in our worthy but humble cause. In the end we'll have our new schoolroom, or we're not fit to be called WASPS!"

Shouts filled the room, nearly lifting the roof off the tiny schoolhouse. Fedelia Yardley had stirred up the biggest stink Wakefield Timber had ever seen.

And it was going to get worse.

20

Hoisting her valises higher, Tess picked her way up the long stairway behind Menson's store. A full moon illuminated the narrow planked landing where she set her bags down at her side. Reaching to straighten her hat, she drew a deep, steadying breath. Could she do this? She could. The WASPS were counting on her.

Before she lost her nerve, she folded her hand into a fist and rapped loudly on the door. Then she cocked her ear and strained to listen. For a few frantic seconds, she wondered if Jake might be out. Maybe he was working late.

No. Don't get rattled. He can't get to Shadow Pine because of the snow. Fedelia Yardley, you are no coward. Jake has to be home. After all, it's nearly eleven o'clock — practically the middle of the night. He's here, all right. He just isn't answering the door, the inconsiderate slug!

She rapped louder. This time she continued knocking until her knuckles stung. Finally, she heard his muffled voice.

"All right, all right! Hold your horses!"

The sound of feet hitting the floor came next. She winced slightly when she heard a loud crash, and then the door flew open, with a disheveled, disgruntled Jake Lannigan filling the doorway.

"I hope you have a good reason for this —"

"Sorry to disturb you, but there's trouble at the bunkhouse."

He reeled for an instant, and then he rubbed the sleep from his eyes to glance at the moon overhead. "What kind of trouble?"

She hefted her bags and said, "Let's take this inside, shall we, Mr. Lannigan? I'm freezing."

He backed up, but not quickly enough. A corner of a hard-shelled valise struck him in the leg when she breezed past him into the dark room.

"Hey, take it easy!" He grabbed his knee. "What's going on?"

"Stop howling and light the lamp. I can't see my hand in front of my face." She dropped her bags and closed the door with the tip of her boot. The short walk from the bunkhouse had nearly frozen her blood, and all he could do was bluster.

More fumbling and muttering, and then a match flared. He adjusted the wick before turning to face her. "Miss Yardley, what are you doing roaming around in the middle of the night?"

"I'm sorry I woke you, but you've always said that if I needed anything I should come to you." She removed her coat and laid it on a chair, her gaze scanning the sizeable room, taking in the washstand, small table, two chairs, nightstand, chest of drawers, pine armoire, and the one narrow, rumpled cot. She could set her room in here and have leftover space.

She noted his anxious eyes scanning the floor, where he had hastily dropped his clothes. He was dressed only in thick white long johns.

"What's wrong at the bunkhouse?" he demanded as he padded over to the bed. "Where are my pants?" He bent, pawing through the mound of clothing.

She averted her gaze to afford him partial privacy. "I hate to tattle," she said, noting that what she'd said made him pause.

He turned to face her, gripping his pants by the waistband. "On who?"

"Your men."

"Did someone step out of line?"

"They were rude to me."

"Rude to you?" He drew his pants on, frowning. "What are you babbling about?"

She removed her hat, carefully brushing the snow from the rows of fabric before setting it on the table.

"Put that silly thing away," he snapped, "and get on with it!"

Lifting her gaze to him, she said coolly, "An emergency's come up."

"Fire?"

"Not the burning sort, but the men are furious with me."

Their anger had everything to do with the way she had wired some of their lady friends in Shadow Pine earlier. She'd been successful in persuading them to join the Wakefield ladies in pursuit of a new schoolhouse.

Folding his arms across his chest, he stared at her through narrowed eyes. "What have you done now?"

"That's not fair. You haven't heard my side, and you're already taking theirs —"

"Nobody has heard anything *but* your side lately. Turn yourself around and march straight back to the bunkhouse. We can settle the dispute in the morning."

She braced herself and said, "I am not going back there. They scare me."

"No one is going to lay a hand on you,

and yes, you *are* going back." He reached for a flannel shirt.

Her chin shot up a notch higher, and smugness touched the corners of her mouth. "Ed said to give you this." She reached into her pocket, withdrew a piece of paper, and handed it to him.

Jake strode to the nightstand, unfolded the note, and held it to the lamp to read.

Big Say,
The boys and I have had all we can take. We left Miss Yardley alone like you said. We behaved ourselves like you told us to, even after she said we couldn't smoke inside.
Now, on account of her, our women won't have nothin' to do with us until we build a new schoolroom. Enough is enough.
If you try to move her back with us, we quit. And we mean it.
                    The Men of Wakefield Timber

Jake's eyes scanned the letter twice.

"I don't know why they have to be so rude," she murmured.

He released a disgusted sigh. "This is just great." He crumpled the letter and tossed it. "I have to hand it to you. In a few short weeks you've managed to turn this camp on its heel. I hope you're happy."

"I wouldn't say that I'm happy, but a new schoolroom would solve most of our problems. Now," she said, glancing about, "where do I find clean linens?"

"Clean what?"

She sighed. "Fresh sheets. I need to make my bed."

"Your bed is at the bunkhouse, Miss Yardley," he said, following the direction of her gaze. "That bed is mine. And you don't really think I'm going to let you stay here."

She crossed her arms. "Then where am I going to stay? From what I understand, you're the only person in camp who has a private residence."

Jake edged forward. "And that, my dear, is the way I intend it to stay."

"I don't see that we have much choice." She upped the ante, her heart racing with anticipation. Would he make her go back to the bunkhouse? "You've exhausted all other possibilities, so until you agree to build a new schoolhouse, and I've decided it really should have adjacent teacher accommodations, we will simply have to share quarters."

"You're not sharing my quarters."

"That's entirely up to you. If you wish to sleep with your men in the bunkhouse, you may. You can even have my room. Now, about those clean linens —"

"This isn't a Philadelphia hotel. Those are the only 'linens' I have!"

She crossed the room, scooting around him. With a flick of her wrist, she gingerly flipped the top sheet up over the pillow and sat down on the edge of the cot. His jaw dropped when she started to remove her boots.

"The women in camp will run you out on a rail!"

Gathering a wool blanket around her shoulders, she smothered a tired yawn. "The women and I have a complete understanding." Removing a piece of chalk from her pocket, she stood, bent, and drew a single straight line across the floor. "If you insist on staying, you may sleep on the opposite side of the room. Don't cross this line. Ever."

She turned down the lamp and stretched out on top of the bed. Leaning on one elbow, she smoothed a quilt over her skirt, and then lay back on the nice, soft pillow. "Pleasant dreams, Mr. Lannigan."

Darkness blanketed the room. She could hear his breath coming in angry huffs. Shortly afterward, she heard him fumbling for a blanket and crossing to the stove. She was moderately surprised she wasn't head-first in a snowbank by now.

Did he intend to actually go through with this?

21

Tess tossed and turned on the hard straw mattress. She was too hot, then too cold. She didn't see how anyone could sleep through such misery, but Jake had apparently slept like one of his logs, rolled up in a blanket beside the stove.

Hours later stiff back muscles screamed for mercy. She rolled to a sitting position when the first light of dawn peeked through the window. Jake had left some time ago. She was grateful it was Saturday. She didn't know what she would have done if she'd had to teach this morning.

She lit the lamp and rose to inspect her surroundings. The furnishings were minimal, but nicer than those in the bunkhouse. She added a few logs to the stove, and after she was dressed she wandered aimlessly about the room.

He wouldn't let her stay, of that she was certain. He'd be back shortly, and then she'd be moving, but she'd made her point. He either had to do something about building that schoolroom or put up with this continued nonsense.

She didn't intend to pry, but she opened the chest of drawers. If he forced her to take the bluff further, she would need room to store a few things. He had jammed his belongings in all six drawers, but she figured if she consolidated his things, she could temporarily use a couple of them.

In no time flat she had rearranged the clutter and put her things inside the two middle drawers. Her gaze focused on the armoire, and she paused thoughtfully. If she scooted his clothes over a tiny bit, she'd have a few hooks in the middle where she could hang her dresses.

The deed efficiently accomplished, she walked to the table where she'd left her hat. The accessory needed a bit of attention. Snow had matted some of the lace, and the feather looked a bit droopy this morning. When she lifted the bonnet, she noticed the table was dusty, and it came to her attention that the whole room could use a good cleaning.

Noises drifted up from Menson's store downstairs, so she assumed that Henry and Grace were preparing to open their shop.

Slipping on her coat, Tess hurried outside and down the narrow stairway. Before she could think twice, she rapped on the store's back door. It took two knocks before Grace finally appeared.

"Miss Yardley, is something wrong?"

"No." She smiled. It wasn't going to be easy explaining to a fellow WASPS what she was about to do, but Grace would be the most understanding. "Why?"

"I'm surprised to see you this early in the mornin'!"

"Nothing's wrong, Grace. I simply need a few things." Tess stepped inside to get out of the blustery north wind.

"We were about to open," Grace said. "What can I get for you?"

"I . . . I." She faltered. Grace was looking at her so strangely — almost as if she knew something unsavory was taking place.

"Come over by the stove, dear, and have a cup of tea. You must be cold from your walk from the bunkhouse."

"I didn't come from the bunkhouse this morning and I can't stay. I need some cleaning supplies. You see, I . . ." Her eyes scanned the store, grateful to note it was deserted. She decided honesty was the only policy at this point. Everybody in town would know she had forced her way into

268

Jake Lannigan's home before the morning was over. "Grace, I'm about to embark upon my plan. You know, the unorthodox one I mentioned in our last meeting?"

Grace's voice was a bit hesitant. "Yes."

Drawing a deep breath, Tess selected a mop and placed it on the counter. "I've temporarily moved in with Jake." The bold act would be short lived. She was confident Jake wouldn't let her remain there another night. She figured he was trying to find other quarters for her, but he wouldn't be successful. The WASPS had taken a stand.

"You moved in with Big Say?" the woman repeated incredulously.

Bending close, Tess said quietly, "Remember, as one of the WASPS you are to look the other way, and proceed with our plan as if nothing unusual is going on."

"Oh, my."

"I don't have a choice. Hard times beg for impractical measures. The men were angry because I convinced the women they cavort around with that, as fellow females, it's their duty to become involved in our fight for the new schoolhouse. Because most of the women are more than tired of the men's superior attitudes, they agreed to help. Dirk Letson somehow made his way back from Shadow Pine last night and told on me. The jacks won't even get to see the women until the roads are passable, but they blew up and told me to leave. Of course, this was my plan, and I intend to see it through for the sake of future generations."

"You'll be living with a man without benefit of marriage —"

"Grace, I've been living with a *hundred and twenty-five men* without benefit of marriage! It seems to me I'll be cutting down my risk of harm significantly by having to deal with just one man instead of all the rest. Besides, Jake won't let me stay here. I think he's out right now looking for somewhere to put me, but the women have to pull together on this."

"I don't like it."

"I won't be in his room past late afternoon, but I have to make him think I'm dead serious."

Grace shifted stances. "I don't know. You may be just plain dead if he has his way. What will the others say?"

Tess shook her head. She was suddenly feeling very alone and inadequate. She needed a friend, an ally, if she was to carry this off successfully. "You must trust me. If vicious gossip spreads, and it will, you must remind the women of our pact."

Grace eyed her with a dubious expression.

"It sounds as though you've put a lot of thought into this, Miss Yardley, but I don't think it's going to work. Lannigan isn't a man to be pushed around. You're playing with fire."

She smiled. "Like I've said before, I'm discovering that I can be dangerous too."

"Not as dangerous as Big Say if you get him riled up." But Grace returned the smile and reached out to squeeze her hand. "I'll go along with whatever you say because we have to bring this dispute to a halt. My Henry is so testy lately I can barely stand him."

Tess hoped she sounded more confident than she felt. "Don't worry. This will all be settled by dark."

"Grace, are you with someone?" Henry's voice drifted from the back room.

"Yes, Henry. Miss Yardley is here."

Tess heard a disgruntled *harrumph,* and then the sound of the door to the storeroom slamming shut. Leaning closer, she whispered, "This is war, Grace, and in war, anything goes. I need a large pail, three bars of lye soap, a pair of sheets, a pillow case, and a can of lemon oil."

Her conspirator glanced toward the storeroom and then back to her. "I hope you know what you're doing."

When her supplies had been gathered, Grace tallied up the bill. Tess waited, relieved to find the woman was going along with the plan.

"Oh, and could you spare some extra bedding? I want to make a pallet."

Grace sighed with relief. "Of course. A place for you to sleep."

"No."

Grace glanced up.

"A place for *Mr. Lannigan* to sleep, should he be even more bullheaded about this."

Chuckling, Grace picked up the bill and read the total out loud. "Six dollars and ten cents." Glancing up, she grinned. "I'll put that on Mr. Lannigan's account."

Picking up the bundle, Tess nodded. "Now you've got it, Grace. Keep up the good work."

22

Lunch came and went. Tess studied Jake's room with a gleam of pride in her eye. The place fairly shone from top to bottom. She had mopped, scrubbed, and dusted everything, and she had even rearranged the furniture to accommodate a pallet she'd made for him beside the stove. The room was austere, and it afforded very little privacy, but it was clean and it meant business.

If he insisted on calling her bluff, she had carefully reloaded.

But she did need a partition of some sort. She didn't know where she'd get a folding screen, but a piece of fabric strung across one corner of the room would certainly disarm him.

She could use some new material for a hat too. It would be rather convenient to live over a store like Menson's. Dusting her hands, she put on her coat and went downstairs for her second shopping trip of the day.

"Let's see now. Five yards of cotton, a spool of white thread, and three cents' worth of peppermints." Henry Menson ordinarily dropped a couple of extra pieces of candy into the sack, but not today. "Is that it, Miss Yardley?"

"Yes. Thank you, Mr. Menson." Henry wrapped the material, thread, and candy in heavy white paper and bound it tightly with string. Handing the neatly wrapped bundle to her, the clerk's customary smile failed to materialize. His thin lips were set in a pinched line and his expression warred with his desire to be polite.

"Right pleasant day we're having."

"It is indeed." She took her purchases and turned to leave. "Please put these on Mr. Lannigan's account."

An exceptionally pretty porcelain bowl sitting in the front window caught her eye, and she lingered to examine it. Her dalliance was merely a tactic to delay leaving. Jake was on the sidewalk outside the store talking to Ed Holman, and she was hoping if she postponed her departure long enough, she could avoid an encounter. He had not been back to the room since he'd left before dawn.

Admittedly, she was starting to worry about his next move. She'd heard the townspeople buzzing, but no one had said a word directly to her about last night's scandalous event.

The bell over the door tinkled, and she glanced up to see Echo enter the store. Tess tensed when she saw that Waite accompanied her this afternoon. She tried to put aside her bias and smiled warmly at her friend.

Echo nodded briefly in Tess's direction, and then she quickly averted her eyes and hurried over to take a seat next to the potbellied stove. The young woman's meek reserve didn't surprise her. When Waite was present, Echo kept to herself.

The big burly jack spotted her. Though he pretended to be interested in a three-bladed cattleman's knife in the showcase up front, she felt his eyes periodically shifting back to her.

Placing the porcelain box back in the window, Tess edged closer to the door. Jake was still deep in conversation, and she knew if she left now he would either confront or ignore her. Her eye caught sight of a new stack of calico and muslins. That would give her something to look at for a few more moments.

Sherman Miller wistfully eyed the barrel of apples, good-naturedly complaining to Henry about his wife Selma's cooking — or the lack of it lately.

"Better get you some of those apples, Sherman. They make a right tasty pie," Henry urged.

"What do I need with apples, Henry? They would sit in my kitchen and turn pithy."

Sherman's eyes coldly skimmed Tess, and she noted that Selma ignored his remark as she picked up a bottle of Doctor Kilmer's Female Remedy and studied the label. *Good for you, fellow WASP.*

"Yessiree bob, there's nothing better after a cold day of being out in the woods than to come home to the smell of hot apple pie bubbling in the oven," Henry agreed.

"A man has a right to come home to that," Sherman made a point of adding. "Especially after he's worked hard for his woman from dawn till dusk."

Tess admired Selma. She casually placed the bottle back on the shelf and moved on.

"I like a thick wedge of cheese on my apple pie. Don't you, Sherman?"

"I don't rightly know, Henry. It's been so

276

long since I had a piece of apple pie that I've plumb forgot what I'd put on it."

Tess wished Henry would drop the subject. Sherman was practically salivating at the thought of the tasty, rich dessert, and the corners of Selma's mouth were getting more pinched by the moment.

"Yessir, women nowadays are something. Don't know their place. That's what it is," Henry decided.

"I agree with you there, Henry. Looks to me like they would know when they're well off." The jack nodded. "I say if a man's good enough to give them a roof over their head and a houseful of kids to run after, they should be grateful enough to make a simple apple pie for him every once in a while."

"Looks like it," Henry sympathized.

"Sherman, you and Henry done been going about this all wrong."

A grin spread across Waite's features, and he walked over to warm up by the stove. Judging from his appearance, Tess guessed he hadn't seen a bar of soap or a razor in weeks.

"A real man keeps his wife in line. Now, take my little woman. She done been fixing me fine meals lately. Extra fine."

Echo glanced up expectantly. "Waite, that ain't so —"

"Hush, darlin'."

She winced when Waite's soft rebuke brought the activity in the store to a halt. Echo's eyes darted to her.

"But I ain't been —"

"No one asked your opinion."

When Waite's harsh look silenced his wife, an uneasy hush fell over the store. Tess longed to intercede for her friend, but she knew any interference on her part would only make the situation worse.

"A woman ought not go against her husband."

"I'm sorry," Echo said softly.

"How sorry?"

"Real sorry, Waite."

"Apology accepted. Now, I think this might be a good time for you to tell the little schoolmarm here that you ain't gonna be in her soo-ciety."

Crimson color flooded Echo's face. "Waite —"

"You don't want to cause a scene now, do you, darlin'?"

"No . . . but don't make me give up my soo-ciety."

Echo's voice trembled, and Tess knew the young woman was close to tears. When she took a step forward, she felt Sherman's hand on her shoulder to stop her.

"No wife of mine is gonna consort with an unmarried woman living with a man," Waite said. "Don't argue with me. Just tell Miss Yardley you're not gonna be able to come to any more of her little after-school powwows. You got a man at home who needs looking after. You don't have time to be running around rilin' up trouble. This town was a God-fearing place until that woman arrived."

Tears rolled from the corners of Echo's eyes. "Waite. I'll . . . I'll start cookin' again, I promise. Don't make me give up —"

"Tell Miss Yardley what I said, Echo." His tone was firm and brooked no nonsense.

Sherman cast a warning look toward the man. "Waite, I think you should settle this matter at another time and place. We've been ribbin' the women, is all. Don't mean any harm, none of it. If they want to have their little society, that ain't gonna hurt no one."

"Miller, I won't tell you how to handle your woman, and you won't tell me how to handle mine," Waite said evenly. "Echo?"

Her head obediently dropped, and she did what he said in a barely audible voice. "I . . . I can't be in your soo-ciety anymore, ma'am. I'm real sorry."

The front door swung open, and Tess's

knees went weak with relief when she saw Jake enter the store.

Waite smiled. "That's fine, sugar pie. Mighty fine."

Taking his gaze away from his wife, he shot Tess a smug reminder that he was still the boss in his household. She watched him saunter back across the room as if the incident had never taken place. She wished she could smack the look off his face, but she knew that was impossible.

"Afternoon, Big Say," Waite said.

Jake nodded and held the door when Echo fled past him like a shy doe, followed by a confident Waite Burne. Tess's heart went out to her friend. She hoped the incident was over and wouldn't continue after the couple got home.

Henry cleared his throat and returned to the Millers' order, his tone seeking to lighten the tension that hung over the room like a pall. "Could be apple pie ain't what it's cracked up to be."

Casting a worried glance at Selma, Sherman said, "Well, won't hurt me none to shed a few pounds."

Tess felt like stamping her foot. Henry was back on the subject of those pies again! But if Sherman still found the heckling amusing, Selma didn't. She quietly moved to the flour barrel.

"Oh, Sherman."

He glanced up. "Yes, darlin'?" He shot Henry a knowing wink.

"Would you step over here, please?"

Sherman obliged. "What is it, love of my life?"

Selma smiled sweetly. "You want an apple pie, darlin'?"

"That would be real nice, dear."

Selma dipped her fingers in the barrel and then calmly flipped flour in her husband's face. "Then bake it yourself, dumplin'."

Sherman was clearly not amused. He sputtered, his large hands coming up to wipe the flour away from his eyes, rimmed in white. Recovering from the unwarranted assault, he spoke in a low tone. "You ought not to have done that, Selma."

Tess couldn't believe her eyes when Selma calmly dipped her fingers in the barrel a second time, and then flicked a wad of flour on the front of Sherman's red flannel shirt.

"Then dry up. Once you and those other baboons agree to build a new schoolhouse, you'll get your pie. Not a moment sooner."

Jake had turned to watch the exchange. Tess noted he was more amused than concerned by the marital dispute. Then she saw Sherman's hand slowly move to dip into the barrel.

"Don't you dare," Selma warned.

Sherman's devilish grin assured her and everyone else in the room that he would indeed dare. Tess backed closer to the door for escape.

Henry glanced up, and his face paled. Hurriedly wiping his hands on the front of his apron, he scurried from behind the counter. "Here now, Sherman, we'll have none of this —"

Suddenly, pandemonium broke loose. Selma screamed when flour hazed the air, and the battle was on.

Jake had stepped to the side, but when apples and oranges started flying, he ducked and headed for the front door. Tess straightened her hat irritably and suddenly felt herself being lifted off her feet and hoisted roughly over the big lumberjack's shoulder. Jake hauled her out of the store like a sack of grain. How dare he! She kicked helplessly as she heard Henry frantically try to put a stop to the broadening fracas.

"Put me down!" she ordered. Jake set her, not too lightly, on her feet on the sidewalk. The clamor of pots and pans flung in anger now came from the store. Henry pleading for Sherman and Selma to stop only added to the confusion.

Jake spoke for the first time. "When are you going to learn to quit butting in folks' business, especially the marriages in this community?"

Tess picked up the bundle of goods and the hat she'd dropped. "It's time someone improves the quality of life around here!" With a sigh of disgust, she began dusting flour off her lovely creation. "And there are *some* marriages that need improving! Take Waite Burne's, for instance. Why don't you fire him?"

"Waite is one of my best fallers. I don't fire a man because I don't happen to like him."

"This is different. He's a miserable excuse for a man! The way he treated Echo in the store was disgusting."

"Did he strike her?"

"No."

"Did he threaten to harm her in any way?"

"No. It was his bossy attitude. I don't like the way he treats her, giving her orders and then running off to get drunk when life doesn't suit him."

"Has she complained about him?"

"Of course not. Echo is too loyal to complain —"

"Unless there's an indication that Waite is mistreating her, you'd better stay out of it.

If Echo needs help, she knows where to find it."

Frustrated, she smashed her hat back on top of her head.

The corners of Jake's mouth twitched. "You know, Miss Yardley, the women in these parts have been raised to know their place."

"Is that so, Mr. Lannigan?"

"They are accustomed to taking orders, and they enjoy the security of knowing that someone is looking out for their best interests."

"Whose best interests? I think that's precisely the issue here. A new schoolhouse would be in the best interest of the entire community. It seems that it's the women who are farsighted enough to understand the problem."

"You'd be wise to keep your thoughts private." He turned on his heel and started off. "This all started in the first place because of you."

"*Me?* What have I done? You weren't in there when Waite made Echo drop out of the WASPS society! It broke her heart!"

Turning, he confronted her again. "Now, you listen to me, young lady. You've been stirring up trouble for weeks over this nonsense about a new schoolroom, and I

284

want it stopped."

"What happened in there is not my fault! If Henry and Sherman would have kept quiet about those silly apple pies, Selma would never have lost her temper and thrown that flour."

"It's not just Selma and Sherman. You have every married couple in camp squabbling. I can't get anything done for the men running in and out of my office whining about the way their wives won't cook, won't wash their clothes, won't talk, and won't — won't do *a blame thing!*" His tone rose at the end, even as he blushed a little.

"Ha! It serves them right!"

His hands shot to his hips. "Ha! That kind of fighting is about as low as it gets."

"If you mean I'm responsible for encouraging the women of this town to use any means they possess in order to have a little say about what goes on around here, you're right, Jake Lannigan! If you and the other men in this town don't have enough pride in your families and your children to see that they have the very best you can provide them, then you can suffer the consequences."

"No one complained until you showed up."

Jake turned and walked off but she fell

into step behind him. Her hair had fallen loose in the scuffle, and she irritably gathered up the strands and tried to shove them back up under her hat. "Don't walk away from me when I'm talking to you! You could put a stop to all this bickering in a minute if you would agree to take a precious few days and ten or fifteen men to build that new schoolhouse!"

"No."

"Yes!"

"You're not getting a new schoolhouse, so you and your fellow hornets had better fly back to your nest. If you think you're going to bring my men down with feminine wiles, you are sadly mistaken."

"WASPS! And pray tell me why not!"

He refused to answer the question. "And you'd best be finding you a new place to store your things. You are *not* moving into my place."

Her chin lifted a notch. "I already have."

"I can move you out just as fast."

She breathlessly tried to match his long-legged strides. Common sense told her to drop the subject. He was obviously not in any mood to rationally discuss the matter, but she couldn't stop now. He was being pigheaded and completely illogical about a serious situation.

"I'm supposed to forget about the school-house and cower down to you like a meek, helpless woman?"

"That would be real nice, Miss Yardley. And, may I add, mighty sensible on your part."

"Well, it isn't sensible to me."

"I can see that."

They had entered the pines now, and the path narrowed. "Haven't you ever wanted anything so bad you were willing to fight for it?"

"Maybe, but I was always smart enough to know when I was licked." He paused at the foot of a large pine and strapped on his safety belt. Then he donned his spikes.

She peered at the tree's towering trunk, and a knot of fear formed in the pit of her stomach. Did he intend to climb to soaring heights in order to end this discussion? "What are you doing?"

"I get paid to work, not to stand around and argue with a wasp."

Her gaze followed the height of the pine. "Are you going to cut this tree?"

"One of the greenhorns left an ax up there this afternoon. I'm going after it."

With rope flying and spikes digging, he began to climb to the top of the two-hundred-foot tree. Tess clamped her eyes shut and leaned against the base to wait. Her heart beat like a jungle drum. If he fell . . .

"I know you have your dreams, Jake Lannigan!" Everyone in camp knew Jake wanted to plant trees as well as harvest them, but the new owner of Wakefield Timber didn't share his vision.

"Not anymore!"

"André told me that once you had hopes of replanting these pines."

Jake paused in his ascent and tightened his safety gear. "André talks too much." His cleats dug deeper into the wood.

"It's true, isn't it?"

"You tell me. You seem to know all about it."

"André said you and Rutherford Wakefield planned to replant the pines, but Mr. Wakefield died before the dream was realized." He had nearly reached the pinnacle now, making it necessary for her to shout to be heard. "Isn't that so?" She wasn't sure if he answered her this time. The wind snatched voices and sent them astray.

"If it is true, why is it so hard for you to understand why building a new schoolhouse is important to me? I won't be here forever, but like your dream, I want to leave something for future generations. It's important to me!" She was a dismal failure at teaching, so she had to leave something behind to prove that she'd been there.

She waited a full five minutes before Jake came back down the tree carrying the retrieved ax in his hand. She breathed a sigh of relief when his feet touched solid ground. "Have you heard a word I've said?"

"About what?" He disconnected the safety rope and let it drop.

"About the trees and the new schoolhouse. Though my goal isn't as lofty as yours, and it won't change the future to any great extent, it's still a worthy endeavor."

"Then get yourself a hammer and a bucket of nails and have at it."

She moaned with disgust. "Why must you be so arrogant?" Jake turned his back, and for a long moment she was afraid he'd simply dismissed the subject until he spoke quietly.

"Did André tell you anything about Tess Wakefield?"

"He said you tried to persuade Mr. Wakefield's granddaughter to keep the land long enough to complete the planting project, but she refused. He said she was expected to arrive in camp to complete the sale of Wakefield Timber to a rival competitor, but she hasn't made it yet."

Jake eyes refused to meet hers. "And?"

"He said you were roaring mad about the sale and that you think Miss Wakefield is a selfish, conniving, unfeeling little witch who doesn't give a whit about anyone's future but her own."

Jake cleared his throat. "I don't know that for a fact. I get hot under the collar when her name comes up."

"Sounds to me that she's all those things and more," she sympathized. "But when she sees what's being done to her grandfather's land, she'll change her mind."

Jake turned toward her, and she saw his gaze soften.

"Maybe."

"She will if she's anything like her grandfather. Would it help if I spoke to Miss Wakefield when she comes? Sometimes a woman can talk to another woman and make her see things from a different perspective. And when you finally agree to build the new schoolhouse, I promise I'll do everything I can to help get the project started." She was surprised to see — what? New recognition in his eyes?

"Is that a fact?" he said. "You think you might convince Miss Wakefield to help us plant trees?"

She sighed. "Well, I can't speak for her,

but I know that I will help. Of course, there's very little I can actually do because I don't personally own the land, but I'll talk to Miss Wakefield the moment she arrives." She nodded, warming to the thought. "Yes, that's exactly what Tip would want me to do."

"Tip?"

Tess glanced up. "Tip?"

"You said *Tip* would want his grand-daughter to replant the trees."

"Oh." Leaning against the tree, she pursed her lips in thought. "That was Rutherford's nickname, wasn't it?"

"Yes, but other than Rutherford's family and closest friends, no one called him that. How did you know it?"

"I don't know. I must have heard it some-where. Maybe André mentioned it." Waving the coincidence aside, she stepped closer, forcing him to take an involuntary step back. "It isn't important . . . and *stop* doing that!"

"Doing what?"

"Always backing away from me. I won't bite you." His mouth curved in one of the unconscious smiles she loved. "And don't do that, either. When you smile that way, it frustrates me all the more that you don't like me."

291

"Who says I don't like you?"

"You do. By your actions in a thousand different ways."

Reaching out to draw her to him, he offered her an arresting smile this time, and the warmth of his hands penetrated her coat. "Well, you're wrong. I was even thinking about asking you to take a moonlit walk with me this evening."

"You were? Why?"

"Does a man need a reason to ask a pretty woman to take a walk in the moonlight?"

"Are you going to try and bully me into dropping my crusade for the new school-house?"

"No. Can't I ask a woman to go for a simple walk without her reading some ulterior motive into it?"

He knew exactly what to do to make a woman's pulse race like a runaway carriage. "You're not going to kick me out in the snow?"

"I can honestly tell you I have never kicked a woman out in the snow, but you're not going to stay in my quarters, Fedelia. Your head injury is interfering with your common sense. Single women do not move in with unmarried men."

"But the women in Shadow Pine —"

"Have nothing in common with the

women in camp. You are not staying with me. When I'm though with work, I'll move your things to Menson's for a few days. Henry and Grace can keep you until I can make other arrangements."

"Did Henry agree to that?"

"I haven't mentioned it to him yet. The arrangement will cramp them, but he will agree."

The world spun lopsidedly when his arm slipped around her waist and his mouth lowered to kiss her.

"Well . . . you need to know I'm going to see this thing through." Her voice had gone all breathy and sweet.

"Good for you."

His mouth closed masterfully over hers, and she thought she would burst from sheer pleasure. She wasn't sure what game he was playing now, and she wasn't about to ask. When their lips parted, Jake gazed down at her with a touch of tenderness shining in his eyes.

"Can we call a truce, Miss Yardley?"

"Would a truce mean I don't get the new schoolhouse, Mr. Lannigan?"

He smiled. "No. It just means we quit nipping at each other's heels for a while."

She returned his smile. "Agreed."

Looping her arm through his, they started

the cold walk back.

"I have some paperwork to catch up on," Jake said. "I'll be back at the room later, and then we'll get you settled with the Mensons."

He'd be surprised with the work she'd achieved this afternoon. At least it wasn't in vain. He'd have clean quarters, but a confession was in order. He might enjoy a good bluff, but she felt he was gradually coming around to her way of thinking. "I didn't really intend to stay with you. Though I don't know who I am, I'm certain I'm not the sort of woman who would . . . well, you understand. I was bluffing. I'm sorry."

"No harm done." The towering pines cast deepening shadows over the frozen ground. "Are you going straight to the room?"

"I want to stop by and see Echo before that. I felt sorry for her today, Jake. She took such pride in being a part of something. Now she has nothing to brighten her life, no cause to get excited about, and no solid reason to feel as if she will ever accomplish anything on her own. Waite will see to that," she added, her voice tinged with bitterness for the man who seemed to wreak such havoc in Echo's life.

"Regardless of your impression of Echo's marriage, you don't know for certain there is any real problem. Marriage is sacred. The Lord meant it when He said that what He had joined together no man — or woman — should set asunder. A lasting relationship takes work, hard work, with one person giving an inch more than the other, and both need the fortitude to work through problems that will inevitably arise when a man and a woman choose to spend their lives as one." He paused. "Don't judge others. That's what Wakefield preached."

"Why, Jake Lannigan." She stopped and looked up at him. "I didn't know you could be so profound." The mention of Rutherford Wakefield brought a lump in her throat, but she couldn't say why. The wise old man must have been a very discerning man. No wonder his employees valued and respected his memory.

Jake's arm circled her waist. "Don't stay with Echo too long.

You haven't got a lantern, and I don't want you wandering around in the dark alone."

Drawing closer to his side, she matched his strides and marveled again at how incredibly safe and contented she felt, secure in the shelter of his arms.

23

The night wind howled when Jake walked home later. He glanced up to see a glow in his window, aware that he was whistling when he climbed the long stairway to his room. It was the first time he could ever remember coming home to a room that wasn't dark, cold, and empty. The thought oddly suited him.

He had misjudged Tess, yet he had no way of telling her he had been wrong unless he told her the truth about who she was. Tip Wakefield's blood ran through this woman's veins. His grit and pure determination still thrived in his granddaughter. When she started making hats, his suspicions were more than confirmed.

Opening the door, he paused when the room's cozy warmth welcomed him. Lamplight spilled across the freshly scrubbed floor. Everything had been moved. His gaze traveled the area, settling on the frilly sheet with rosebuds strung across one corner of the wall.

"You like it?" Tess asked. She stepped from the shadows to help him remove his coat.

"What have you done?" His eyes searched what had formerly been a man's domain. Fire crackled in the stove, and on top of it a whistling tea kettle made a racket. His gaze shifted to the pallet on the floor, one he'd never seen before. An assortment of bottles and a silver-handled brush and comb sat atop his dresser instead of his razor and shaving mug. And on his nightstand, where he threw his pocket change, sat a bowl of some kind of dried leaves.

"Do you like it?" she prompted again.

"What's that smell?"

Tess lifted a porcelain bowl that had formerly been in Menson's front window. "Dried rose petals. Don't they smell lovely?"

"Where's my stuff?" Jake's brows knit together tightly. His personal effects were not where he had left them this morning.

"Here . . . all neatly in place."

"You *cleaned?*" The word came out more like an accusation than a compliment. He started to circle the room, trying to assess the damage.

She nodded, grinning. "Took hours, but

I've rearranged drawers. I threw away a lot of useless things in the process."

His brow lifted. "Useless?"

"You know — worthless stuff you had lying around. Doesn't it look better?"

"I didn't have anything worthless lying around." His eyes searched for the stack of journals beside his bed. They were missing. "If you were going to get rid of something, why didn't you pitch your useless things?"

"Are you angry with me?"

"Fedelia . . . where are my journals?"

"Under the cot. It's much better to store them there where they'll be out of sight," she reasoned. "You don't mind, do you?"

"Mind? No. I'll just crawl across the floor like a snake when I need to make a notation."

Her face clouded. "You are angry."

"I'm not." His words said one thing; his tone, another. He fixed on the dainty pillows tossed on the hard wooden chairs. Her eyes traced his. "You have to admit the chairs are much softer with cushions."

He glanced back to the pallet.

"It's quite comfortable," she said cheerfully.

"Ah. And if you weren't moving downstairs, who would have the pleasure of sleeping on it?"

"You, of course. A gentleman would never ask a lady to sleep on the floor."

"Not in Philadelphia, perhaps, but you're not there."

"A gentleman is a gentleman, Jake, no matter where or what his circumstances."

"You're my mother now?" Jake sighed, shaking his head. "Put it all back, and then we'll get you settled downstairs."

Tess shook her head, stifling a yawn. "It's so late, Jake." She sat down on the cot, loosened her hair pins, and dropped her head on the pillow. "I think the room looks lovely."

"Oh, no you don't. We already talked about this. You're going to the Mensons' *tonight.*" He grabbed her hand and pulled her upright.

"Oh, all right. If you insist." She stood and reached for a valise. "But I'll have to pack."

"Why haven't you done that already?"

"In case you can't see, I've been working. Your quarters are as shiny as a new coin."

"You'll have to get your things tomorrow." He opened the door. "Ladies first."

Though he was more than a little irritated at the changes she had wrought in his simple bachelor's quarters, she was so beautiful he couldn't help but smile at the

299

pouting look on her face as she started down the stairs.

By late morning the next day, Tess had gathered her belongings and was settled, in a closetlike room, in back of Menson's store. Grace, for one, was openly relieved about her change in residence.

"It's better for everyone this way."

"Much better," Tess agreed. Yesterday she'd been certain she was getting through to Jake, but now she suspected that no woman would break through his tough barrier. All she knew was that she had to keep trying.

Echo glanced up when Waite kicked the heavy door open and entered their one-room shack.

"Clean this," he snapped, pitching the carcass of a wild turkey onto the table.

She moved from the stove, where a pot of beans and a skillet of potatoes and onions were simmering. She picked up the bird and carried it to the sink.

Waite sat down at the table, and thrust one foot out. "Take off my boots, honey."

Wiping her hands, she knelt beside his chair.

Staring down at the top of her head, Waite remarked. "You're not mad at yore man, are you?"

"No. I love you, Waite." Her eyes refused to meet his as she began to untie the strings.

"No reason to be mad, girl. You know that soo-ciety ain't fittin' for a woman like you. You're a pleaser, sweetheart. You don't need the likes of Fedelia Yardley gettin' you all stirred up."

"The potatoes need turning, Waite," she murmured. "Let's not start an argument."

He rolled his eyes toward the ceiling. "My, my. Ain't we actin' uppity lately. 'The potatoes need turnin', Waite.' You learn that from the schoolteacher?"

Echo remained silent.

"Cat got your tongue?" He nudged her with the tip of his boot.

"No."

"Then answer me, darlin'."

She rose and walked to the stove.

"Ain't you gonna answer me?"

"Leave me alone, Waite," she said. "Go sleep it off."

"I still got my boots on, and you're frettin' over potatoes. 'Course, appears that you're cookin' again. That's an improvement."

"Your boots are untied," she said. "Slip them off."

"That's your job."

"You're liquored up. Go to bed."

He got out of his chair, groping for support with one hand. "You embarrassed me in front of Sherman Miller and Henry Menson, Echo. No one embarrasses Waite Burne, least of all his woman. Say you're sorry for embarrassing me."

"I'm sorry I embarrassed you."

He paused, holding on to the sink. "And I'll hear no more about that silly soo-ciety. You quit and you're gonna stay home and take care of yore man liken' you're supposed to do."

Echo lifted a shoulder.

"I want to hear you say it, woman."

"I said I wouldn't go anymore."

"And you're gonna stop associatin' with that uppity Fedelia Yardley. From now on, you're not to see her or go near that school-house unless I say so. You got that?"

She met his eyes. "I'm not deaf. I got it."

As suddenly as the argument erupted, it stopped. "That's my woman. If I hear of you seeing her again, you'll answer to me." He pointed toward the sizzling skillet. "My supper's burnin'. Hurry up. I ain't got all day," he muttered. "I'm gonna eat, then me and Ben's goin' to try to get to Shadow Pine for the night . . . gonna play some cards. He's got a right nice sleigh that takes the deep snow real fine."

Echo slowly turned to face him. "Then why don't you and your card-playin' buddy eat over there?"

"What'd you say?" His frown deepened. "That Yardley woman has ruined you. She's turned Big Say into a regular sissy pants and you into a sassy little twit."

"She's my friend."

He got to his feet and swayed unsteadily. "Well, I'm leavin' and I might *stay* gone. You'll be on your own. No way to feed yourself, no one around to protect you from the other jacks. How would you like that, Miss High-and-Mighty?"

"I don't want you to leave, but you got a mind to do what you want. The Good Lord will help me make it if you don't come back."

"You might think different once you've gone without fresh game or a regular pay-check," he sneered.

"Might be, but things have to change, Waite. I don't mind giving up the soo-ciety, but I want to be friends with Miss Yardley. You got no call to make me give her up."

"Change?" He threw back his head and hooted. "Over my dead body, woman. I like the way things are." He glared at her. "Or I did until now."

He reached for his coat and slammed out
of the house with his boots untied.

24

Tess trudged through heavy snow to school, her mind still on Jake and his moody behavior. Her room at the store was tiny but comfortable, but she was crowding the Mensons and the arrangement could only be temporary. Modeen wasn't happy with the schoolteacher staying in her home.

The store was an active place with folks coming and going. Grace had her hands full filling orders and cooking. She couldn't be bothered with a guest, even though Tess looked after herself. The telegraph machine hummed before sunup this morning, and poor Grace took the message and then called to Henry that she was going in search of Jake or André. Most likely an emergency had risen in one of the jacks' families.

Approaching the schoolyard, Tess was dimly aware of raised voices. She drew closer and the loud tones grew more pronounced.

"Miss Yardley's set her cap for Big Say," King Davis declared. "My pa says so!"

"She has not!" Tirzah yelled, defending her teacher.

"Tirzah, you're such a baby. You don't know what it means for a woman to set her cap for a man."

"It means you're sayin' bad things about Miss Yardley, and it ain't so!"

"Well, it is so if a woman is chasing a man like a common strumpet!"

Tess gasped. King would only know hateful accusations like that if he heard them at home.

"You take that back, King Davis!"

Tess broke into a run, covering the last few steps in a dash while other students stood in the snow watching the scene. "Children! Stop this right now!"

Tirzah was near tears and not in a mood for reasoning. "King is saying *bad* things about you, Miss Yardley, and I'm not gonna stand for it." The girl's hands grabbed a chunky piece of wood and held it threateningly.

Tess stepped between the two students to put an end to the fracas. She held up a finger. "I said —" She stopped speaking when a sharp pain exploded in her temple, and then she crumpled to the ground, unconscious.

"Holy Moses! Look what you done, Tirzah!"

Tirzah broke into sobs. "I didn't mean to, King. I was throwing that log at you!"

King dropped to his knees beside the teacher, placing an ear to her chest. He shushed for silence and listened. "I cain't tell if she's breathing."

"Tirzah's done gone and kilt the teacher," Quinn whispered.

The youth straightened after a few moments. "She ain't dead," he declared. "She's jest out colder than kraut."

"I oughta go git someone to come and see about her," Scooter said.

"No, we knocked her out. We'll get her on her feet again. Pud, help me carry Miss Yardley inside the schoolhouse."

The two boys lugged her inside and laid her on the floor beside the stove. Tirzah spread a cloth on the teacher's forehead while debate raged over what to do next.

The pounding in her head was almost unbearable when Tess tried to open her eyes. The first thing she saw was nine worried faces staring down at her.

"I'll help you to your chair, Miss Yardley," Tirzah offered.

"Miss Wakefield," she corrected drowsily.

"Tess Wakefield." Why did the children look at one another, shaking their heads?

King broke the silence. "I think you'd better rest awhile, Miss Yardley. That knock on your noggin has you plumb confused."

"Please help me sit up."

The young man obeyed, lifting Tess gently to a sitting position. Her eyes traveled slowly about the room as pieces of her memory started to return. Gradually, in bits and snatches, she recalled her life in Philadelphia, Talbot, and the moments before the wagon accident.

Modeen bent down to stare at her. "Are you all right, Teacher?"

"Yes. I'm fine, children." Getting to her feet, Tess walked slowly to her desk, her head swimming, and sat down, staring vacantly at her class.

I am Tess Wakefield. I am not Fedelia Yardley. Fedelia was swept downstream with poor old Walter Fedderson and the others.

The children scrambled for their desks and opened their math books without her having to ask them. Tirzah was the most concerned, and before going to her seat she approached the desk to check one more time on her teacher.

Tess smiled reassuringly at the girl. "I'm okay, Tirzah. Really. Please continue with your work."

Talbot. What is Talbot thinking? He must assume I was the woman swept downstream in the accident. I have to wire him immediately.

A new, more sobering thought came to her as the children worked quietly at their desks.

Does Jake know my identity?

With a muffled sob, she fumbled in her pocket for a handkerchief.

"Suppose I oughta go for Doc?" Pud whispered to King.

"Those snowflakes are gittin' bigger," he said. "If you're goin', you'd better start now, or else someone should go with ya."

Tess glanced up, her head clearing. "That won't be necessary, King. I'm going to be fine. Just a tiny knock to my head."

"You sure? You look all white and pasty — like you're gonna spit up."

"I'm not going to spit up. And, children, I'd rather none of you mention the incident to anyone." She needed time. Time to decide how she was going to handle this startling turn of events.

"It's all right with me," Tirzah readily agreed. "If my pa heard I throwed a log and hit the teacher in the head, I'd get a whippin' when I got home."

"It's threw, not throwed, Tirzah." Tess was

surprised at how natural it felt to correct the child. She truly was the teacher, even though she had no right to be.

By early afternoon, Tess knew she'd suffered more than a mild hit. Her head ached and her vision was blurry. The weather was becoming beastly, and in another hour it wouldn't be safe for the children to walk home. "Class, I'm going to dismiss school early today. King, I would like you to see that everyone gets home safely."

She was given no argument. The children scattered like leaves in a heavy gale. The room emptied, and Tess dropped her head into her hands. Wood popped in the stove. Outside, snow fell like a thick blanket, and the wind howled around the schoolhouse eaves.

Jake, how will you react when you discover I am Tess Wakefield and not Fedelia Yardley?

She had so many questions, but there was one thing she knew for sure. She wouldn't have the slightest chance of winning his love when the mistaken identity was revealed, if a chance had ever existed. Why hadn't she given serious thought to his dream to replant trees?

Now the plan seemed so logical, so noble. Then it had been impractical and frivolous to both her and Talbot, but she had witnessed firsthand the pine's destruction and seen what man was doing against nature.

Will you ever forgive me, Jake? Is there a way I could convince you that if I had known the true problem I would have readily agreed to the replanting, even been here to help?

God, forgive me. If I had only known, I would have respected Your land more, Your earth.

Lifting her head, she knew she had to talk to someone. Echo would tell her what to do.

She rose, banked the fire, grabbed her coat, and closed the schoolroom door behind her.

Snow was falling in blustery sheets by the time the Burnes' cabin was in sight. Coming here was foolish. Tess should have gone directly to her room. The storm was worsening, and it appeared the area was in for a heavy blizzard.

Deep drifts covered the timber roads. Tess struggled to maneuver the growing banks, her boots sinking deep into the terrain.

An angry wind hurled snow through the tall pine as she struggled toward the log shack. Tears were frozen on her cheeks, and she realized her life was a sham.

Earlier she had started to resent the crude logging town, the hard life, the endless snow, and the heinous children. She thought of Jake. Now she longed for the familiar, the sane. This way of life would be taken from her when the truth came to light.

How could she return to her prior life now that she had experienced the sweetness of falling in love? She loved Talbot, but she knew it was different than what she felt for Jake. Maybe it was appreciation for what he'd done for her over the years, but she was definitely not in love with him.

And her hat boutiques? The stores she had borne like children? After seeing the land left stripped and barren, how could she return to making hats for customers so vain and sheltered that they never gave the environment a thought?

She was so caught up in her thoughts that she wasn't paying attention to the path. Her hands shot out to break a fall as she tumbled headlong into a snowbank. She hadn't noticed the fallen log blocking her way. Snow blinded her as she struggled to regain her footing. A sharp gust of wind snatched her bonnet and sent it whirling into the storm.

Pulling herself to her feet, she glanced down, realizing she hadn't tripped over a log.

She'd tripped over a body.

25

With a strangled gasp, Tess recognized Waite Burne. Her heart jumped into her throat as she reached out to touch him. Drawing back, she realized he was frozen stiff.

"Oh, Echo," she whispered, her head swimming. Where was Echo? Tess made a quick search of the area, satisfied that Waite was alone before she started to run, her boots covering the remaining distance to the cabin. Collapsing against the door, she lifted her fist and pounded twice. Echo answered the summons, her eyes lighting up when she recognized her visitor.

"What are you doing here on a day like this?"

"You . . . have to . . . come . . ." Tess gasped, reaching out for her friend's hand as she struggled to catch her breath.

"You're near froze, ma'am. Come in and let me fix you a cup of tea —"

"Waite . . . he's . . ."

"He isn't here. Really, it's all right to come in. I'm so happy to see you, Fedelia." Echo drew her inside, and then she filled the teapot with water from the pitcher. "I never dreamed you'd pay a visit on such a worrisome day."

Tess's head was swimming from the earlier blow and the shock of finding Waite's body in the snow. Echo's voice sounded as though she were speaking from a drum.

When she didn't respond, Echo turned to glance at her. "Won't be no trouble at all. I was about to make a cup for myself when you knocked."

Tess closed her eyes. Jake. She had to get Jake, but he had told her last night that he would be way over on the south road, working.

The smell of supper cooking lent the appearance of normality. A lantern burned on the table, casting its warm rays over the sparsely furnished room. The table was set for a couple: two plates, two cups, two forks, two spoons, two knives. Fresh coffee perked on the stove. Everything was as it should be, yet Tess knew that nothing about this day was normal.

"It's frightful out there," Echo remarked as she carefully measured tea from a jar into two cups.

"Echo, please listen to me." Tess finally caught her breath and crossed the room to grasp the young woman's shoulders. "Something's happened to Waite."

"Let's see. You take sugar in your tea, don't you?" Echo picked up the teakettle to pour hot water into the cups. "I like three teaspoons — sometimes four. Waite says I have a terrible sweet tooth."

"Echo." Why wasn't she listening? It seemed she wanted to avoid any mention of her husband.

"Waite's gone," she admitted. "And I don't care. I plain don't care anymore. He was liquored up when he left. If he got hurt in a fight, there's not a thing I can do."

Tess's voice was barely above a whisper. "It's more serious than that."

"What happened?"

"I'm not sure, but he must have fallen . . . Echo, he's dead."

"Dead?"

Tess nodded. "He's lying out front so cold . . . and so quiet . . ."

Echo turned and placed the two cups of steaming tea on the table. She didn't appear to comprehend what Tess was saying.

"Echo? What should we do? We can't leave him out there."

Finally, her friend looked up. "Waite's dead?"

Nodding, Tess said softly. "He's not far. When did you last see him?"

"Last night. He was mad at me and left the house. Said he was going to Shadow Pine."

"He must have started out, fallen, and hit his head. When did he leave?"

"Just before supper. He told me he was leavin' and not comin' back — but I didn't believe him. He's always saying mean things like that."

Tess moved to comfort her friend. "Oh, Echo, you should have come for me. Have you been alone since then?"

"Yes, but I'm always alone, except for my Bible and the dogs."

Sinking into the nearest chair, Tess tried to think. She had to go for help. She couldn't handle this alone. She sensed Echo putting a cup of tea gently between her fingers. "Drink this, Fedelia. You'll feel better."

The hot liquid seared Tess's throat, but she drank it anyway. Her mind refused to function, Waite lay dead in the snow, and Echo was acting as though they were having a tea party.

Finally, Tess summoned the strength to

push the cup aside and murmur, "I have to find Jake." Mechanically she got to her feet. The entire day had been a nightmare. First she was hit in the head, then her memory returned, and now she had found her friend's dead husband. "He's over on the south road. It'll take a while."

"No need to hurry." Echo took a sip of her tea. "Waite's not going anywhere."

It occurred to her that the woman was in shock, which would explain her bizarre behavior. Resting a hand on Echo's thin shoulder, she prompted gently, "Get your coat and come with me."

"I'll stay here and keep the fire going. You go on."

Shocked by her refusal, Tess shook her head. "Please, Echo, you can't stay here alone." What if she were to wander outside and find Waite? "Get your coat. You're coming with me."

"I'll be fine. You take the lantern and bundle up real tight." Echo stood up and went to the cupboard. She returned and lifted the lantern's globe to trim the wick. She lit it and then replaced the globe. Handing the light to Tess, she said, "Tell Jake that if he hasn't eaten yet I'll have extra."

"Yes . . . all right." Tess edged toward the door. This was another bad dream.

Echo smiled. "I think I'll sit a spell and read my Bible."

"That's good." Her fingers fumbled blindly for the latch on the door. "I'll be back as quickly as I can."

"All right, ma'am. I'll be here."

Outside, Tess sucked large amounts of bitter-cold air into her lungs. Despite the rest and tea, her head was still reeling from the earlier blow and the now shocking events, but she had to get help. Jake would know what to do. She struggled over mounds of deep drifts in the thickening darkness. Blizzard winds howled.

The wildly swinging lantern cast distorted shadows over the disappearing path. Ordinarily, she wouldn't consider taking this remote road alone, but she barely noticed the grotesque shapes of branches and limbs that eerily reached out and threatened to snatch her. Her blood pounded, and her lungs filled with the scent of the resinous pine.

What would Echo do? Waite Burne was a pitiful human being, but he had fed and clothed her, and provided a roof over her head.

Straight ahead, Tess detected a faint light and the sound of men's voices. "Jaaaake!"

■ ■ ■ ■

Jake glanced up when he heard Tess's voice mingle with the yowling wind. His brows drew together in a frown, and he watched her wading through snow toward him.

"Jake!"

Sliding down a hillside, he moved quickly to meet her. "What's wrong?"

"It's Waite!" she gasped. "You have to come now!"

"Waite?" Jake's frown deepened. "He didn't show up to work today. What's he done?"

"He's dead!"

"Dead? Where?"

"He's lying in the snow, some yards from his house. Oh, Jake, it's awful!" She knew her voice bordered near hysteria, and she threw herself into the safety of his arms. Hugging him tightly, she felt the familiar sense of security wash over her. It didn't matter that she wasn't Fedelia Yardley. She was oblivious to everything except that she loved this man, and she wanted him to make her world right again.

He held her close for a few moments, soothing her, and then he pushed her back by the shoulders, keeping his hands on her arms to steady her. "Are you hurt?"

"No, no, it isn't me. It's Echo . . . and Waite. He's dead, Jake!"

"Where is Echo?"

"She's back there in the cabin . . ." Tess broke off sobbing, but then she took a deep breath and forced herself to go on. "She's acting so strangely. She just sits there drinking tea as if nothing happened!" Closing her eyes, Tess relived the horror of the terrible scene she had witnessed.

"Anything wrong, Jake?" Fred called from a waiting sled.

"Trouble at the Burnes' cabin. You and Joe had better come with me." He turned and set Tess's feet back in motion. "Are you sure Waite's dead?"

"Yes!"

"Do you have any idea what happened?"

"Echo said he'd been drinking. He must have lost his footing."

"One of the men said he saw him over in Shadow Pine early yesterday afternoon, drinking heavily."

"Echo said he didn't come home last night." Tess broke out in fresh tears.

"Get in!" Fred pulled the sled up beside them. As soon as they were onboard, it zipped off.

When they reached Waite's body, Jake

rolled the jack face-up and searched for a pulse. "He's been dead for hours," he murmured. Then he stood and walked to the house.

Echo answered the door at the first knock. Tess saw her open Bible on a footstool beside the fire. She met Jake's eyes. Tess had never seen such pain as she saw in their agonized depths.

"Waite's gone," she said.

Reaching for her hand, Jake said quietly. "You're going to be all right, Echo."

"He said he was leavin' me, but I knew he didn't mean it. I knew he'd be back. See." Her gaze swept the set table. "I've cooked for him and made all his favorite things. Fried potatoes and onions . . ."

Jake reached out to cup her face with his fingers. "You were a fine wife, Echo," he said. "Waite was a blessed man."

Their eyes met, and Tess witnessed a strange but unmistakable message pass between the two people. The message of understanding flashed in Echo's eyes.

"He's not comin' back, is he?"

"No. He isn't coming back." He squeezed her hand.

She reached out and touched his face. "I know you will be worryin' about me, Jake, but you don't need to. I'll make it fine without him."

He nodded and stepped to the door. He opened the latch and called, "Fred, you need to take the body back to camp. Joe, you head on over to Doc's place and tell him he's needed out here. I want him to look at Echo."

"Yes, sir."

"Right away, Big Say."

Tess gently placed a cool cloth on her friend's forehead. Echo tried to smile, but tears rolled from the corners of her eyes. It was the first emotion she had shown, and Tess found the sign encouraging.

The dam burst then, and the young woman's shoulders heaved. The silent gesture tore at Tess's heart. The passing of her husband was finally sinking in, and Echo was trying to deal with it the best she could.

Sinking down beside her, Tess cradled her friend, and they shared a good cry together. When the heart of the emotional storm passed, they held each other tightly. She knew Echo was frightened. The woman had no one now.

"Don't worry. I'll take care of you," Tess promised. "You don't ever have to be afraid anymore."

"I . . . love . . . you . . . so . . . much," Echo said, and her voice reminded Tess of the day that she had held Juice Tetterson in her arms. The young seven-year-old had been crying and sniffling that afternoon because she'd fallen and scraped her knee.

"One good thing. At least now I won't have to . . . lose . . . you," Echo said.

Smoothing back her friend's hair, Tess whispered, "You will never lose me."

There was so much to share with her friend. Her true identity, and how she had selfishly and thoughtlessly fought Jake on replanting the pines, but now wasn't the time or the place.

Now, like the Good Book said, was a time to cry.

26

Jake told Tess that the sheriff had to be summoned when a death occurred. He left to
comply with the notice. She was relieved
when he also suggested that she dismiss
school for the rest of the week. Not only
because of the weather, but because he
wanted her to stay with Echo. Grief had
rendered her senseless.

Tess spent the night with her. It would
take hours for the sheriff and deputy to
make the arduous trek to Wakefield Timber.
One more heavy snow burst and all travel
would come to a halt again.

Now it was late morning, and she sat with
Echo beside the stove, listening for the occasional sled, its runners squeaking as it cut
through the deep drifts. Large wet flakes
swirled beneath a slate-colored sky like
feathers from a torn pillow.

Occasionally Echo left her chair to check
the turkey roasting in the oven. A mouth-

watering aroma filled the small cabin. Tess had tried to persuade her to forget about cooking anything substantial, but she insisted that the sheriff and his deputy would appreciate a hot meal before they made the trip back to Shadow Pine. Nothing Tess said could penetrate Echo's fog.

She got out flour and sugar. "I think I'll make a cake. Waite liked my cakes."

Tess stepped into the kitchen to help her. They worked in companionable silence and had just put on the last of the sugar frosting when a knock came at the door.

Echo wiped her hands on her apron. "I'll get it. That's probably Jake and the sheriff."

Jake and two other men were standing outside when she opened the door. Her heart skipped a beat when she heard Lannigan's deep voice.

"Afternoon, Echo. This is the sheriff from Shadow Pine. He took a look at Waite."

Opening the door wider, Echo said, "You men come on in out of the cold."

They stepped inside and the sheriff shook his head. "I don't know what else to say, ma'am. We're mighty sorry your man is gone. He sure enough hit his head hard when he fell down. It was purely an accident."

"Thank you, sir. I appreciate your coming

all the way out here."

"You're welcome, ma'am."

Nodding, she motioned to the set table. "I would like to feed you dinner and a piece of cake before you leave."

"Much obliged. It's a long ride back."

Tess helped her dish up food and fill coffee cups. The authorities ate heartily and then immediately left for home, while Jake disappeared to the lean-to to build a pine box for Waite's burial.

Tess found the contrast between Echo's husband and the camp foreman overwhelming. Jake was a good, honest, hardworking man. Waite had been the exact opposite.

Tess had deliberately caught and held Jake's eyes when she handed him the bowl of potatoes during dinner. If she had failed to capture his love, this would be one of their last meals together, and the knowledge nearly broke her heart.

A full moon rose, and silence settled over the Burne place. The old clock ticked away, as if somehow by continuous labor it could erase the sorrow that had taken place. Everyone but Tess and Jake had left. Tess felt comforted that he'd decided to stay the remainder of the night with them. The weather wasn't fit for man or beast.

It was rather unsettling that the box with Waite's remains was in the lean-to close by. It was draped in heavy canvas and awaiting a spring thaw for burial.

Echo fitfully tossed on the bed she had once shared with her husband. Around one o'clock, Tess warmed a pan of milk and added a dollop of the sleeping powder Doc Medifer had left earlier.

Echo drank the potion. "I'm sorry I'm so much trouble, Fedelia."

"You are no bother. Rest, my friend." She walked toward Jake. "Try and get some sleep," she whispered to him as she sat down in her chair.

"I'm all right." He stifled a yawn. Deep creases of fatigue darkened the corners of his eyes. "We should both try and get some rest," he said softly. "We can hear Echo if she needs anything."

Tess nodded and got up to get an extra blanket. She noticed a smile touching the corners of his mouth as she tucked it up snugly around his shoulders. She cocked her head. "Is something funny?" If it was, she'd failed to note it.

He took her hand and pulled her close. "Nothing's funny. I was just thinking that I always ask a lady for permission before I kiss her."

"You don't have to ask." His lips briefly touched hers, and she closed her eyes, drawing deep of the faint aroma of pine in his plaid shirt.

"I'm proud of you." His fingers rearranged the loose tendrils of hair around her face.

"What have I done?"

He slowly shook his head. "You've been good to Echo. She hasn't had much love in her life, and to have a friend like you means everything to her. She'll never forget you."

"I love her, Jake, and there'll be no need for her to forget me. I'll always be in her life."

She would be there for him too, if he asked, though she had given her promise to another man. Would Jake resent her when he learned the truth? That she knew she was not Fedelia Yardley and hadn't told him? She needed time before she faced the truth. Time to sort out the emotional turmoil that wound around her heartstrings like a vine. Would his feelings change when he learned that she was the primary source of the molten anger that seethed in his soul day after day?

Their mouths touched a second time and the kiss lingered until Jake set her aside, despite her disenchanted murmur. She didn't want the moment to end.

"It will be morning soon, and I have a crew to run."

"You sleep, and I'll sit beside you." She would gladly forfeit a meager hour or two of rest for the pleasure of his company. Her life was in complete upheaval, but her desire for him remained strong and unmistakable.

Had she ever truly loved Talbot? The emotions she felt right now suggested she was merely infatuated with her fiancé. He was a good man, but Jake was the love of her life.

Big Say gave a lopsided grin that caused her stomach to knot, and then he kissed her briefly again — with enough mastery to make her wish he found sleep highly overrated.

"Go to sleep," he said.

She accepted the dismissal without further argument. She had a lot of thinking to do. She felt his hand close over hers. Tonight she'd seen in his eyes what was in her heart every time she looked at him, but from the depths of her memory came the knowledge that she might never have him as her own because she was promised to another.

Tess thought about Talbot's genteel manners, his kindness, his thoughtfulness, his patience. She struggled to remember the feelings his kisses had evoked. They had been sweet, chaste, and proper, but they hadn't felt like Jake's. They had never left her breathless.

The light wind outside lulled her weary body to relax. Logs snapped and popped in the stove. Though her heart ached for Echo, when she was close to Jake like this, she couldn't help feeling grateful. God worked in mysterious ways. That's what Tip always told her, and tonight she believed it.

It occurred to her in that drowsy state between sleep and awareness that she could have adjusted to being Fedelia Yardley. The mistaken identity didn't bother her. Fedelia was a lovely but lonely woman. How long could she go on pretending she was the schoolteacher?

If she remained silent and told no one of the mistaken identity, she could stay here with Jake until Talbot decided to come and investigate the accident, which he surely would when the thaw came.

Thinking of the prospect of his arrival was too alarming for her to consider. She would never leave Wakefield Timber. This was her land, her rightful heritage. She might have promised her future to Talbot, but her heart belonged to Jake.

An ache throbbed in the back of her neck. She was torn. Torn between the past and the present, and the future looked too dismal to consider, but instinct told her that no matter how fast she ran, she couldn't outrun the truth.

27

Tess awoke to the touch of warm lips brushing her forehead. The mantel clock struck four.

"I'm leaving now," Jake whispered.

"Mmm . . . so soon?"

Kneeling in front of her, he smiled. "Cookee will be sounding the horn soon. I need to stop by my place before I start the crew."

"You've had so little rest." She sat up and wiped sleep from her eyes.

"I'll catch up tonight. Why don't you walk with me?"

Coming fully awake, she glanced up to check on Echo, who appeared to be sleeping soundly. Pushing the blanket aside, she accepted his invitation. "She'll sleep a while longer. I can be back before she wakes."

Jake lit the lantern and loaded the stove with firewood while she splashed cold water on her face. Going to the bed, she tucked the blanket around Echo more securely and then leaned down to kiss her cheek.

She momentarily stirred. "Is it morning?"

"No, go back to sleep. I'm going to walk with Jake to camp. I'll be back before dawn."

Nodding, she drifted off.

A thick cloud bank hung to the east as Tess and Jake stepped out of the cabin. Darkness covered the earth, and the snow showed signs of letting up. Only a thin white powder sifted from the sky. The wind had died down, and a peaceful silence blanketed the frozen earth. Bitter-cold air heightened the scent of pines, and she stepped closer to the man she loved.

She knew the road monkeys hadn't had time to clear the path, and their footprints left deep tracks in the snow as they walked around the deep harbor. In the distance, a dog barked, momentarily shattering the frozen stillness.

"I think it would be a good idea for you to stay with Echo a few more days," Jake said.

Her steps fell in sync with his as they followed the lantern rays spread out before them. The light flickering against the stark white drifts cast a warm yellow glow. "I'll stay for however long she needs me." She glanced over and smiled. "It isn't as if I have a home of my own."

He chuckled. "You have had your problems."

"I'm glad you noticed. When I wake up I'm never sure where I am." He paused, and Tess sensed that he wanted to say something, but apparently he changed his mind and picked up the pace again.

"If you stay with your friend, then the problem is solved."

"Or," she ventured boldly, "we could court for a proper time and then marry." His kisses had more than assured her that he shared her deepest affections.

"Now you're talking crazy."

"Brazen, perhaps, but not crazy." She swallowed her last ounce of pride. "Jake, by now you know that all you have to do is ask me, and I'll marry you so fast it will make your head swim."

Desperation fueled the compulsive outburst. If they married quickly, they could outrun the past that was slowly eating its way into their lives. It was foolish for her to propose, but if he didn't marry her soon, Talbot would come.

How long had she been here? Time had lost its meaning. If she were married to another man when he came, he couldn't insist that she honor their agreement. She wasn't proud of her duplicity, but Talbot deserved a woman whose heart could be truly his, not someone who was in love with another man.

Jake's jaw firmed. "We can't marry."

"For goodness' sake, Jake, why not? I know it's sudden and the marriage might lift a few brows, but we're in love with each other, and I would marry you today if you asked." A sobering thought gave her pause. "Are you in love with that woman in Shadow Pine?"

She wasn't fully convinced the rumors about various men frequenting those women were even founded. And everything she'd seen Jake do or say indicated he was a man of principle, and she had no reason to doubt that included his taste in women.

"What woman in Shadow Pine?"

"Marcy Wetlock. I've heard that you . . . visit her now and again."

A frown deepened. "What has André told you about me now?"

"It isn't just André. There's been . . . talk." The subject was most uncomfortable and inappropriate. Tess suddenly realized she had no right to bring his personal life into the conversation, however the matter concerned her. She regretted she had brought the matter up.

"Oh? Did anyone happen to mention how often I take a bath?"

Heat crept up her neck. "Of course not, but you bathe twice a week."

"And how do you know that?"

"Women know, all right?" One didn't have to stand around a jack long to determine their bathing habits.

They circled the pond, and she huddled deeper into her outer wear. "Well?" she prompted.

"Well, what?"

"Are you going to ask me?" Urgency compelled her. She intuitively felt that if she didn't solidify this relationship now, it would slip away forever. Her past was breathing close on her heels. She could feel obligation tightening around her heart like stubborn tentacles. If she didn't make this effort for freedom and the liberty to choose the man she adored, Jake would slip away.

"Ask you to marry me?"

"Yes. What else have we been talking about?"

"I would if I could." He paused, turning to take hold of her shoulders. Their eyes met. "I've never said that to another woman. It's important for you to know that."

She smiled. "I'm so glad." Her mood

brightened. He didn't think her horribly impertinent, and he had as much as said he was in love with her and wanted to marry her. And even if she were Fedelia Yardley, he had fallen in love with the woman, not the name. She would eventually have to tell him she was Tip's granddaughter, but he couldn't resent that. "Then let's get married. The sky pilot will be here Sunday. There's not one single reason to wait."

He smiled down at her as they resumed walking again. "In a hurry?"

"As a matter of fact, I am. I love you, and I don't have time to wait."

"Brazen too?"

"No. Only deeply in love for the first time in my life." She leaned up to kiss his cold lips.

His features sobered. "You don't know what you're asking."

She tilted her head. "What's that supposed to mean? I do know what I'm asking."

Menson's store loomed in front of them, soft lantern light spilling onto the snow-packed ground. Tess's hands and feet were numb with cold. As she was about to enter the store, Jake reached out to stop her. Drawing her back to the privacy of the porch, he said softly. "We need to talk."

"Can't we talk inside? My teeth are chattering."

"This won't take long."

The sudden seriousness in his tone stopped her, and she allowed him to pull her deeper into the shadows. He kissed her softly and so sweetly that she thought she might burst with her love for him. When he broke the kiss, she gazed into his eyes.

"What I'm about to tell you will break your heart."

Her heart thumped in her chest. "You don't love me."

"Oh, I love you, Tess. I have from the moment André dragged you out of that freezing river."

She leaned in for another kiss. If he loved her, then nothing else mattered. But as her lips brushed his, the given name he had just used sank in. He'd called her Tess.

Pulling back, she met his gaze in the soft lantern light. "You called me Tess."

Releasing his hold, he stepped away from her. "I did."

"But you meant Fedelia."

"No, I said the proper name."

Emotions ricocheted through her. Physical pain, disbelief, and then slow recognition. "You knew all this time that I was Tess and not Fedelia?"

"Not for certain. All of the physical evidence indicated Fedelia was the one who survived, but it wasn't long till I had a good hunch that it might have been you instead. When you started making hats and using fancy words, I knew."

"And yet you didn't tell me."

"I'm not proud of it, but . . . no, I didn't tell you."

He stepped closer, reaching for her again, but she jerked away. He had deliberately perpetrated a fraud. He had put her through the agony of those camp children — she, who couldn't make one plus three equal four! Was he out of his mind? Insanely mad!

"Why, Jake?"

"When I first met you, I didn't like Tess Wakefield or what she was going to do with Wakefield Timber."

"Well . . . that's a *sick* answer!"

"Granted. I wasn't thinking straight at the time."

"How could you do such a thing? Especially later, when you knew me, when you knew I was falling in love with you."

"If I told you, I knew you would leave right away. I didn't want that. It was a stupid thing to do, and I'm paying the consequences."

She slowly backed away. "You said you

loved me."

His gaze softened. "I *do* love you, Tess. I'm in love for the first time in my life."

She shook her head. "I thought you respected my grandfather."

"He was one of the finest men I've ever known, and I have no excuses. I did a dim-witted and selfish thing, and as stupid things often do, it's caught up with me. I'm sorry. Deeply sorry."

Hot tears sprang to her eyes, and it hurt to breathe. She couldn't cry now. She had every right to grieve this loss, yet at the time he misled her, he had every right to resent her.

She had rejected his pleas about replanting those pines, and her chickens had come home to roost. And they were every bit as ugly and spiteful as his stupid mistakes. And she couldn't deny she was just as guilty of the same treason by not telling him she remembered who she was.

Her voice caught on a sob. "I . . . I've known who I am since early yesterday morning. I wanted everything to settle down before I told you, and I needed to make sure you loved me so I wouldn't lose you." A sudden thought occurred to her, threatening to stop her heart. "Oh, Jake, if you know I'm Tess, then you know about Talbot."

"Yes, I do."

Menson's front door opened, and Henry stuck his head around the screen. "Jake, hate to bother you —"

"Then don't. I'm busy right now, Henry."

"Some man hopped the last sleigh able to make it from Shadow Pine. I guess they had a rough time and almost didn't get here. He's over at your office waiting to speak to you."

"I'm busy. Tell him I'm unavailable."

"He's insistent."

Tess shook her head. "Go. He's probably desperate for a job. I'll stop by the office in a bit. I need to get my things if I'm going to be staying with Echo."

He stepped closer. "Will you be all right?"

She was so confused. Who was most in the wrong? Jake, who knew she might not be Fedelia Yardley? Or she, for knowing the truth and shamelessly going after him when she was betrothed to Talbot?

She would have to answer to God for her actions, but Jake had all but lied about her identity for months, to everyone, and that she didn't think she could forgive. If he'd only been truthful, all of this might have been avoided.

"At the moment, I don't think I'll ever be all right again, Jake."

28

Dawn slowly lit the sky. Rays of sunshine topped the rim of the pines and blanketed the camp, promising a clear day, when Tess opened the door to Jake's office. At the moment, she didn't care about her appearance or even that she needed to hurry back to Echo. All she could think about was that she had been betrayed by the man who meant the most to her.

André glanced up when she stepped in on a cold rush of wind. His expression this morning was masked.

"*Ma chère.* We have been waiting for you."

"Good morning, André. Jake." Her eyes skipped immediately to Big Say, who didn't look an ounce better than she did. Suddenly, her heart shattered in tiny pieces. She longed to kiss away the anguish she so clearly recognized in the slump of his shoulders, in his rumpled appearance. For once, he didn't have the last word. He stood at the window, his back turned to her, lost in the sunrise.

She took a step toward him before she noticed that another man was sitting in the room. She paused and focused on the city clothes, the new hat, and the high-buttoned shoes with bulldog toes. She blinked twice, trying to adjust to the bright light. Talbot? He was here? She looked up when he slowly rose from his chair and extended his hand, relief evident in his eyes.

"Tess. Thank God."

He was really here, standing right in front of her. She couldn't believe her eyes. He cautiously took a step toward her, both his hands extended now as though he feared she might dissolve in a mist.

"I was afraid to believe it . . . even though I've dreamed of this moment. I never abandoned hope that you were the one who survived. Thank You, God. *Thank You!*"

Joyful tears rolled from his eyes and streamed off the tip of his nose. Tess withered inside. Talbot had forged his way through the icy Michigan woods to find her. She glanced expectantly at André, who kept his head down and remained silent. Her gaze shifted to Jake. His broad back, tense now, partially blocked the golden rays of sun streaming through the windowpanes.

She thought of the arms that had engulfed her so dearly not long ago on Menson's front porch. Welcoming arms, tender, loving arms, the exact arms she wanted to hold her forever. She could forgive him anything. "Jake?" she prompted softly.

He slowly turned, and her heart throbbed when she witnessed the raw torment that filled his eyes. *Please, no* . . . her gaze mutely pleaded. *Love me enough to fight for me.*

Jake's answer was barely audible. "Tess . . . I'm sorry."

It was his tone that told her. It was over. She used the pain inside to fill her eyes, and beseech him to not let her go this easily. "There's nothing more you want to say?" she whispered.

Reaching for his coat, he pulled it on and left the office. A cold wind from the open door swept her, chilling her bones.

"Tess, my love, I know this is upsetting," Talbot said quietly. "Mr. Lannigan has explained about your memory loss —"

"*Ma chère* . . . he does not know what he says," André consoled. "He is angry with himself."

Lifting her eyes to the man she was to marry, she said in a flat voice, "Talbot, I want to go home."

He sprang to assist her. "Of course, my

344

love. I'll arrange for a sled. Once you're back in Philadelphia we can put this whole unfortunate episode behind us."

André cleared his throat. "I am not sure a sleigh will make it back to Shadow Pine. Though the snow has stopped, the roads will be very dangerous."

"I want to go now, André," she murmured, still dazed by Jake's rejection. "Can you arrange for the sled promptly?"

Addressing André, Talbot said, "Please, do as the lady asks." He turned back to Tess. "Pack your things. The sled will be waiting. We'll be detained in Shadow Pine for a few days until the train is running again."

"I don't have anything, Talbot. I only have Fedelia Yardley's personal effects." She brushed by André on her way out. "Please tell Echo I love her and that I will send for her soon. She can visit me in Philadelphia . . ." She paused, tears rolling down her cheeks. "Will you purchase a train ticket for her, André? I will reimburse you . . ."

"*Oui, ma chère.* I will take good care of your friend until she can join you."

"Someone needs to notify Bernice. She'll have to fill in for me."

André nodded. "This I will do, but I will not enjoy it."

"Oh . . ." she paused, blinking tears. "I've

345

made each of the WASPS a small gift —
Coburn bonnets. Will you see that they get
them?" At the last moment she had discarded frivolous in favor of common sense.
The bonnets stacked in her room were
colorful and practical, and she was sure the
women would love them.

"This is most kind of you, mademoiselle."

"And don't muss them, André. They're
serviceable but delicate." She didn't know a
woman alive who didn't appreciate a little
oomph in her fashion.

"Oui."

Tess opened the door, wrapped her scarf
around her neck tighter, and led Talbot out
of the office.

Jake stood on a high ledge and watched the
big sled pull out of camp. He'd felt pain
before — the bite of the ax, frostbitten toes
and fingers, night sweats, and even a concus-
sion one winter — but the hurt inside him
now overrode anything he'd ever experienced.

Why had he done that to her?

Tip's voice rang in his mind. They had
been crosscut-sawing one afternoon on the
south rim when the man first mentioned his
beloved granddaughter. He'd voiced how
he'd missed out on much of her life because

346

of his thirst for adventure. And it worried Tip.

Giving Jake a history lesson, Tip had told him that back in the day, men and women came by canal boats, paddle steamers, sloops, wagon trains, and clipper ships, looking for limitless stands of the coveted *pinus strobus* — that lofty, graceful, aromatic evergreen known as the eastern white pine.

Still a young man, he had barely been eking out a living for his family on a small piece of land in the Midwest when timber fever spread like wildfire across the eastern states. Jake could still see Rutherford's powerful arms pulling the crosscut saw back and forth. He'd loved that old man.

That had been years ago, but now he loved another Wakefield. His eyes followed the sled carrying Tess away. At one time he thought he loved the pine more than he could ever love anything. Now he knew he was wrong. He loved Tess more than life itself.

Are You paying me back, God? Should I have done more? Talked less? Worked harder?

For twenty years he'd taken part in the land's desecration. When he was a boy of fourteen, J. Basil Lannigan had set him behind a pair of Percherons, and he'd

347

worked as a teamster, dragging logs out of the woods to the skid ways. He was taught how to build roads and how to use an ax and a crosscut saw. He'd worked at every job in the timber field, from pin whacker to ink slinger, and he'd learned his job well.

He'd worked as hard as any man, saying little and trying to ignore what was being done to the earth, but it was clear to him that no one cared what was happening, certainly not his father or the men whose livelihoods depended on the pine. But the day came when Jake took a long, hard look around him and could no longer avoid the appalling truth.

The land was being savaged in a cold, callous, premeditated act, and he knew he could no longer, in good conscience, ignore his responsibilities to his future children and his children's children. He ached for something to offset the madness systematically destroying the countryside.

He had tried to get his father to understand what was happening, but he'd failed. J. Basil refused to see the problem.

Around that time Jake had heard Rutherford's son was killed in an accident and the man was looking for a foreman. Still clinging to the hope that he could persuade at least one timber baron of the madness of the destruction, he had left Lannigan Timber to accept a job with Wakefield.

The decision to leave his father's business had been a painful one, but at least Rutherford had taken the time to hear what he had to say. Tip had sat before the fire one cold night, quietly listening as Jake explained his dream of planting acres of young pine to give new life to a dying land.

When he finished, Rutherford knocked the ashes out of his pipe before repacking it from the tobacco can sitting beside his chair. "Your dream is a mighty tall order, son."

"I know, sir, but it can be done."

Rutherford's eyes had studied the young man before him, and Jake recalled the smile that fixed at the corners of his mouth.

"I don't doubt that you can achieve whatever you desire. This is a dream for all mankind. A dream God would approve of."

Jake recalled the rush of relief he'd felt after Rutherford's quiet acceptance. For the first time in years, he felt a resurgence of hope that the pine madness might begin to subside. "Then you'll authorize me to begin replanting?"

The old man nodded. "I've taken more than my share from the land. Together, we'll see that the pine lives on. Once a stand is cut, you put a crew to replanting what we've taken."

Months later, Tip had mentioned his granddaughter again. "It's a real shame my Tess can't marry a man like you, Jake. Her mother took her off to the city when she was young. She's about to marry the son of a wealthy carriage maker. I guess he's good enough — but I worry about her."

"She's your granddaughter, Tip. She'll do fine."

And then, just a few weeks after that, while trying to bring a skid of logs out of the woods, Rutherford had keeled over dead, and Jake's hope for the future dimmed. And now it was gone, and with it the only woman he'd ever loved.

He could go after her. Nothing was stopping him — except for the knowledge that she belonged to another man. She once accused him of having too much integrity. He supposed she was right, as she'd been so often.

Integrity. The notion got a little tight when practiced, but he knew the word's meaning. A firm adherence to a code of moral or artistic values. Honesty.

And Tess had honestly never belonged to him.

29

Tess stared out the window of the coach. She was on her way back from another endless shopping expedition. Philadelphia had much to offer: restaurants, haberdasheries, exquisite seamstresses, and store-bought clothing fit for royalty.

"Are you comfortable, my dear?"

"Yes, Talbot, thank you."

He smiled paternally, and she was glad when he turned his attention to her friend, who sat with her nose pressed eagerly against the carriage window.

"And you, Echo? Is there anything I can do for you?"

"No, sir, Mr. Wellington-Kent. You've done too much for me already."

"Call me Talbot, please, and it's entirely my good fortune to have two such beautiful ladies under my protection."

Tess's wan smile did little to encourage his compliments, and her attention strayed back to the passing scenery. The events of the past few weeks had rendered her numb. Learning that she was Tess Wakefield and not Fedelia Yardley had come as a shock, but it was Jake's releasing her to Talbot so easily that she found so heartbreaking.

A hysterical giggle rose in her throat, but she quickly forced it down. If Jake Lannigan had wanted to hurt her, he had certainly accomplished his goal. The knowledge that he was willing to let her marry another man was beyond the realm of punishment.

She promised herself one thing. She would never again be the same trusting, gullible fool Jake had proven her to be. Even his quietly spoken, humble apology had done little to ease her hurt. If he had so much as hinted that he wanted — needed — her to stay, she would have swallowed what remained of her pride and broken Talbot's heart.

If only Jake had taken her into his arms and assured her that his words were not a lie, that he loved her without remorse, she would have forgiven him.

Biting her lower lip until she tasted blood, she vowed she would not let Talbot see her cry again. The poor man had listened to her sobs, showing her incredible patience, even though he'd completely misunderstood the reason for her abject misery.

Had he noticed the love in her eyes when she'd looked at Jake Lannigan that last morning? If so, he had far too much breeding to question her about it, and he had gone out of his way to console her, sending for Echo as soon as the roads were clear enough for safe travel. The young woman could stay for as long as she wanted. Talbot had been most gracious.

Get a grip on yourself, Tess! Her self-control was on another downhill slide. A sob escaped her, bringing Talbot and Echo's conversation to an abrupt halt.

Echo leaned over and cooed sympathetically. Talbot quickly extracted his handkerchief from his breast pocket. "Your emotions are clearly askew, dearest. Don't despair. The doctor assures me you will be better soon. You've had quite a disquieting experience."

"Thank you. You're too good to me, Talbot." Tears spilled down her cheeks.

Tess saw Talbot and Echo exchange helpless looks, but she couldn't stop her emotions from welling up inside. Leaning forward, Talbot placed his hand over her fingers. Staring at his hand, she was reminded how different his slender, pale fingers were from Jake's large, nut-brown, work-callused hands.

"I know how much all of this has upset you, but soon you will resume your normal life, and then I'm certain you'll find joy again." Talbot peered at her hopefully. "Do you remember your former life in Philadelphia, Tess?"

She nodded. "It's coming back in bits and pieces."

"Then you will not think of your accident. And you will enjoy life as you did before."

Talbot had spent hours filling her in on her childhood. Her mother had married a lumberjack when she was seventeen. The love of her life had died when a logging chain tangled with his foot and dragged him to his death when Tess was three. Her grief was too much for her mother, and she blamed the timber industry and Tip for Hugh's death. Tip sent his only daughter and grandchild to a second cousin in Philadelphia, where she lived until pneumonia took her life seven years ago. Tip then appointed Talbot her legal guardian until she reached the age of eighteen, and two years after that the young carriage maker had asked her to marry him — but the information wasn't new. She recalled it all. She remembered the past, but now it bore no relevance to the future.

He hesitantly withdrew his hand, drawing in a deep breath as he settled back against the seat. "Well, you're not to be concerned. I will see that you have the finest physicians money can buy. I'm sure the superb medical facilities we have at our disposal will help to see you through this crisis, and the moment you find a ring you fancy, we'll replace the lost one."

Tess's tearful gaze fell on the bare third finger of her left hand, and she vaguely recalled the engagement ring she had been wearing the day she'd left for Wakefield Timber.

"I'm sorry about your ring, Talbot."

"My dear, material possessions are the least of my worries. My only concern is that you are well and happy." Turning back to Echo, he smiled. "And we're going to provide both you and Tess with new clothes, young lady. Entire wardrobes. Coats, hats, shoes, dresses, lingerie, and anything else your heart desires. You and Tess shall make a holiday of touring the dressmakers to your hearts' content!"

"Oh, I don't know what to say, Mr. Wellington-Kent. I know I'm going to wake up tomorrow morning and find that this has all been an exciting dream!"

Tess's friend was in complete awe of the

generous man. Talbot had taken to Echo immediately, and they had formed a close bond in a short time. She listened as they began to rattle on about the proposed shopping expedition as if they were two children planning a day at the circus together.

She sighed, returning her gaze to the window. Talbot was little more than a polite stranger lately, yet in a matter of weeks she would be his wife. The day they left Michigan, he had informed her that once they reached Philadelphia, after a reasonable time of adjustment, their wedding would proceed as planned. The unnerving thought brought the handkerchief to the corners of her eyes again. She should be grateful that such a man of wealth and prestige would still want her for his wife.

Through the past few dark days, she had found Talbot to be an honorable and gentle man. He had stood by her, permitting her to lean on him when her world had fallen apart. If only he knew that what she really ached for was Jake to take her into his arms and beg for her forgiveness — but Jake had left Talbot to dry her tears of disbelief.

Tess recalled how, when their sled passed through a grove of dense pines, she had seen Jake at the top of a ridge, watching from a distance. He'd stood alone. Deep inside, she still believed he cared for her, yet he'd done nothing to stop her departure.

Echo quietly pressed a fresh handkerchief into her hand. Smiling in mute gratitude, Tess dabbed at the moist corners of her eyes. She knew her friend understood. Drawing a deep, ragged breath, she willed her mind to cease dwelling on her memories of the timber camp and its foreman.

"Isn't it the prettiest thing you've ever seen?" Echo floated into the study and whirled about the room, modeling for Tess a stunning silk gown of Federal blue.

Winter had finally come to an end, and the first tender buds of spring were popping out on the trees lining the cobblestone street in front of the Wellington-Kent mansion. Turning from the window, where she'd been staring at the tiny crocuses that had pushed their heads above the ground to make their first appearance, Tess smiled at the young girl.

The past few weeks had brought about a miraculous change in Echo. Under Talbot's dedicated care and tutelage, she had become quite a lovely young woman. Her earlier gauntness had disappeared into nubile curves, and her sallow complexion had taken on a warm, healthy glow. Tess had never seen her friend more beautiful.

"It's breathtaking, Echo. I see you and Talbot have been shopping again this afternoon." She watched Echo's smile rapidly turn to one of immediate concern.

"I hope you don't mind."

"Don't be silly. Of course I don't mind. Now, show me what you've purchased." Tess's closets were overflowing with silks and satins that she couldn't possibly hope to wear even if she lived to be a hundred.

"Well, all right, but Talbot wanted me to remind you that the seamstress has arrived for the final fitting for your wedding gown. And you simply must see the rose crepe de chine we found in a marvelous little shop near the center of town. You're going to adore it!"

"I'm sure it is in excellent taste."

"We have to hurry, though. Talbot says he's taking you to the opera tonight!"

"I'll be along shortly. I have a letter I want to finish." Tess returned to the Louis Quatorze writing desk and resumed her seat while Echo pirouetted happily around the room, trying to catch occasional glimpses of her gown in the large gold-framed mirror hanging above the fireplace.

Tess brought her hand to her forehead and murmured, "Echo, I was wondering if you would mind accompanying Talbot tonight. I have developed a ghastly headache."

"Oh?" Echo's satin slippers paused, and she instantly turned sympathetic. "Another one?"

Tess made her smile as wan as conceivable. "Yes, I'm afraid so. Would you mind terribly going to the opera in my place?"

"Not if Talbot doesn't mind."

Tess knew Echo would do anything she asked, and she felt a twinge of conscience that this was the fourth time this week she had asked the girl to fill in for her, but she simply was not up to a social outing tonight.

Since her return to Philadelphia, her schedule had been exhausting. With the balls and the formal teas and the endless succession of parties and social gatherings held in honor of her forthcoming marriage, Tess had not been able to catch her breath.

She realized she had been wretched company for Talbot. A constant depression accompanied her, and she knew he was growing more puzzled by the day with her continuing lethargy.

During dinner one evening, he had casually mentioned Wakefield Timber and encouraged her to talk about the time she'd spent there, but she had quietly refused. Anything that involved Jake was still far too painful to discuss, though she knew Talbot was only following doctor's orders. She had excused herself from the table early and gone to her room without dinner that evening.

She didn't want to hurt his already bruised feelings. He had done everything short of a miracle to make her happy, but nothing could ease the constant ache in her heart. If it hadn't been for Echo's company, Talbot would have been as bereft as he had been when he'd thought she was dead.

Echo sighed. "They had to bury Waite last week. André sent a message."

"I'm sorry, Echo."

She shook her head. "He's where he should be."

The door to the study opened, and Tess's betrothed entered. "There you two are. Miss Perryworth is waiting in the solarium for you, darling."

Tess nodded without glancing up. "I shall be along momentarily."

Strolling toward the fire, Talbot and Echo exchanged shy smiles. "You look lovely in that color, little one," he said softly.

A flash of pain seared Tess, and her hand trembled. *Little one.* Jake had called her that in the magical time an eternity ago . . . or had it really been only a matter of weeks since she left him standing on a rise, watching her leave? Did he ever think of her? Were his nights as endless with memories of her as hers were with memories of him?

"Thank you, sir."

Tess watched the young woman smile as she dipped demurely, a rosy blush flooding her cheeks. "Echo, why don't you run along and change for dinner? I would like to speak to Talbot in private."

"Yes, ma'am."

Would her friend ever stop calling her "ma'am"? Echo curtsied again, and then she ran happily out of the room.

"There's something you wanted to discuss with me, dear?"

Nodding, she rose from the chair. "I wanted to make my apologies, Talbot. I fear I have a dreadful headache coming on, and I have asked Echo to accompany you to the opera tonight."

"Oh. That is most unfortunate. Shall I have Freda prepare a toddy?"

"No. I'll take some powder later."

Patting his vest, his gaze skimmed her. "I do hope you're planning to have dinner with us tonight. You've grown extremely thin of late."

She smiled. "You worry too much about me."

His expression softened. "I care very deeply for you, Tess."

"As do I for you, Talbot."

"I don't want to push you, but there are so many wedding gifts pouring in." He shrugged. "They must be opened and tagged soon."

"Can't the servants do that?"

"Of course. I just thought you and I might want to personally open them."

She nodded modestly. "Then I shall try to oversee the opening of gifts very soon."

"Thank you. There are those in my family who would be deeply offended if they thought someone other than the bride had opened their offerings."

"Of course. Perhaps this weekend." Opening wedding gifts and trying on her wedding dress were the last two things she felt like doing. However, she knew both tasks were inevitable, so she'd have to somehow manage them.

"What of your hat business? You've barely visited the boutiques, and your customers are asking for you."

"I'm sorry, Talbot. I have not the slightest interest in hats."

"But once you loved them."

"Perhaps. An eternity ago."

Drawing a deep breath, he said, "Mother

wishes our company this Sunday for brunch. She has invited a few of her closest friends to dine with us."

Her head throbbed. "Very well."

He checked his pocket watch and then snapped the gold case shut. "Was there anything else?"

"Yes." Tess folded the letter she had been writing, and then slipped it into an envelope with her initials embossed in silver. "Some days ago I received a letter from Sven Templeton, asking that the sale of Wakefield Timber be completed."

"I'm sure Mr. Templeton is most anxious to get on with his plans."

"I'm sure he is," Tess murmured, remembering the unspeakable carnage she had witnessed under the hand of uncaring timber barons like Sven Templeton. "I've written to inform him that I shall be keeping my grandfather's business after all."

The surprise that flashed briefly across Talbot's face didn't go unnoticed by Tess, but he recovered his composure admirably.

"Well, darling, that is entirely up to you, of course, but do you think it is wise?"

"Yes, and I've also decided that for every tree Wakefield Timber cuts, one shall be replanted." Tess's chin firmed. "There shall not be another pine cut from Wakefield land that isn't replaced."

Talbot met her determined gaze thoughtfully. "That is quite a large and costly undertaking, wouldn't you say?"

"It can be done."

"And Jake Lannigan? Will he be in charge of this vast replanting?"

Tess's gaze dropped to the letter in her hand. "I have no idea what Mr. Lannigan's plans are." He had not written or wired since she left. She could only conclude that his plans did not, nor would not, include her.

Talbot stepped to the window and lifted the curtain to look outside. "And if he should refuse to stay on as foreman of Wakefield Timber?"

There was the pain again, deep and searing as ever. "That will be Mr. Lannigan's decision. He doesn't consult me on such matters."

Talbot sighed. "I see." Letting the material drop back into place, he cleared his throat. "Let's not keep Miss Perryworth waiting."

He crossed the room and bent to kiss her. Tess casually averted her face, and the kiss landed benignly on her temple.

"Would you rather I stay with you tonight? The opera is not important."

"No," she said, hoping he would go. "Echo will enjoy the performance."

"Is that what this is about? Do you feel that Echo and I have been spending undue time with each other?"

"Goodness, no." She offered a genuine smile. "I'm ever so grateful you have taken her under your wing, Talbot. I love her as I would a sister."

Drawing a deep breath, he nodded.

He was so kind. Why couldn't she love him the way she did Jake? "I'll be along soon, I promise," she murmured.

"Thank you, my love." Talbot smiled warmly at her before gracefully leaving the room.

The moment he left, she suspected Talbot only let the issue drop because he didn't want to upset her. She knew he wanted to forget that horrible chapter in their lives and move on, but she couldn't forget. Jake Lannigan was seared in her mind.

And time would do nothing to change the matter.

30

"Jake! Do you have some sort of death wish lately?"

He felt André reach out to jerk him back to safety just as a pile of logs broke loose and spilled out into the thawing waters of Lake Huron.

The spring river drive was on, and the time had arrived for the shanty boys to discard their shoepacs and rubbers for corked boots and peavey poles. Harvested logs were broken out and driven by the white-water men down the crowded strip of water to the sorting booms at the booming ground.

Melting snow and heavy rains made a turbulent sight this morning. The pandemonium of thousands of logs dumped from neighboring logging camps — all massed together and floating down rivers and streams — was a nightmare to the inexperienced.

Jake had been through it many times, but his mind was on something else. No, not something. Someone. "I'm sorry. I wasn't thinking."

"On the contrary, you have been thinking too much lately."

"Let it drop, Montague."

"I cannot let it drop, Jake! *Alors!* You will be killed if you don't snap out of it!"

Jake turned to walk off, but André grabbed his arm and spun him around. He met the angry eyes of his friend.

"If you can't get Tess out of your mind, then do us both a favor and go after her!"

"I can't go after her."

"Why not? She's not married to Wellington-Kent yet, is she?"

The facade Jake had been struggling to carry for weeks was momentarily discarded, and for the first time since Tess left, he had to pause and gather his emotions. He hadn't had a decent night's sleep in months, and he couldn't think straight anymore. "I don't know if she's married, and it would only make matters worse if I did know, so drop it." André gripped his shoulder tightly, and Jake saw mute understanding in his eyes.

"Then I beg of you, *mon ami,* put an end to this madness. Make the trip to the city. Tell her you have been an imbecile but you love her."

Jake smiled. André did have a way with words. "If it were that simple, I would never have let her leave." He swiped at moisture that welled in his eyes with the back of his hand. A grown man crying wasn't a pleasant sight, and if André ever spoke of the incident he'd fire him. Then hire him back. The Frenchman was not only a comrade, but irreplaceable to Wakefield Timber.

"It would seem that you are making this harder than it needs to be." André's tone softened. "You are blindly in love with this woman, Jake. How often does one's true love happen along? I beg you, go after her."

The muscle in Jake's jaw tightened. "I've done enough to disrupt her life. I refuse to do any more."

"You do not think she is also grieving?"

Shrugging off the hand André had placed on his shoulder, Jake pulled his red wool cap down tighter, reached for a pike pole, and started toward the riverbank.

"Don't be a fool, man! It is not too late!"

Jake continued on, ignoring the words. The last thing he wanted was to cause Tess more grief. She was to be married or already was, and he wouldn't interfere.

"Jake, you are not thinking straight. Please go back to the office. I will take care of things here."

"No one does my job for me, Montague," Jake shouted above the roar. "Get to work or I'll dock your pay."

The Frenchman's sober expression didn't escape him. A river hog's job was nothing but danger this time of year, and André was justifiably worried. Jake knew he'd been taking too many chances lately. Did he think by deliberately asking for trouble, he could somehow bring some missing ingredient back into his life? All he knew was he wanted the pain in his heart to stop.

He spotted a large jam forming at the sharp bend leading out into the channel. One of the jacks shouted, and he bound across the rolling logs to locate the one causing the problem. The deafening roar of timber breaking away reverberated around the hillsides as several old-timers worked to break up the jam. The poles rolled and jabbed and hooked logs on top of each other in an effort to unclog the stubborn mass. Overhead, the sky was a bright blue, though the air still had touches of the last vestiges of winter.

André had stayed back to watch the men trying to free the jam.

Suddenly, the log causing the trouble broke loose and shot down the river, followed by hundreds of logs under the immense pressure of the moving water. Jake jumped back to regain his footing, but the log his foot had been aiming for moved to join the others in its mad rush downstream.

André took a step forward. "Jake!"

Jake glanced up and his boot slipped. He dropped into the roiling water and was immediately sucked out of sight beneath the churning mass of pine.

The Frenchman broke into a run, cupping his hands to his mouth, shouting, "Man down! Man down!"

Jacks appeared from every direction, with poles poised, eyes fixed on the churning waters for the victim to surface between the milling logs.

A red woolen cap bobbed to the surface, but its owner failed to follow.

André's boots raced along the riverbank, and then he abruptly turned and attempted to plunge into the swirling mass of water. A jack grabbed him, blocking his efforts to reach the approximate place where Jake had gone down.

"Let go!" André bellowed. "Jake's out there!"

"You can't help him, Montague!" The jack shouted above the roar of the churning water. Others gathered around, their eyes searching the milling logs for signs of life.

"He'll wash up downstream somewhere," someone said.

But minutes passed, and Jake wasn't anywhere to be seen.

"He's a goner," someone else in the crowd said, voicing what every man was silently thinking.

"No!" André said tightly. "Please, my friend," he urged to thin air, "hang on."

On a Saturday afternoon, April twenty-first, soft strains of organ music filtered beneath the study door of the oldest Methodist church in Philadelphia, Pennsylvania.

It was a fitting spring day, and if Tess were to judge from the sounds of the birds' merry chatter coming through the open window, everything was right with the world.

So why was nothing right with hers?

She stared at the image of the stranger standing in the floor length mirror, and wondered for the thousandth time what Jake was doing. Was he well? Was he eating properly? Was he dressed warmly enough?

The apparition looked intently back at her in a lovely tulle-and-lace wedding gown of pristine white, embellished with hundreds of tiny pearls. The creation had been hand-sewn by the finest seamstresses in all of

Philadelphia and would be the envy of a queen.

The woman in the mirror looked familiar, but surely it wasn't her. This person was about to walk down the aisle with a man, who, though very, very kind, was not the one she wanted to spend her life with. So, if this was supposed to be the happiest day of her life, why did she feel like running out and flinging herself off the nearest bridge?

The door opened and Echo entered the room. The cloying, sugary smell of lilies and roses followed her, the sweetness threatening to make Tess "spit up," as King Davis would say.

"I have never seen so many people in my entire life," the woman confessed, breathless. "Such fine carriages and fancy clothes. I do declare it's like living in a palace. You can absolutely smell the money packed into those pews."

Taking in a deep breath and then slowly letting it out, Tess picked up her wedding veil and slipped it carefully on her head. "That's nice."

"Oh . . ." Echo's hand came to rest on her heart. "You look like an angel."

"I don't feel like an angel," Tess grumbled when Echo stepped over to assist her. "You know, my sweet friend, Talbot and I want you in our home for as long as you care to be with us."

"Thank you, Tess. I will stay for a little while, but I want to go to school. I want to learn."

The young woman's eyes brightened. Tess could barely discern a trace of the waif from a remote logging camp in Upper Michigan who didn't own a decent coat. Though sad, Waite's death had freed his wife.

"That's good, Echo. I'm so proud of you. Have you spoken to Talbot about your desire to further your education?"

"Many times, and he insists that he wants to fund my adventure, but I can't let him." She smiled. "I want to find work and pay my own way."

Tess's gaze returned to the mirror. This is not what she wanted. "Echo, I feel sick."

"Wedding day jitters." Echo fussed with the bride's veil. "Talbot will be so proud of you."

"Talbot deserves better than me."

"That's not true! He's the luckiest man in the world to have you, and he knows it."

A soft tap at the study door signaled that the ceremony was about to begin. Tess pressed her hand against her stomach. Could she do this? Echo stood back, peering at her with a knowing look. Her friend's voice was soft when she spoke.

"Try to be happy, my friend. I know your heart still yearns for Big Say, and I ache for you, but Talbot loves you so very much . . . and he is such a good man. He will do his very best to make you happy."

Tess was mildly surprised by Echo's quiet declaration. She'd never dreamed the girl perceived the real reason for her heartache, but the young woman wasn't stupid. Reaching out to touch the tip of Echo's nose gently, she said softly, "Talbot would be far better off with someone like you."

"But he doesn't want me," Echo said simply.

"And if he did?"

Her friend's gaze softened. "Talbot is a wonderful man. You are most blessed that he loves you."

The organ music swelled, and Echo went to open the door. Tess's stomach tangled in a million knots.

"Hurry now . . . he's waiting for you."

Tess lifted the hem of her dress in her hand and stepped into the foyer. The dimly lit hallway was teeming with five giggling, breathless young women, all dressed in long flowing gowns in various hues of the rainbow and wearing matching wide-brimmed hats.

She felt worlds removed from women who had been close childhood friends. Smiling faintly, she moved to stand at the head of the sanctuary doorway. The five attendants reached to adjust the pool of silk and satin that tapered to a long train.

Taking a deep breath, she closed her eyes. The massive sanctuary was filled to over-flowing. All of Talbot's family, friends, and business associates were gathered to witness the exchanging of vows between Miss Tess Wakefield and Mr. Talbot Wellington-Kent.

"Miss Wakefield?"

Tess glanced up to find one of Talbot's manservants extending a yellow piece of paper to her. A wire?

"This just arrived for you." His eyes met hers. "I know this isn't an ideal time, but I thought it might be important."

"Oh?" Debating whether to open the wire or not, she decided she should. Handing her bouquet to Echo, she unfolded the page, her eyes hurriedly scanning André's brief message.

The first of her bridesmaids started down the aisle. Tess slowly lifted her gaze. The wire fluttered to the floor as the room started to spin.

The bridesmaids stepped out to walk with measured grace one behind the other, the gathered guests smiling as the procession of dresses moved down the aisle. Blue, yellow, pink, green, violet . . . Organ notes rang out, and Echo's turquoise gown blurred in front of her as the woman moved to take her place at the doorway. She turned to look at Tess.

"Are you all right?" she whispered. "You look as though you've seen a ghost."

Tess shook her head, unable to find her voice. A chord sounded — Echo's clue to start her slow descent down the aisle. Tess saw her maid of honor step out hesitantly.

"Are you coming?"

The music switched tempo. The crowd swelled to their feet when the organ pealed out Mendelssohn's "Wedding March."

Staring sightlessly ahead of her, Tess woodenly started to move. One foot after the other. Left. Right. Left. Right. Down the polished floor leading to the massive altar, she walked with hot tears rolling beneath her kohl-darkened lashes.

The music expanded and filled the room even as her tears came faster. She could barely make out Talbot's tall figure waiting for her, looking so fine and handsome dressed in dark trousers and waistcoat. His best man and childhood friend was by his side, and beyond them stood five more groomsmen, their top hats tucked neatly beneath their arms. Through her tears Tess saw seven men smiling their admiration and encouragement as she walked toward them.

It seemed like hours before she reached the end of the incredibly long aisle. She was vaguely aware of Talbot extending his arm to her.

The music slowly died away, and the official, in his long white robe, began to pray. "Most heavenly and divine Father . . ."

The orchid bouquet in her hand trembled.

"We are gathered today to ask Your blessing on this man and woman . . ."

Her whole body began to shake, and her tears flowed like wine. Talbot glanced at her from the corner of his eye, and she felt him squeeze her hand reassuringly.

"This holy and sacred union is not to be entered into lightly, but . . ."

A loud sob tore from the depths of her soul, and she began to openly weep, long racking sobs that shook her frame and filtered softly to the gathered audience. The guests began to uneasily shuffle in the pews and whisper among themselves, clearly mystified by the strange outbreak she could do nothing to control.

The official glanced at Talbot, and he held up his hand to interrupt the service. Heaving a resigned sigh, he turned her, lifted her veil, and tipped her face up to meet his. His voice was almost hushed, but she heard his words clearly.

"It's Jake Lannigan, isn't it?"

Speechless, she nodded, her face wet with tears. Talbot calmly reached into his breast pocket and handed her a handkerchief, a gesture that had become almost habitual between them since her return.

"Are you that deeply in love with the man?"

She nodded again, realizing what an embarrassment she must be to him. His friends and family were looking on, completely mystified by what was taking place.

Her voice came out barely above a whisper with words that broke her heart. "He's been gravely injured in a logging accident."

Talbot's eyes briefly closed. "I see."

"He's — he's not a bad man, Talbot."

"I gather not, but is he the man you want to share your life with?"

"Yes. Oh, Talbot, I love him more than anything or anyone in my life. I *ache* to be with him."

"And does he return your love?"

The audience and official looked on as they all waited for her answer.

"It doesn't seem so . . . but deep in my

heart I believe he does. He knows I belong to you . . . and he knows he deceived and hurt me."

"Yet you would give up everything I offer you to be with him?"

Tess's tearful eyes met his. "I don't care about *things,* Talbot. All I know is that my life is miserable without him. I would rather spend one hour living in squalor with him than live the rest of my life spending your money." She caught herself, not wanting to hurt him. She glanced at the guests. "Please forgive me. I am aware that wasn't put very diplomatically, but it's true."

"Then go to him, Tess," Talbot urged softly.

A sob tore from her throat. She dabbed at her eyes again. "What about you? I love you in so many ways, but I don't think — no, I am quite certain I could never make you completely happy. You deserve better."

Talbot gazed at her affectionately, and in the depths of his eyes she recognized understanding. And complete forgiveness.

"I knew the day I brought you home this hour would come."

"Talbot — I am so sorry."

"Go to the man you love, my dear. And may God bless your union."

Smiling, she rose on her tiptoes and

placed a kiss on his lips. "Thank you." She turned away, and then she hurriedly whirled back and leaned close to whisper something in his ear, causing him to chuckle.

"Truthfully? I would be most honored."

Nodding, she turned to smile at Echo, and then to face the sea of stunned faces in the crowd staring back at her. "I'm sorry, but if you'll all keep your seats, the ceremony will continue in a few moments."

Talbot calmly turned to the stunned bridesmaids and smiled when his eyes met Echo's. Her face was pale when she stared back at him, wide-eyed and uncertain.

Clearing his throat, he said, "Echo, it has been brought to my attention that you would make a more suitable bride for me than Miss Wakefield."

Echo's jaw dropped. "Me . . . sir?"

He smiled and went on. "I know this is a bit out of the ordinary, but I must admit that the thought has occurred to me on more than one occasion recently. Even before Tess brought it to my attention a moment ago, I realized you are an exquisite creature . . . one with whom I would be extremely pleased to spend the rest of my life, if you will have me."

"Are you talking to me, sir?" Echo repeated. A gasp of disbelief came from the

Wellington-Kent pew.

"Yes, you, madam." He threw his head back, and his laugh was jovial. Tess knew she'd done the right thing for all of them. She saw happiness shine in Talbot's eyes for the first time in a long while.

"But as my wife, you must stop calling me sir."

Echo nodded. "Yes, sir."

He laughed again and extended his arm. "If you would be so inclined?"

Tess's heart sang. Everything would be okay in Philadelphia without her. She swiftly hugged her friend before turning and running down the long aisle that had seemed endless only minutes ago, her decision crystal clear.

She was going home.

31

"Shadow Pine comin' up!" the conductor sounded.

Tess sprang to her feet and ran to the back of the car to watch the train pull into the station. Stepping onto the back platform, she felt a warm, southerly breeze brush her cheeks as if to say, "Welcome home, little one."

Drawing a long, appreciative breath, she luxuriated in the spicy smell of white pine. She had missed these sights and the scents.

Every morning while she'd been away, she had awakened before sunup. Long before the household servants rose, she'd lie beneath the rose-colored canopy above her bed and listen for the sound of the Gabriel horn to summon her to breakfast. At times she had longed so badly to hear the familiar call that she'd imagined she could make out quite clearly the long, doleful bale echoing across the frozen hillsides.

The engineer pulled a couple of loud toots on the whistle, and steam poured out of the engine's smokestack. She ran back inside to gather her luggage. She wanted to be first in line when the locomotive finally ground to a halt in front of the depot.

After stepping down from the coach, she hurried across the street. She saw no familiar faces, but the town appeared to be nearly empty today. The spring thaw had melted away the mounds of snow, and the air was delightfully mild for April.

No one knew she was arriving, so she searched for a wagon to hire. One sat vacant, and her eyes fixed on the rig. She approached and carefully circled the conveyance, inspecting the workmanship. All four wheels appeared to be in good shape and the structure sound, so she paid the driver and climbed aboard. "Wakefield Timber camp, please."

When the wagon rolled into camp, she spotted Bernice coming out of Menson's store. Hoping to catch her attention, Tess stood and waved. The stout woman paused, shock registering on her features. Tess couldn't help but grin. It was good to see the cantankerous ol' schoolmarm wearing one of the bonnets Tess had made.

"Fedelia . . . uh, Miss Wakefield. What on

earth has brought you back here?"

Moments later, Tess set her valises down on the planked sidewalk and tried to catch her breath. "Well, I own this land, Bernice."

The woman cleared her throat. "Oh, yes, of course."

"Where is everyone?"

Bernice glanced around expectantly. "Who?"

Tess smiled and reached to remove her hat — a simple straw one that wasn't at all pretentious. She glanced up at the clear blue sky, unable to recall the sun ever being so welcome and warm. "The men. Where are they?"

"Most of the jacks are at the loading pens. The ones who aren't are over in Shadow Pine drinking liquor that would grow horns on a horse and recklessly gambling their hard-earned money away. If they can't accomplish that, they'll be spending it on the loose women." Bernice sniffed self-righteously. "Bunch of heathens."

"Where's Big Say?"

"Jake?" Bernice's forehead drew into a frown, and she clucked her tongue sadly. "Poor man."

Tess edged closer, her breath catching in her throat. "Where is he, Bernice? He isn't worse, is he?" Her heart threatened to escape her chest. If he had died from his injuries before she could get to him — she couldn't bear it. She just couldn't.

Lord, You wouldn't let this happen. You saved me from the river. Please save the man I love.

"He isn't worse. Doc says he's going to make it, but he's in a pitiful state."

"Is he in his quarters?"

"Oh my, no. He's not up to that yet. He's still at Doc's —"

Bernice's voice faded behind her as Tess bolted in the direction of Doc Medifer's house.

"Miss Wakefield, your luggage!"

"I'll get it later!"

"Thank you muchly for my hat! I shore like it!"

"You're welcome, Bernice!"

It took only moments to cover the ground to Doc Medifer's house. Tess bounded up the front steps and pounded on the door, trying to catch her breath. Panic seized her and she pounded harder. What was taking so long? Why didn't someone answer the door?

She banged loud enough to wake the dead, and the door was opened abruptly by an irate Doc Medifer. "What in tarnation is goin' on out here?"

Rushing past him, she nearly knocked the elderly gentleman off his feet. "Good morning, Doctor. I'm here to see Jake, please."

The doctor took a startled step backward. "Miss Yard — Miss Wakefield?"

"Please . . . Jake? Is he improving? Will he live? I'm here to help."

Closing the door, Doc fixed on her flushed features with open amusement. "My goodness, young lady, did you run all the way from Philadelphia?"

With her hat in her hand, she self-consciously smoothed her hair. She knew she must look a fright — she could feel tendrils hanging down both sides of her face. She tucked them quickly behind her ears. "I'm sorry. It's just that I've traveled a very long way to see him." Her eyes brimmed with unexpected tears. "It's very important that I be with him."

Medifer's smile was so kind, it made it even harder for her to control her urge to break down with exhaustion and weep.

"My dear, the whole town had been thinking that you would be very good for Jake right now. Follow me. I'll take you to your young man."

He turned and she followed him down a short, familiar hallway to the small room that she had occupied only a few months earlier.

André was closing the door behind him as they approached, and she broke into fresh tears when she saw the tall, handsome Frenchman. With a smile he held out his arms, and she gratefully went into them.

"I came as soon as I heard," she said, sobbing quietly.

"I am most grateful, *ma chère*."

"Is he worse?"

"He is . . . not so good. The man's heart is very sad."

Tess pulled from his embrace. "I want to see him."

André gently restrained her, his eyes troubled. "I do not know if he will let you."

"Why not? I love him. He needs me."

"It will come as a great shock to him to see you here," André confessed. "He believes you are on your honeymoon with your new husband."

Tess searched André's eyes for some sign of hope. "He doesn't know about the wire you sent?"

André shrugged. "He will not be surprised when he learns what I have done. I felt certain you would want to know."

Her frown softened into a smile. "I would have wrung your neck like a chicken if I had found out he'd been injured and you hadn't contacted me. But now I must go to him and tell him how very much I love him."

"But your husband?"

"I didn't marry Talbot, André."

André closed his eyes. "This is very good news. But Jake is a stubborn man, *ma chère.* I fear he will resist your help now . . . but perhaps the sight of you will give him the will to heal."

"What do you mean? Once he hears that I'm not married, why would he hesitate to accept my help?" Nothing could keep her from Jake Lannigan — certainly not Jake.

"One of his legs was injured in the accident and infection has set in. It's possible the leg will have to be removed. Doc isn't sure. You know Big Say. He is proud, and he feels that if his leg is taken, he will be less of a man," André said gently.

"Less of a man — Jake Lannigan? That's nonsense!"

"We have tried everything we know to encourage him," Doc interjected. "But he is a willful man."

"Is he strong enough to go home yet?"

"He has the strength of ten men, but the uncertainty about his leg has defeated him," Doc admitted. "I'm afraid he thinks his life is over. He refuses to eat or wash or even get out of bed. Nothing we say has helped. He's made up his mind that he wants to die."

Her back stiffened with resolve. "I'll get him out of that bed!"

"*Ma chère,* it will take a firm hand to pull him out of it."

She was up to the job, even if it didn't sound as though it would be easy. She knew if it meant otherwise losing him, she'd have Goliath strength. "You just let me handle him from now on."

André breathed a sigh of relief. "Gladly."

"I'll tell him you're here," Doc said, "but I fear he'll be none too happy."

"Pride goes before a fall," she reminded them. Her hand came out to block the doctor's entrance into Jake's room. "I'll tell him I'm here myself." Her chin lifted. "I can match Lannigan stubbornness any day of the week."

André grinned. "You are very brave, my little friend. I must warn you that he is not in the most sociable mood."

Tess reached for the doorknob and turned it. "Good. Neither am I."

Her heart pounded at the thought of finally getting to see the man she loved. She couldn't wait one more minute. She slowly entered the gloomy room, her eyes trying to adjust to the dim light. Although the window was open a crack to let in some fresh air, someone had drawn the shade. Jake lay on the bed with his eyes closed.

Taking a deep breath, she let her gaze move to the area beneath the sheet where he was resting his injured right leg. Catching her breath softly, she bit her bottom lip as compassion coursed through her. Drawing a second deep, cleansing breath, she moved silently toward him, relieved to have the first shocking sight over with. She was glad she had been warned. He looked pale and beaten.

He had always been such a vital force, so tall, so proud, so very much his own man — and he would be again. The Lord was faithful. He had allowed him to survive, and now He had answered her prayers to reach him.

The task that lay ahead would not be a simple one, but she knew, now more than ever, that she would be his unending source of strength. She vowed to stay by his side, no matter what.

"Who is it?"

The familiar sound of his voice sent goose bumps racing down her spine. "Come to empty yore slop jar, sir," she said in a soft drawl.

His eyes slowly opened. "Tess?"

She moved swiftly to his side. "Yes, my love."

Taking his hand, she gazed into the depths of the most troubled hazel eyes she'd ever seen. For the briefest moment, she caught a glimpse of his intense pain.

"What are you doing here?" he whispered.

"Where else would I be?"

Heartbroken, she saw tears rolling from the corners of his lids. "Why . . . why did you come back now?"

"Because we are in love, and we should be together."

"No." He turned his head away.

She placed her hand on his cheek and turned it back gently but firmly. "Yes."

"I'm going to lose my leg. I don't want you to see me like this."

"Listen to me, Jake Lannigan, a leg wouldn't matter to me — do you understand? No matter what happens, even if someone chopped you into tiny pieces, that wouldn't change my love for you."

"Go back where you belong. I don't want you here."

"You can't make me."

"There's nothing here for you now."

"You are."

Rolling to his side, he turned his back to her.

With a sigh she pulled a chair up beside his bed. It was clear he thought he'd given the final word. "All right. I'll permit this maudlin act for a while longer. I know the accident has been a terrible shock, but I won't let you roll over and die, Jake. Someday very soon we will have to get on with our lives."

"Go away."

"Not as long as there is breath left in my body."

"Where's Talbot?"

"Um, I think he and Echo are on their honeymoon. Europe. A two-month cruise. Very urbane."

His head lifted ever so slightly from the pillow and he frowned.

"Go to sleep, grump. There's too much to explain right now."

He refused to answer.

And that was how they went on. For days Jake refused to speak or eat or bathe. And when the days had turned into a week, Tess finally began to lose patience with him. He was drowning in self-pity, and she realized she had to take matters into her own hands.

One morning at the beginning of May, she

entered his room with a tray loaded with bacon, eggs, flapjacks, and hot coffee. The pleasant aroma drifted through the room as she set the tray beside his bed and stepped over to open the window. "Good morning, darling!"

He barely glanced at her before he rolled over and presented his back to her, just as he'd done many times before. Today, however, was going to be different.

She walked to the bed, lightly smacked him on the rump, and taking him firmly by the shoulders, she eased him over onto his back. After tucking a napkin under his unshaven chin, she brought the first forkful of eggs to his mouth. "Open wide."

He refused, staring back at her with a stoic, silent resentment, but she calmly held the fork to his lips. When he opened his lips to complain, she quickly put the food into his mouth. At that point, he was forced to chew or strangle.

Before he could catch his breath, a forkful of pancakes followed, and then more eggs, and then a strip of bacon.

"You're choking me!" he sputtered.

"I've given it serious thought," she agreed, "and you're not out of the woods yet, but if you'll eat three more bites without me hav-

ing to manhandle you, I'll spare your life —
today."

"Miserable pest!"

"Oatmeal next?"

She heard his stomach growl when she
brought another bite of pancakes to his
mouth. "See how good this is? Mmmm."

"Put more butter on those things," he
grumbled. "Hay tastes better."

She smiled. "Put it on yourself."

The next morning she carried a basin of
water and fresh towels into his room. "Good
morning, sweet thing." As usual, she was
met with stony silence, but she walked to
the window and threw the curtains open
wide.

Jake's hand shot up to ward off the deluge
of bright sunshine. "Don't you have anything else to do but torment me?"

"No, I've made that my life's goal." She
loomed over him menacingly. "Guess who
gets to give you a bath this morning?" His
eyes widened, and she almost laughed at
the horror she saw in them. "The doctor
tells me you refuse to do it yourself, so I'm
thinking maybe I'll give it a try. And that
beard definitely has to go."

"Over my dead body!"

"I'm not looking for trouble, but if you
want it, mister, you've got it." She reached

out to unbutton his nightshirt. His hands shot out to stop her. She was surprised to find that his strength had not diminished much over the weeks of convalescence. He was as the doctor had said — strong as ten men.

"I would hate to floor you, lady."

"Not half as much as I would hate to be floored." She shoved his hands aside and continued with her work while he stared at her in disbelief. "What's going on with the schoolhouse?" she asked. "Any progress?"

She knew he wasn't going to answer her, so she thumped him gently on the ear and asked again, "Have you built a new schoolhouse?"

"King Davis burnt the old one to the ground the day you left," he snapped.

"Well, good for King. Now you'll *have* to build a new one if you haven't already."

Peeling off his shirt, she let her eyes linger momentarily on his broad chest before she dipped the cloth into the warm water and lathered it with soap. His hand moved quickly to block her efforts, and their gazes locked in a stubborn duel, but she refused to back down.

"You are not going to wash me."

"You're too sick to stop me."

"I am not sick. I'm an invalid, and you're

not going to wash me."

"You're an invalid then. You can't stop me. You can't get out of bed. Once I'm through with your torso, then I have to wash your legs and your feet. Doc said so."

His expression turned from irritated to wounded feelings. "I can get out of bed. I don't happen to want to get out of bed."

"Then you will have to endure being bathed like an infant every morning," she said simply. "You're not going to make everyone else suffer because you're too lazy to wash." She slapped the cloth to his chest with enough force to take his breath away. Her eyes openly defied him to stop her. "And if you don't pipe down and let me get this over with, tomorrow morning I'll start with your bottom first."

A deep red color crept up his neck. "Where is André? Tell him to get in here!"

"André's busy." She was happy he was getting so riled up. It was the most life she'd seen in him since she'd arrived.

"Doing what?"

"Running my business, of course. Because you're too irresponsible to do your job, he's doing it."

"You're letting André do my job?"

"Well," she shrugged, "someone has to see that Wakefield Timber runs smoothly."

When she went to draw the sheet back, he reached out to jerk it back angrily.

Steeling herself, she grabbed it back and hung on until she dislodged it from his deathlike clutch. Thrusting it aside, she saw the neatly bandaged leg he had been trying so hard to hide from her.

A tense silence fell between them. The sight was one she would gladly have forfeited, but she knew it was one more milestone that had to be faced. Willing her features to remain expressionless, she began to carefully clean around the bandage.

"It serves you right," he accused.

"What serves me right?"

"Seeing my leg. Are you happy now?"

She realized he was embarrassed, and she ached for him. "I wish it was well," she said softly, "but since it isn't, we have to deal with it. If it can be saved, so much the better. But if you lose it, Jake, well, it will only make me love you that much more."

"I don't want your pity!"

She draped the sheet neatly back in place. Meeting his accusing gaze, her temper flared. "Pity! You think I *pity* you? On the contrary, you infuriate me! You pity yourself, Jake Lannigan! I'm here because I love you, not because I feel sorry for you." She closed her eyes and fought to get her emotions under control.

She was met with silence again. After rinsing out the cloth, she lathered it up again and lowered her voice. "You might as well get used to me being here. I'm all yours. My hopes, my hurts, my fears, and most of all, my love. Now, I can wash the remaining area or you can. Which will it be?"

"If it's washed, honey, you'll wash it."

She shrugged and flipped back the sheet. He grabbed the fabric and stared at her. "So help me, I'm getting out of this bed —"

"God helps those who help themselves, so I doubt that He has time to listen to an otherwise healthy man like you whine all day." She met his gaze. "He has been very good to you, Jake. He's given you a fine strong body and a woman who loves you more than anything on earth. You should be ashamed of the way you're acting." She picked up a container of cornstarch and opened it. "This will make you more comfortable during the warmer weather." White powder fogged his head as she dusted away.

"Stop putting that girlish stuff on me! You *read* to Frank Kellier when he was injured! Why are you torturing me?"

"You are torturing yourself." She gathered the basin and towels and walked out, leaving him to rant and rave for as loud and long as he wanted. But she smiled when she recalled that he remembered and apparently resented her visits with Frank.

When she entered his room the next day, he was sitting on the side of the bed waiting for her. He was cleanly shaven, and everything on his breakfast tray had been eaten.

"Good morning, my love."

"Just leave the soap and water."

"Sorry, I can't do that."

"I'll bathe myself this morning."

Her eyes locked with his. "Well, that must mean you're feeling better." Finally, he gave her a brief nod and then turned his back, but she didn't dare smile. "Good." She walked over to arrange the basin and soap before turning and straightening the bed. "Looks like your appetite's returning."

"I'm only eating to get enough strength to get away from you."

"You couldn't possibly eat that much."

"Humph!"

"It's a lovely day. Why don't we go outside? A little sunshine will do you good."

"How am I supposed to get out there? Crawl on my belly like a lizard?"

She turned to look at him. "What are those wooden things propped next to your bed?"

His eyes snapped fire when he reached for the sticks and then flung them angrily across the room. "Crutches! I'll not use them!"

Tess calmly walked across the room, picked them up, brought them back, and stood beside his bed. "Think again."

32

Days slowly passed, but Tess was pleased that eventually Jake began to regain his will. His pride was slower to heal, but she started to see small signs that it, too, would mend. They spent their mornings sitting in the sun talking while she sewed. Minor skirmishes inevitably erupted, but they came with less frequency now.

"You know, it really burns me up the way you keep doing that to me," Jake complained.

"Doing what to you?"

"Jake, you're going to eat — no, I'm not — yes, you are. Jake, you're going to wash — no, I'm not — yes, you are. Jake, you're not an invalid — Jake, use your crutches. What kind of a way is that to treat a man in my condition? Are you trying to humiliate me?"

Tess continued to sew. "Well, you've guessed it. The moment I'd heard you might lose your leg, I told Talbot I'd have to interrupt my wedding and come quickly so I could make fun of you. He was most understanding. Actually, he's a swell person."

He glanced at her. "I don't find that amusing."

"When are you going to stop feeling so sorry for yourself? You could be in worse condition. Look at poor Frank. He did lose a leg. What if you'd lost both legs in the accident? And while we're on the subject of what's amusing and not, I didn't happen to find it very funny when I was the one involved in an accident. I was the one who lost her memory, and you told me I was the new schoolteacher. Ha-ha. *Not* funny."

"I didn't tell you that."

"You didn't bother to tell me otherwise."

His eyes refused to meet hers now. "I've already told you I'm sorry for that. It was a rotten thing to do, and you have every right to be upset."

"Jake, aren't you the least bit curious about why I didn't marry Talbot and decided not to sell Grandfather's business?"

"No. It's no skin off my nose if you wanted to sell and invest your money in ridiculous hat stores. The land is yours, not mine. And you're not mine. I had that mixed up for a while."

402

"You really don't think I have a gift for making lovely hats, do you?"

"I refuse to comment."

Ignoring him, she continued. "Well, I'm going to tell you regardless. I only knew my grandfather through the letters we wrote to each other. As you know, I left here when I was very small, and then I only saw him occasionally when I was a young girl." She placed her newest creation in her lap. "I remembered how tall and lovely the pines were, but this land was worlds away from Philadelphia. Mother was in ill health most of her life, and we only made the long trip to visit infrequently. I grew up aware that Tip owned a timber business in Michigan, but I didn't have the slightest idea what that meant.

"When he died I had already accepted Talbot's marriage proposal. Because I knew nothing about running a logging camp, Talbot thought it best to sell the company and reinvest the money in my hat shops. Had I known what I know now, I would have willingly kept the land. I share your dream to replant the pines, Jake. I've seen what man is doing to the earth, and it saddens me."

He stared off into space, but she knew he was listening. "I'm sorry I didn't know. It might have made things different between

403

us," she said softly.

He slowly shook his head. "We would have never met if you hadn't come here to finalize the sale."

"True, but sometimes I wonder if that would have made any difference to you. I can't seem to reach you whether I'm Fedelia Yardley or Tess Wakefield."

"That isn't how it is."

"You didn't come to see me off that morning," she said quietly.

"I couldn't." His voice turned oddly uneven.

"Why not? Because you were afraid it would hurt too much?"

"It hurt. More than you'll ever know."

"More than I'll ever know? Are we ready to compare hurt? Because if we are, let me tell you how much I hurt all the months I was in Philadelphia. Every time the mail came and I didn't hear from you, I hurt. Every time I thought about the way you let me go that morning without a fight, I felt incredible pain."

"Do you think I wanted to let you go?"

"I don't know, Jake. Did you?"

"You know better than that."

"No, I don't." She gazed at him, her eyes pleading for the truth. "You tell me what you felt that morning."

His face clouded. "I felt helpless anger and guilt for what I'd done. Suspecting who you were and not telling anyone. Hurt? Oh, I hurt, all right. The pain that filled my heart because you belonged to someone else was overwhelming at times."

"I've belonged to you from the moment we met. How much clearer could I have made my feelings?"

"Tess, you weren't aware that you were engaged to another man. I knew or strongly suspected. I should never have lied to you."

She willed his beautiful hazel eyes to look at her. "Do you ever think about the good times we shared? We had a few."

"Yes."

"Often?"

"More than I care to."

"I thought of you every day, every hour, every moment."

His eyes shifted away again. "I had no right to take what belonged to another man."

Tess sighed and turned back to her hat. "Talbot's a good man. After the honeymoon, he's bringing Echo back here to visit Waite's grave. I got a letter from her this morning."

His grunt told her he didn't care to hear about Talbot.

"He would have made me a fine husband."

"I suppose he had a good laugh when he heard about my accident. Probably thought I got what I deserved."

"Talbot doesn't like to make fun of people the way I do," she mocked. "I imagine that he and Echo are very happy together."

"Talbot and Echo. It's kind of hard to believe."

"When I told Talbot that I couldn't marry him because I loved you, he married Echo instead. Isn't that romantic?"

He sat up straighter. "Tess . . . who broke the engagement?"

"We sort of both broke it." She mechanically drew the thread through the fabric.

"Because of me?"

"Don't be so arrogant. It was because of me. I never loved Talbot, Jake. Not the way I should have."

"How do you know for sure? What about your memory?"

"Now you're forgetting. My memory returned the morning I found Waite's body in the snow. I'd accidentally gotten hit in the head at school. But whether I'd ever regained my full memory or not, I couldn't possibly love another man. You're the one, Jake. God has made that abundantly clear in my mind."

He rolled his eyes in disbelief. "You knew you were Tess Wakefield before Talbot arrived?"

She nodded. "I told you that morning. Have you lost *your* memory?"

"I tried to forget that day." He turned toward her. "I can't believe you knew who you were."

"I did, but what I couldn't be sure of was if you had known it all along."

"I suspected." He shook his head. "And I didn't do a thing to help you. In fact, I hurt you."

She lifted her eyes to find him staring at her. "But don't you see, Jake? *I* knew exactly who I was when I asked you to marry me."

His gaze held with hers, softly caressing. "But I lied to you. I don't lie, Tess, ever. Only I did to you."

"You did, and I didn't like you very much for a while, but I've never stopped loving you. Not even once. Nothing you can do or say will change that — unless you'd run off with one of those Shadow Pine women."

Shaking his head, Jake said softly, "Did Talbot know about us?"

"I hardly see how he couldn't have known. He's an observant man, and he offered his blessing for me to come here."

Pulling in a deep breath, Jake settled back

in his chair. Sunlight warmed the porch. "So Echo married Talbot."

"That's right."

"Tess, if I didn't know you better, I'd swear you were making that up."

"I don't lie, Jake. Ever." She watched a slight grin cross his handsome face. "It was apparent to me after a few weeks that Echo and Talbot were meant for each other. You should see them together. They laugh and giggle like two adolescents. Talbot isn't stuffy when he's with Echo, and I've never seen her so happy."

Jake stared off in the distance thoughtfully. "The good Lord knows she deserves a little happiness."

"Echo's wealthy now beyond her wildest dreams, and she has a devoted husband who will give her the love and respect she's worthy of."

"And when was all of this decided?"

"The day of my wedding — at the altar. As a matter of fact, they married the instant I left." She shrugged and then flashed him a sheepish grin. "Why waste all of those wedding preparations?"

When he continued to stare at her, she leaned over and laid her hand on his. "Stop fighting it. It's really all very simple. Fate and the B&O Railroad brought me back to you."

Jake grunted. "What do you people do up there in Philadelphia? Change fiancés like we change socks?"

"No." She took his face in her hands and met his gaze. "We follow our hearts."

Darkness had fallen when she slipped into his room later that night. They had spent the day together, but tonight she felt lonely, so she had left Menson's for the time being, and walked back to see him.

"Jake, are you asleep?"

"No. What are you doing here?"

"I missed you." Her eyes grew accustomed to the darkness, and she saw him sitting in the chair next to the bed.

Smiling, he held out his hand to her. "Come here and keep me company, little one. I can't sleep either."

Little one. Ever so slowly, he was returning to her. She scurried quietly across the room to perch on the side of the narrow bed.

"We have to be quiet. We don't want Doc to hear us." She giggled. It felt as though they were doing something naughty.

"Doc wouldn't hear it if they reenacted the Civil War in his backyard. Listen." They fell silent, and Tess heard snores coming from another part of the house.

The warmth of his hand went all the way to her heart. She stood and then knelt on the floor beside his chair. They gazed at one another in the moonlight streaming through the window.

"Why can't you sleep?" she whispered.

"Because I lied again. I *am* glad you came back," he confessed.

Her fingers reached to lovingly trace the contours of his face. She longed to kiss away the pain and the fear she still saw shining from deep within his eyes. "I know that. I didn't believe a word you said to me."

"Go back to Philadelphia, Tess."

Her heart sank. "Why?"

"I have nothing to offer you. I don't know what the future holds."

"I don't either, and that's a good thing, but I have enough money to last us the rest of our lives," she reminded him.

"I couldn't take your money."

"It would be *our* money."

"And what happens if you find yourself saddled with a cripple? You'll regret giving up Talbot and his Wellington-Kent fortune, and you'll end up resenting me."

"I understand your health issues —"

"I still could lose my leg. Don't you understand what that would mean? If I lost my leg, then I couldn't harvest timber. And if I can't do my job, I can't support you, and if I can't support you, I would never consider myself a man."

"I pray none of those things will happen, and if we pray together, and ask for compassion, I believe God often grants such wishes. And even if the worst happens, André will run the crew."

"No. I could never be happy letting another man run your company."

"*Our* company. Don't kid yourself, Mr. Lannigan. You will be so busy replanting trees, loving me, and being a papa to our children that you'll have no time left for all of this self-pity."

His eyes slowly met hers. "Are you serious? You really want to replant the pine?"

She stood and then sat on the knee of his good leg, bending down to rub her nose against his affectionately. "Every last one that Wakefield Timber has harvested over the years, but I'll need your help. I know nothing about running a timber business, and you know everything. You will have to marry me or else I shall be forced to run off and marry Sven Templeton."

He chuckled, his voice breaking. "You're bribing me?"

"I'm loving you." She bent closer. Their

gazes locked. "With my heart and soul."

"I love you, Tess. Too much to saddle you with an invalid."

"I know," she said simply, and rested her head on his chest. "I will strike a bargain if you will permit it."

"What sort of bargain?"

"I won't come around or bother you anymore until you've had time to come to grips with your injury. Deal?"

"You would be content to step back and give me room to think about what's happened and where I'm going?"

She nodded. "I'm not going anywhere. I have a timber operation to run."

"What if I decide I can't marry you and I eventually go back to my father's business? It's what both he and my mother want."

"That will be up to you."

"All right," he said finally. "I accept your terms, but I can't promise anything. I'll see that your trees are planted, but it could be a long time before I can think about the future."

She smiled.

"What's going on in that devious mind of yours?"

"Nothing, darling." She looked at him. "I'll wait for you however long it takes."

"All right." He drew her mouth slowly to

meet his, whispering, "I'll hold you to your word."

As long as he held her, that was good enough.

EPILOGUE

Exactly two days later . . .

The spring rain pattered on the eaves of Jake's roof. Tess turned to gaze up at her new husband.

Leaning on his crutches, he nuzzled the warmth of her neck. "Why do I feel as though I've just been snared like a rabbit?"

"Do you feel like a captive?"

"No. I feel like the luckiest man on earth."

She tilted back her head and winked. "Why, Big Say, I'm surprised it took you two whole days to come to your senses. The jacks had a pool. Almost all agreed on twenty-four hours. Tops."

Chuckling, he kissed her soundly. When he pulled back, he said, "You knew, didn't you?"

"That you loved me and you were going to marry me? Yes. But I wanted you to comprehend your situation and fully accept it. No one knows what tomorrow brings, and aren't we fortunate for that grace?"

"Situation? You think it was André's idea to contact you?"

"Jake!"

He flashed a smug grin. "You'll never know, will you? The office does have a telegraph wire. And you did ask me to marry you. I figured you were a woman of your word."

"Why, Big Say." She kissed him softly. "You astound me. I think we're going to have a very interesting life together."

Grinning, he nudged the door shut with his shoulder. "I don't plan to disappoint you, Mrs. Lannigan." He held her close, gazing deep into her eyes. "Welcome home, darling."

DISCUSSIONS QUESTIONS

1. Tess Wakefield was a different woman at the start of this book than she was at the end — or was she? Do you think people can change, or does the worst often bring out the best in people? Do you think God might intend that to sometimes be the case?

2. Do you think Jake's anger toward Tess was justified? Should he have told her right away that he suspected she was Wakefield's granddaughter and not the new schoolteacher? Why or why not? What would you have done under the same set of circumstances?

3. André is Jake's right-hand man. Though he is interested in the schoolteacher, he puts his friendship with Jake first. What did you think of him as a counterpoint to Jake and a possible love interest for Tess?

4. Have you ever had a situation where you wanted revenge? Is revenge ever worth the pain and sorrow it can bring?

5. Can you name one thing that actually changed about Tess? Can you name two good things about her?

6. Relationships are often made difficult by the slightest misunderstanding. A word not said, a hug not given. Can you think of a time when you were able to work out a difference with someone and go on to form a solid friendship?

7. What do you think about inherent personal qualities shining through, even if someone were to forget their identity? If you lost your memory, what traits do you think would still be part of who you are? Tess's breeding, perseverance, and creativity showed up even when she had no idea of what her past consisted of. Do you think that was portrayed realistically in the story?

8. Talbot and Echo demonstrate how truly nice people can touch the lives around them for the better. What did you think of the way the story ends for them?

9. Jake worried about losing a leg. Should he instead have been more concerned about his actions — for not fighting for Tess's love and letting Talbot take her away?

10. Tess discovered what she really wanted to do with her wealth and life. Do you think we all have opportunities to change the direction of our lives this way? Do you think that is something God can help us do?

ABOUT THE AUTHOR

Lori Copeland is the author of more than 90 titles, both historical and contemporary fiction. With more than 3 million copies of her books in print, she has developed a loyal following among her rapidly growing fans in the inspirational market. She has been honored with the *Romantic Times* Reviewer's Choice Award, The Holt Medallion, and Walden Books Best Seller award. In 2000, Lori was inducted into the Missouri Writers Hall of Fame. She lives in the beautiful Ozarks with her husband, Lance, and their three children and five grandchildren.

The employees of Thorndike Press hope you have enjoyed this Large Print book. All our Thorndike, Wheeler, and Kennebec Large Print titles are designed for easy reading, and all our books are made to last. Other Thorndike Press Large Print books are available at your library, through selected bookstores, or directly from us.

For information about titles, please call:
(800) 223-1244

or visit our Web site at:
http://gale.cengage.com/thorndike

To share your comments, please write:
Publisher
Thorndike Press
10 Water St., Suite 310
Waterville, ME 04901